THE LADY WHO KNEW TOO MUCH

Agents of Desire Book One

ALYSON CHASE

Cover image by Dar Albert.

Visit the author website: http://www.alysonchase.com

ISBN-13: 978-1-944802-26-4
ISBN-10: 1-944802-26-6

Chapter One

London, 1819

One would think that being a woman on the run would be an exciting adventure. One heart-pounding moment after the other. In truth, Lady Juliana Wickham had never felt so dull in her life.

She tugged at the rope holding the window's curtain back. The drape fell closed. She didn't want any views of the outside world. Or her own reflection. Neither sight gave her solace. She rose and paced Hyacinth's bed chambers, the room she hadn't left for nearly a week.

Admittedly, it was a large room, with a wide fireplace and a bed big enough to comfortably sleep Juliana and Hy. With just the smallest amount of blunt, Juliana had bought the silence and aid of her friend's maid, who smuggled meals up to Juliana each day.

It was the loveliest of prisons.

Still, a prison it remained. That it was one of her own choosing did little to assuage her irritation.

She eyed the portable desk Hyacinth had smuggled into her bedroom for Juliana's use, but even that didn't interest her. She'd already spent too many hours hunched over the thing, spilling her innermost thoughts, trying to organize them into persuasive arguments. Even if her essays convinced society of the folly of its ways (which she was certain they would), well, even world-changing philosophers needed a respite now and then.

She flopped to her back on Hyacinth's bed. Her feet

tapped along to the beat of the music resonating from the ballroom below. Turning her head, she met a scornful green-eyed gaze. "What do you say, Mr. Blake? Shall we dance?"

She reached for the tabby, picked up his wriggling form, and scooted off the bed. She waited for the next melody to start and fell into step, curling the cat close to her chest.

He swatted her jaw, his claws stinging.

"Lawks!" She dropped him on the bed and rubbed her chin, watching as he stalked away. Even her friend's cat was too busy to entertain her. She plopped onto a stuffed armchair. Her next essay would be a treatise on what to bring when on the run.

More books, definitely. While Miss Hyacinth Butters had many fine qualities, a sufficient library wasn't one of them. Juliana had fled Bluff Hall with naught but a satchel full of clothes and what funds she could gather.

Juliana stared at the curtained window. She'd been at her friend's house for five days now. The first day she'd been quite happy to languish in Hy's bed. That attack had...well, it was best not to dwell on such unpleasantness.

Even better not to think of the man who had occupied a starring role in her dreams since he'd saved her that night.

She closed a door in her brain, shutting out a pair of broad shoulders and a set of piercing blue eyes.

The second and third day at Hyacinth's she had begun plotting her next steps.

And come up with nothing.

Then she'd written, a pleasant enough pastime, but it didn't serve to take her mind off her troubles.

Hy had tried to entertain her, but as her parents didn't know Juliana was hiding in their house, her friend couldn't very well spend all her time in her bedroom without drawing suspicion. When the carriages had begun arriving for this evening's rout, Juliana had felt the excitement of the evening's festivities to her very bones.

She longed to be among the dressed-up ladies, dancing

across the parqueted floor, and as she wasn't much of a dancer, that was saying something.

Being on the run wasn't for the faint of heart.

Nor the listless of spirit.

She should be thinking of new ways to uncover the truth. She was a smart woman. She plucked up the poker and jabbed at the dwindling flames in the fireplace. Her father hadn't spared a second thought on providing his daughter with as thorough an education as he'd given his son, untraditional as those educations might have been. And at two and twenty, Juliana credited herself with having enough sense and experience to solve life's problems.

Yet it had been almost a fortnight since she'd fled home. Nearly a week since Mr. Pickens, her father's secretary, had been arrested. Two weeks, and she'd yet to learn anything more about his motivation. Whether he'd worked alone or not.

Whether her father was finally safe.

She pushed that disquieting thought from her mind. As Rodger Rose, the great modern philosopher and poet, said, thoughts become words, words became deeds, and deeds became reality. In order to create the reality you desired, it was necessary to keep your mind clear of negative thoughts.

Which was much easier said than done.

The door eased open, and before Juliana could dive behind the bed, Maisey, Hyacinth's maid, slipped inside the room.

She dropped a hasty curtsy. "Begging your pardon, miss, but I saw this on the butler's tray and brought it here straightaway." She held out a familiar envelope, and Juliana's shoulders slumped.

This was the third letter that had been returned unopened. Was her father's butler in on the plot, too? His new secretary? Someone was preventing her letters from getting to her father, even when she'd gone through the subterfuge of making it look as though the letters came from a third party.

She took the missive, tracing the letters of her father's name. It had been written in her friend's hand, and if Mr. Butters questioned why he was franking letters from his daughter to the Earl of Withington, he had not yet spoken of it.

"Thank you, Maisey." Her mouth went dry, and she swallowed. Her father was in danger. She felt it in her bones. But what good was her certainty when no warning could reach him?

Not that he'd heeded her previous warnings. He'd laughed when she'd pointed out his horse's girth strap had been deliberately cut, causing him to tumble. Chucked her chin when she'd urged him to send for the magistrate after a section of parapet had fallen from the roof of Bluff Hall, nearly killing him as he walked below. And the last attempt on his life...

She pressed her hand to her abdomen. He had been so ill, she hadn't thought he would survive. She'd said he was poisoned. He patted her hand and said Mrs. Bailey hadn't cooked the lamb sufficiently.

But now that his secretary had been arrested, surely he'd heed her warnings. It was true that Mr. Pickens had yet to confess to any attacks against her father. From the little she'd read in the papers, the blackguard had only been charged with assaulting her, because she'd uncovered him stealing from her father the theory went.

But her evidence was mounting.

If only her letters would reach her father.

She tossed the missive down on the side table. She should travel home, speak to her father in person. Icy dread filled her at the thought. It was the same feeling that had gripped her each time she stepped across Bluff Hall's threshold in the past year. Something was deathly wrong in her home. She didn't know whether she'd survive her return.

"Do you want to send another note?" Maisey asked. "I can tell Bobby to give it to a maid instead of the butler. I'm sure she could get it to your father. We know how to get things done."

Juliana smiled. "Yes, probably." What other choices did she have? "But not tonight. Go. I know the servants are having a party of their own down in the kitchens. Enjoy yourself."

Maisey gave her a conspiratorial grin. "Bobby did promise me a dance. But are you all right up here? Can I bring you anything?"

Juliana waved her away. "I'm fine. Enjoy a drink for me."

The girl turned for the door. "I'll enjoy one for myself, as well. And one for Miss Hyacinth, and one for—"

"Don't get too carried away." Juliana chuckled. Though maybe Maisey had the right of it. A bottle of wine to drown her worries tonight wouldn't go amiss. Or even a dram of whiskey. Her father kept the best whiskey, and never scolded his children for indulging in a glass or two.

"Have a good evening, miss." Maisey silently pulled the door open an inch, peered out, then slid through the opening, closing the door behind her.

Juliana sank onto the bench at the foot of the bed. She couldn't remain hiding in her friend's bedroom. Hy's parents were bound to find out, sooner or later. And she was merely delaying her problems by remaining hidden instead of resolving them.

The string quartet Hy's parents had hired turned their instruments towards a waltz. The music was muted but skillful, and the wistful melody had her feet sketching the dance's pattern on the carpet.

Yes, she needed to determine if someone still wanted her father dead, but it wasn't going to happen tonight.

She rose and faced her friend's floor-length mirror. She imagined a tall, burly figure, and dipped a deep curtsy. "Why yes, I would love to dance."

A hard blue gaze flashed across her imagination. Those eyes belonged to someone completely inappropriate, but this was her fantasy, so she let them linger in her mind. She closed her own eyes and began to sway to the music. She raised her arms, as though holding her imaginary man, and fell into the rhythm of the dance.

The hem of her skirts whisked across the carpet. She hummed along with the music and wondered what it would feel like to have such strong arms wrapped around her body. The men of her acquaintance were all slender and sensitive.

Perhaps she should expand her acquaintance beyond philosophical societies. The male members were all kind and intelligent, but none of them sent a shiver straight down her spine with merely one glance. Perhaps—

One thick band, hard as iron, wrapped around her waist. One rough hand gripped her own, engulfing it.

Her eyes flew open.

The pair of piercing blue from her imagination met her gaze.

A shiver raced down her spine.

"My lady." Mr. Brogan Duffy, inquiry agent and the man featuring much too prominently in her dreams, inclined his head. "I'll take this dance."

Chapter Two

She was soft in all the right places. A fact that was of no consequence to his purpose, but still, Brogan noticed.

Her plain face gazed up at him, mouth open wide with shock. A bit of pride unfurled in his chest, replacing his irritation. She should be surprised. It had taken some doing discovering the Lady Juliana Wickham's location. His employers at the Bond Agency for Discreet Inquiries would be pleased. He had only worked there four months, and finding Lady Juliana was the first case he'd been assigned to as principal agent.

A fortnight to resolve an investigation seemed like an effective resolution...if his employers ignored the fact that he'd found her once before and she'd manage to slip away. The back of his neck heated.

She stumbled, and her full bosom pressed against his chest. She jerked away as though scalded, and he tightened his grip on her waist.

"I'm not...what are..." She blew out a breath, a strand of her brown hair lifting and drifting back to her cheek. "How did you find me?"

"I had a man watching Bluff Hall. He saw your letter to your father. Or should I say, Miss Butters's letter to your father." And he'd seen Lord Withington's butler refuse delivery. Because it was from an unknown sender? From a chit he thought would write nothing but nonsense? If he knew Miss Butters was a friend of his missing daughter's, wouldn't he welcome any correspondence?

No matter. His job was to deliver Miss Juliana, not

analyze her father's correspondence habits. "Would you like to finish the waltz or are you ready to leave?"

She tried to step back, tugging at his grip. He thought about holding on, but restrained or free, she was no match for him. She would go where he wanted. Hopefully without kicking and screaming. He disliked causing a scene.

He released her, and she took a quick step back. She rubbed her arms. "Leave? Why would I leave?"

She was going to be difficult. He sighed. He'd only laid eyes on her that one night, but he'd known she was trouble right away.

The case should have been easy. A brother worried about his missing sister had hired an inquiry agency to find her. Brogan had discovered her first at the apartments of a set designer she'd befriended. From the intelligence he'd received, Lady Juliana adored the theatre, and tracking her from there had been simple.

Attempting to be kind, he'd allowed her to remain with her friend until the next morning when Brogan would deliver her home. She'd needed comforting after the attack by Mr. Pickens.

He should never attempt kindness. It wasn't a trait he excelled at.

"An unmarried woman of your station doesn't just flit about London without supervision. It isn't proper." She should know this. He reached for her arm. "Let's go."

She skittered away, putting the bed between them. She crossed her arms under her bosom, giving him an arch look. "Proper? You're going to have to give me a better reason than that. In fact, if you want to discuss propriety, how proper is it for your agency to accept a commission from a lady's brother when it is my father who is my legal guardian. If he takes no issue with my 'flitting about,' then my brother can't, either."

Brogan inhaled sharply. It was her eyes. That was how he knew she was going to be trouble. Much too assertive than a lady of her years should be.

"Your father isn't well." According to his peers, he hadn't been for quite some time. After the death of his wife, he'd become disinterested in affairs of state. Taken on some queer ideas. Let his children run wild. At least so said His Grace, Duke of Montague, one of the co-founders of the Bond Agency. And the result of such poor parenting was a daughter running about London like a harridan.

"Your brother worries for you." A fact Lord Snowdon had seemed eager to impress upon him. He most likely didn't want his sister to embarrass the family. His reasons were his own. Brogan circled the bed. "Now, we go."

She hopped up on the mattress, scuttling to the center. "You'll have to carry me, kicking and screaming through the ball. Mr. Butters will stop you."

"Mr. Butters doesn't know you're here." Brogan planted his hands on his hips. He wouldn't have to take her through the ballroom. He'd ascertained all the possible exits. The one through the kitchens would work best.

She flushed. "That is irrelevant. You can't be such a monster that you'd abscond with an unwilling woman, taking her back to her doom."

He glared at the ceiling. She would have to be dramatic, too. Consorting with aristocrats was going to be an annoying corollary to his new job. "You're safest with the people who love you best. Your brother. Your father. I don't want to argue about this."

She picked up a pillow and held it to her belly. "Someone tried to kill my father."

"There is no evidence of that." More dramatics, he presumed. Perhaps it was a natural reaction for one of her kind to have after her ordeal.

His stomach hardened, remembering her cowering before her father's secretary. The man had deserved a much worse thrashing than he'd received for attacking a woman. But what reason would he have to kill his employer? He'd admitted to being a thief, no more, and his attack on Lady Juliana had been an attempt to escape detection.

And having a passing acquaintance with the woman, Brogan could understand the impulse to throttle her.

Her brother had given him some hints of her character. An indulgent father had led to a spoiled upbringing. She looked upon her flight as some grand adventure. Even now her eyes sparkled with excitement.

He held out his hand. "Take it up with your brother."

"Snow doesn't see what's happening." She huffed. "You're an investigator. Can't you help me find the truth?"

"No." If he was found indulging a chit's delusions, he'd never hear the end of it at the Bond Agency. Although the five founders of the business never made mention of it, Brogan knew they weren't the usual toffs. They each had backgrounds assisting the Crown in delicate operations. Word in the agency was they'd saved the prime minister's arse on more than one occasion. Brogan wouldn't embarrass himself in front of them, not when he had a decent job for the first time in his life.

"Lady Juliana, if you do not come—"

She struck him on the side of the head with the pillow. "I am a grown woman. This will be kidnapping."

A grown woman wielding a pillow as a weapon? She acted more like his ten-year-old sister.

She smacked him again.

"Desist," he gritted out through clenched teeth.

"No. Not until you—"

He snaked his hand out and grabbed the pillow. He yanked it away, causing her to fall to the mattress in front of him. He gripped her wrist and hauled her to seating. "Now, it is time—"

"Juliana!" A distressed gasp dragged his eyes to the doorway of the bedroom. Miss Butters, clutching her ruffled ballgown, gaped at them. "What are you doing with this man in my room? On my bed?"

Lady Juliana shoved his chest, and he stepped back, giving her room to climb from the bed. "I am trying to impart the seriousness of my situation to this...man." She scowled at him. "He isn't taking liberties. He's trying to take *my* liberty."

"Don't worry, Miss Butters. There is absolutely nothing untoward going on here," he hastened to add.

For some reason, that only caused Juliana's scowl to deepen.

"Now if you will excuse us, Lady Juliana is going home." He took her elbow, careful not to hurt her but with enough strength she wouldn't be going anywhere but where he willed.

"How can you be so heartless?" the lady in question asked.

"Am I the heartless one?" He nodded at Miss Butters. "You've placed your friend in an untenable position. What do you think will happen to her if you are discovered?"

Miss Butters paled. "My mother would kill me."

"And have you no thought for your brother?" he asked. "The man is out of his mind with worry for your safety." Out of his mind was an exaggeration, but Brogan would take any advantage he could get. "And your father..."

Brogan sniffed. Her father didn't seem concerned his daughter was traipsing about unsupervised. The man did have a lot to answer for in the raising of his children. "Well, if your suspicions about your father are true—"

"All right. I'll go." Lady Juliana pointed to a coat hanging over the back of a chair. "But we have to leave unnoticed. I won't have Hyacinth in trouble for aiding me."

He released her to fetch the coat.

"Thanks, Juliana." Miss Butters blew out a breath, her shoulders sagging. "Of course, you're welcome to stay as long as you need, but..."

"But it would be easier if I left." Lady Juliana gave her friend a smile. "You've done more than I have any right to expect. I can't thank you enough, Hy."

Miss Butters hustled over and gave her friend a kiss on the cheek. "Take care of yourself."

Lady Juliana gave her one more smile before leading Brogan from the room.

He guided them to a back staircase. "She doesn't know of your suspicions."

"That someone is trying to kill my father?" She slid into her coat and buttoned it. "No. Hyacinth is very sweet, and very simple. She wouldn't understand."

"Plus, if you convinced her there was a killer afoot, she might not have allowed you to stay in her room." No girl was that daft.

Lady Juliana sniffed. "She's a *friend*. Of course, she would have let me stay." She turned left at the bottom of the steps, and Brogan took her arm and guided her right.

"Friendship doesn't extend that far," he muttered.

She waited as he peered around the corner of the hallway. "You clearly don't have any true friends if you believe that."

He grunted. This discussion was pointless. He led her toward the kitchen, heard the sounds of a party from within, and switched direction. He found the door to the side garden and pushed it open.

Her feet planted themselves in the entryway, and he practically carried her across the threshold. He gritted his teeth. "*Lady* Juliana—"

"Is that the problem? Do you have so little care for my safety because I have a title in front of my name?" She planted her hands on her hips. "You wouldn't be the first person I've met who despises those of a different rank." A yellow cat circled about her ankles, and she bent to pick the beast up.

The back of his neck prickled. What was she on about? It was the aristos who looked down on his kind, considering them inferior in birth and taste. Was she trying to act the victim with her title? "Your rank has nothing to do with it. This is my job. I only receive payment if I complete it. And I was only pointing out how unladylike you're acting."

He ran his gaze over her. "You don't even look like a

Lady Juliana." Other women of her class wore their fancy clothes like armor, starched and adorned to meet standards only they cared about. Those women wouldn't look him in the eye as Lady Juliana did. Wouldn't deign to argue with someone such as he. If Brogan hadn't recognized the quality of the silk of her gown, he would be hard pressed to think of her as the daughter of an earl.

Lady Juliana looked...touchable.

She looked away, her shimmering eyes catching the moonlight. "Very well, if it's money you care about, I can pay you. To not return me to Bluff Hall. To investigate who is trying to kill my father."

Brogan scraped his palm across his jaw. She didn't give up.

He relented. Somewhat. "When we arrive at your home, I'll speak with your brother again. I'll impress your concerns upon him. You will be safe." And hopefully he could do so in a manner that wouldn't anger the viscount to such a degree he'd leave a bad reference with Brogan's employers.

Juliana buried her face in the cat's fur. "That's a kind offer for you. And I'm sorry."

"Don't be." He took a step closer. "Though you did lead me on a merry chase, this is my job, after all."

She laughed. "That wasn't what I was apologizing for."

He frowned. "Then what?" It wasn't her fault she was irritating, not really. She'd been given free rein her whole life. She'd—

A mass of fur and claws flew at his face.

"Gah!" He caught the cat as it scratched at his throat. It hissed, completely ungrateful that Brogan hadn't just batted the beast aside. "Lady Juliana," he thundered, "you..."

A shimmer of blue silk swished around the corner of the house.

"Son of a bitch." He dropped the cat and ran after the infuriating chit. When he hit the front of the house, he paused, chest heaving.

She was gone.

He turned a circle. Carriages lined the street, awaiting their ball-goers return. A hansom cab slowly wheeled out of sight. A driver tossed his cheroot to the ground.

But no infuriating young lady met his eye.

He clenched his hand. He'd told Wilberforce, the manager of the Bond agency, he'd have her tonight. That he should expect payment from Lord Snowdon in the morning. And now he was returning to the office empty-handed.

Again.

He cracked his knuckles.

When he did find her, he was going to wring Lady Juliana's neck.

Chapter Three

"Thanks, Bertie." Juliana shifted the large screen so it no longer blocked the narrow bed from view. "I truly appreciate you letting me stay here again." Especially as the last time she'd been at his apartments, her father's crazed secretary had roughed him up trying to get to her.

Bertie Huddleson folded a blanket and tossed it on the sofa he'd slept on last night. "After all you've done for me? I owe you my life."

Juliana shook her head. Introducing the set designer to the manager of Covent Gardens when he'd needed employment didn't qualify as life-saving, but theatre people tended to be dramatic.

"What are you going to do, Jules?"

She plopped onto the foot of the bed. "I don't know, but I can't keep hiding." Especially not with Brogan Duffy on her tail. The man would give her no respite. He refused to listen, to even try to understand her side, and there was little she detested more than a closed mind.

"The monthly meeting of the Rose Salon is today." She adjusted the cuff of her gown. She'd left Hyacinth's without any of her clothes, and she was looking a bit wrinkled this morn.

Another reason she didn't resemble a Lady Juliana, she supposed. She sniffed. She knew she didn't have the grace of her peers. The sloping shoulders and delicate cheekbones. The trim waist and deferential attitude. Such things had never mattered to her. They didn't matter to her friends and acquaintances in the societies she belonged to.

But because of Mr. Duffy, for the first time, she wished she had a bit more grace. More beauty. Something to stand out from being the plain daughter of a lessor earl.

"Are you planning on attending?" Bertie's eyebrows drew together. "Your brother might be there."

"Yes." She pulled her slippers from under the bed and slid her feet inside. "I think it's time to speak with Snow. He might think me mad, but in a room full of our acquaintances, he's hardly likely to try to drag me home. I need to convince him that father is still in danger."

And have him call off his dogs. She couldn't very well investigate with Mr. Duffy one step behind.

Bertie rubbed the back of his neck. "Uh, do you want me to come with you? I will if you want me to, you know I will, it's just that..."

"There is someone there you'd rather not face." She stood. "Hiding from him isn't the answer."

"Neither is facing him and getting my heart broken. Again."

"Bertie—"

He jumped to his feet and grabbed her coat. "I know you want me to face my problems head-on, Jules, but I can't. Not now, not with him. The world doesn't always provide the happy endings you think it does."

She pressed her lips together. The world had plenty of happy endings, but they wouldn't come unless a person worked for them. Sitting at home sulking would accomplish nothing.

But Bertie had to lead his own life. One thing she'd learned from her father and brother, no matter how much guidance she provided, men would make their own decisions. Poor as those decisions might be.

"Will you be coming back here after?" he asked.

"I don't know." She chewed on her lip. "It depends on Snow. If I can convince him, he might put me up at our normal London lodgings, if they're available." Unlike many of the aristocracy, her father didn't own a home in the city.

He preferred the country and Bluff Hall, and didn't see the need for the added expense of a London residence.

That, and his banker wouldn't give him a loan to purchase one.

She bussed Bertie's cheek. "I will speak to you later, regardless. Save me a seat at the performance tonight?"

He grinned. "Always."

She hustled out of his rooms and down the uneven staircase. The meeting of the Rose Salon was on the other side of town. The hansom cab dropped her in front of a neat row of townhouses, and she made her way to the one with the blue-checked awning.

She knocked, and the butler opened the door, nodding. "M'lady. Everyone is in the back sitting room."

"Thank you, Mr. Watkins." She handed him her hat and gloves. "Do you know if my brother is arrived?"

"Not yet, m'lady."

She nodded and made her way to the back of the house. A group of fifteen or so attendees lounged on every available seat, glasses of liquor in many hands, lit cheroots in others.

She received a warm chorus of 'Juliana's!' but no one seemed surprised to see her. Which meant Snow had kept her running away quiet. Or else this lot saw nothing remarkable about a daughter of an earl striking out on her own. As eclectic as this group was, either was equally possible.

She poured herself a small drink and sank onto a cleared side table, the tension in her shoulders easing.

This salon had become like a second home. Founded by Rodger Rose, he held monthly meetings discussing anything from his latest poem to politics to philosophy. Her father had encouraged her and Snow to join, wanting them to be exposed to unorthodox ideas and people.

A man with paint-stained fingertips and a glass of green liquid rolled onto his stomach on the carpet. "And I say it's possible. Once we find a way to reach the asteroid, it will take us on a journey through the stars."

Her father had certainly gotten his wish when it came to introducing her to unorthodox people.

She leaned over to the woman next to her and whispered, "What are we discussing?"

"We were talking about the Herschels and which sibling deserved the most credit for their astronomical discoveries, but the discussion has degraded into fantasy."

Rodger Rose twirled his unlit cheroot between his fingers. "We were originally discussing the riots in Stanhope last year. I don't know how we got to space." He frowned. Juliana knew he didn't like when discussions became disorderly. From his expression, this one bordered on being just that.

She bobbed her leg up and down. She'd sent Mr. Rose one of her essays, but he likely hadn't received it yet. Would he enjoy it? Find it shallow and banal?

"Sibling rivalry," another guest, James Masters, said. He gave Juliana a familiar smile, one that used to warm her insides. Now she compared his face to the stern visage of another. The image of Mr. Duffy's set jaw made her stomach flutter. The inquiry agent probably didn't know how to smile.

James crossed one leg over the other. "There were rumors that one of the miner's sisters urged him on to start the rioting, which led to a discussion of other sisters who were trouble for their brothers, which led us here."

"And is it only the sisters who are culpable in these instances?" Juliana asked mildly. "I personally know that brothers can be just as incorrigible."

The room laughed.

"Especially when it's your brother," Mr. Rose said. "Where is Snowdon anyhow? Has he become too good for us now that he's found a new crowd of friends? I haven't seen your father in what feels like ages. Am I to lose the society of the son, as well?"

"His new friends?" Juliana ran a jerky hand over her

hair. She needed to speak with Snow. If he wasn't attending their usual salons, she didn't know how she was to talk to him without going to their home, which was something she very much wanted to avoid. She needed the safety of acquaintances about them when they spoke. Snow wouldn't dare try anything in public, not if his actions would cause a stir.

"I saw him at the Turk's Head Tuesday last when I went for my morning coffee. He was surrounded by an unwashed group of louts, and didn't bother to acknowledge my presence." Rose's voice was all amusement, as though being snubbed by a viscount was a common occurrence.

Which was why Juliana enjoyed the man's company so much. Aside from being brilliant, he truly didn't care a whit how people liked him. His poetry wasn't for the faint of heart, and had made him infamous just as much as famous. But it was his new debate society that Juliana truly admired. As soon as this business with her father was resolved, she would double down on her efforts to be invited onto it.

"It was Wednesday, and I was trying to be kind." Snowdon swept into the room, running a hand through his shaggy, dark hair. "If those blighters had known I was acquainted with *the* Rodger Rose, they would have swarmed you like locusts on wheat. And expected you to buy the next round of coffee and cake."

Her brother's gaze landed on her, and he stilled. "Juliana."

Giving him an even smile, she stood and crossed to him. She kissed his cheek. "Good afternoon, brother. I hope you are well."

A muscle ticked in his jaw. He wrapped his arms around her and crushed her to his chest. "I was so worried."

Feeling too many pairs of curious eyes on them, Juliana grabbed her brother's hand and tugged him to the door. "Do you mind if we use the front sitting room?" she asked Rose. "We'll just be a moment."

The poet waved his hand. "Go, go. Have your secrets.

Perhaps we'll be past talk of traveling the stars by the time you return."

She tugged Snow down the hall and enclosed them in the empty room. She smoothed the stomach of her gown and put some space between her and her brother. Now that she had an audience with Snow, she didn't know where to start. "How are you?"

"How am I?" He fisted his hands on his hips. "How bloody am I? I've been worried sick wondering how my sister fares, or if she was even alive."

"I did write." She narrowed her eyes. "It was most unseemly of you to send out detectives to hunt me down. I'm a grown woman."

"You are my sister, my responsibility." He paced the room. "And after Pickens went mad and attacked you, I wanted you back home, safe where you belong."

"Father is still head of this family," she pointed out.

Snow snorted. "In name only, as you well know. He spends nearly all his time with those damn chickens, leaving me in charge of Bluff Hall."

Juliana chuckled, both at the picture her brother created and at her brother. Their father was inordinately proud of his chickens, though, to his credit, his breeding program had created some fine birds. But for Snow to think he managed Bluff Hall was equally laughable. Their father wasn't the most attentive steward, but he did his duty.

Her brother enjoyed the appearance of his duty rather than the work itself.

"Come home." Snow stepped forward and took her hand. "We've missed you."

"Have you questioned the servants? Made any attempt to discover who wants father dead?"

He shifted his weight. "Come now, Juliana. We've indulged your imagination too long. No one is trying to kill father."

"And Mr. Pickens's attack on me? Just a coincidence, I suppose."

"He was stealing from us," Snow said. "With all your ravings about murderers, he most likely thought you had discovered his thefts. Now that he's in prison, all is well."

Then why did her skin crawl just thinking about returning home? She wasn't one normally subject to flights of fancy. But she also wasn't one to discount her inner convictions.

And her convictions were telling her something was very wrong at Bluff Hall.

"No." She rubbed her arm. "I'll continue staying with friends." Hopefully out in the open. No more hiding in bedrooms. "Now, about this detective—"

"You're coming home, Juliana." Her usually easy brother's face was drawn in stern lines. He strode to her and took her arm. "No more nonsense. Come along."

She sputtered as he propelled her forward. "What are you doing? Unhand me this instant."

The door swung open. James peered in, a frown creasing his face. "Is everything all right, Juliana? We've started discussing Mrs. Siddons. I know how you enjoy her performances."

Snow loosened his grip on her arm. "Everything is fine. Juliana isn't feeling well and I'm taking her home."

She pulled free. "I'm feeling much better. Hyacinth's family will see me home when I'm ready to return." She gave the men a bright smile, knowing Snow wouldn't want to cause a scene. "I'll be home when the diversions of London have ceased to entertain me. Goodbye, Snow. James. It was lovely to see you again." And she flew from the room.

"Juliana!" her brother called.

The low voice of James followed her down the hall. "Snowdon, now that I have you, I've been meaning to ask..."

She gathered her hat and coat and hurried from the townhouse. She owed James a gift for that bit of diversion. He'd always been able to read situations and people well.

She hailed a cab. She used to think she was good at reading people, too. Unconventional though it was, she'd thought her brother considered her his equal. A confidante, a friend.

Not someone he could order home like a dog.

But Snow wasn't a man who stood on principle. For him, the means justified the ends. And if he truly feared for her safety, perhaps his heavy-handedness could be excused.

But his refusal to see the danger their father was in bordered on unforgiveable. If their father scoffed at his near-death events, and her brother refused to acknowledge them, then it was solely down to her to catch a killer.

And for once in her life, Juliana didn't know if she was up to the task.

Chapter Four

Brogan's knife whisked over the bit of silver birch in his hand. The blade caught the Bond offices' lamplight, a subtle flash every time he scraped downwards. He didn't know what form would appear from this carving; the wood hadn't told him yet.

Two fellow agents laughed from their desks in the corner of the open main office. *They'd* just concluded their latest case, successfully he might add. Their laughter was most likely over him, his failure in capturing one small, strange woman.

A pair of scuffed boots entered his field of vision. Brogan looked up, into his boss's face. He nodded. "Wil."

Wilberforce, the manager of the agency, looked at the hunk of wood in Brogan's hands, at the row of carved figures lining the edge of his desk, and raised an eyebrow. "I didn't realize we had so little to occupy you that you turned to whittling."

"Helps me think."

Wil nodded. He grabbed a nearby chair and pulled it up to Brogan's desk, his left foot dragging slightly with each step. The manager had never told Brogan how he had been injured to suffer the limp.

And Brogan had never asked.

"We've had another message from Lord Snowdon," Wil said. "He's in London. He saw his sister at some philosophical meeting at a Mr. Rodger Rose's home, but she ran again."

After making an obscene amount of money writing frilly

poems, Rodger Rose had turned to more intellectual pursuits, creating a salon for open conversation in many fields. As uninterested in the lives of the Beau Monde as Brogan was, even he knew of the man's influence. "Did Snowdon know she was a member of the Rose Salon?"

Wil ran a hand through his black hair. "Apparently they're both members."

"And he didn't think to tell us this when we asked about her interests?" Brogan snorted and tossed his wood and blade on his desk. "Does he still want us to bring her home?" His gut swirled. If the agency lost this job because he was too slow to get his woman, that could be the end of his employment.

He stretched his right hand, feeling each ache from the lesson he'd had to give a man that afternoon. If he lost this job, his hands would be feeling a lot more pain. He'd have to go back to boxing.

"Yes." Wil picked up the swan he'd carved last week. "His note was adamant. He wants her home."

Brogan nodded. That was good. He still had a chance to redeem himself. He drummed his fingers on his thigh. So why were his insides still twisting about like eels in a bucket? "The sister..."

"Lady Juliana? What of her?"

"Could there be a valid reason she shouldn't return home?" He flexed his hand again. "There's something about the brother I don't like."

Wil stared at the scrapes on Brogan's hand. "He's a jackanape, but his concern for his sister seems genuine. It isn't safe for a girl to be wandering about London alone."

"At two and twenty, she is no longer a girl." He shifted in his chair. Her bosom was exceptionally womanly, and he pushed thoughts of it pressed against him out of his mind. "But, I agree, ladies have no place on the streets. Especially this one."

Wil rested his elbows on his knees. "Why do you say that?"

"She still believes someone is after her father." He shook his head. "Part of her is scared, but part of her sees this as a game. She's a spoiled, rich girl playing at intrigue." He could see it in her eyes. A hint of excitement lit them up, turning the drab brown to a beautiful mahogany.

"Her father isn't wealthy. Not for an earl. Summerset was surprised the family hired us."

Brogan arched an eyebrow. Most gentlemen would be considered lower class compared to Lord Summerset, one of the founders of the Bond Agency. Brogan didn't know if he trusted Summerset's judgment on who was wealthy or not.

"All right," Wil conceded. "Compared to our kind, she's got blunt." He rubbed his chin. "But just because she's playing at intrigue doesn't mean intrigue doesn't exist. That secretary did come after her."

"The magistrate found that the man was trying to hide his thieving from being discovered. There is no deeper conspiracy." But still, something about this didn't feel settled. "She has reached the age of majority. If she doesn't want to return home, do we have the right to force her?"

Wil blinked. "She's an unmarried lady. If she decides to live apart from her family, it would be a serious act of rebellion. She would be cast out of society. Besides, how would she support herself?"

"This woman would find a way," Brogan grumbled. "The way she talks, she could convince Prinny himself to give her a job."

Wil stilled. "When did you speak with her?"

Brogan's shoulders drew toward his ears. Damn. This was why it was better to remain silent. Words only caused trouble. "I had her." He cleared his throat. "Last night." He waited for his employer's reprimand. He'd had a small, helpless gentlewoman in his grasp, and she'd escaped. It was too humiliating. When he could stand the silence no more, he added, "She's damned slippery."

The edges of Wil's eyes crinkled, but his mouth

remained flat. "Ah. Well, any plans to catch her again?"

Brogan picked up his knife and sheathed it. He shoved it in his pocket. "Yes. Tonight. I have Samson watching a house for me." Samson was the agency's errand boy. Wil had found him in the streets and taken him in, and so far the boy's transition from petty thief to general lackey seemed successful.

Brogan stood and reached for his coat on the back of his chair. It was time he relieved the boy. He had been fortunate Samson had been available so Brogan could take care of his own family business.

He flexed his hand again. "I'd best get going. Can I use the office tonight?"

Wil's forehead furrowed. "Of course. Why?"

"It will be too late to leave for Bluff Hall, and I can't take Lady Juliana to my place or a hotel."

"She can use the cot in my office." Wil pushed out of the chair. "And when you drop her off, make sure to get payment upon delivery. I don't trust Lord Snowdon's credit."

Brogan nodded as he shrugged into his coat. His first case as primary investigator was coming to an end. It hadn't gone as smoothly as he'd hoped. The satisfaction he'd expected to feel wasn't there. But he wasn't going to be the only one who was disgruntled. Lady Juliana would be none too happy come tonight.

But she'd put herself into this situation. She'd have to deal with the consequences of her actions, just like everybody else.

Chapter Five

Juliana leaned forward, peering at the stage. "Is that Miss DuBois in the breeches role?" she whispered. Their seats, the last row in the house, were far unlike her usual in a box near the stage. She wondered if it was even worth watching *The Country Girl* from such a distance. But as a set designer for Covent Garden, Bertie could only take what spots were left available.

"Yes, she joined our theatre but recently." He sighed. "She's marvelous. And delightfully wicked. She entertained us all with lines from the original play, *The Country Wife.* Absolutely scandalous. No wonder it's been banned."

Hmpf. Juliana settled back. Fortunately for her, her father disagreed with the government's enforced morality laws as much as she, so she'd had access to the original play to read it for herself. Still, it would have been nice to be able to see it performed. If she could see anything from such a distance.

"How did you fare this afternoon?" Bertie asked. "Did your brother see reason?"

Juliana gave her neighbor an apologetic look. She lowered her voice, hoping Bertie would follow suit. Since he worked in the theatre, he didn't seem to hold its customs, like keeping quiet during a performance, in the same regard. "Of course, he didn't see reason. This is Snow. Once he has something in his head, he doesn't let it go. And he has it in his head that I should be home."

Damned, infuriating man. Treating her like a child. She crossed her arms over her chest and glared at the stage. The actors were but fuzzy blurs. Perhaps it was time to look into those spectacles her father nudged her about.

Bertie patted her knee. "Well, you can stay with me as long as you want." He shifted and snatched his hand away. "Don't look now, but we have our own audience."

Juliana craned her neck about. "Who? Where?"

"I said don't..." He sighed. "Two rows down, ten seats to the left. The man who is glaring positive daggers at me. Though I do say, he looks handsome angry."

She looked where he indicated, her breath stalling in her lungs when her gaze clashed with Mr. Duffy's. "How on earth did he find me?" she said, then winced as her neighbor glared at her. She lowered her voice to a whisper again. "I have to get out of here, Bertie. Cause a distraction."

He dipped his chin. "I'm not that type of friend, Jules. Besides, the play is enough of a distraction. Wait until the interval and slip out with the crowd then. Though why you want to get away from that man, I don't know."

She slid down in her seat, hoping to disappear from sight. Or at least from *his* sight. His glare did funny things to her stomach. Things she attributed to fear of being caught and sent back to Bluff Hall, but worried might actually be from another cause.

She wouldn't be attracted to Mr. Brogan Duffy. Yes, he was handsome in a blunt sort of way. And if her father wasn't in danger, if her independence wasn't at risk, then the idea of him pursuing and catching her for a whole other purpose could be...diverting.

But her father *was* in trouble. She *was* vulnerable to having her agency stolen away. And having been raised by a father who'd told her she could do anything her male counterparts could, that thought was particularly intolerable.

As soon as the lights went up, she pushed her way down her aisle, in the opposite direction of Mr. Duffy.

She didn't see him in the crowd of theatre-goers surging for refreshments in the lobby, no matter how often she peered behind her.

But she could feel him.

Tracking her.

Hunting her.

And even though she didn't want it, a small kernel of excitement blossomed in her chest. It was with something almost like regret that she burst through the front doors of Covent Garden, like a cork from a bottle of champagne, and waved down a hansom cab.

The driver stopped. He raised his eyebrows in surprise, but tipped his cap at the solo female just the same.

She climbed inside and blew out a breath. As exciting as Mr. Duffy proved himself to be, he had left her in a bit of a pickle. He'd seen her with Bertie; she couldn't spend the night at her friend's apartments. Where should she go? What were—

The door sprung open just as the cab started to move. Mr. Duffy clambered inside, his face an emotionless mask, and slammed the door behind him.

He settled next to her, facing forward, saying nothing.

Juliana twisted her fingers around her pocket-book. Her skin went clammy, then hot.

"Where to?" the driver called down to them.

She bit her lip, sliding Mr. Duffy a sideways glance. Even if he wasn't here, she'd be hard-pressed to answer that question. But his answer would be worse than anything she could come up with.

She opened her mouth, but Mr. Duffy cut her off. "Vincent Street. A block north of St. Mary's."

The address wasn't familiar. It definitely wasn't her family's usual London lodgings. "Where are we going?"

He grunted.

"How did you find me?"

"I followed you from Mr. Huddleson's home." He glanced at her from the corner of his eye. "You don't have that many friends."

"I have plenty of friends!" Her face flushed. But most of

them were also Snow's friends.

She glanced at the door opposite.

Mr. Duffy gripped her elbow. "Don't even think of it."

"Jump from a moving cab?" She sniffed. "I wouldn't dream of it."

He arched an eyebrow.

She grumbled. Well, she wouldn't think of it, not when he held her arm so tightly. "I could always scream," she said.

"You could," he agreed. "Why haven't you?"

She chewed on her lower lip. She didn't think she'd ever screamed in her life, not a full-throated help-I'm-being-murdered kind of scream. She didn't know if she could force the sound from her throat, not without feeling foolish. "Would it be effective?"

He snorted. "Definitely not."

She lifted her hand, palm up. "Well, there you have it." She cleared her throat. "Besides, I spoke with my brother just this afternoon. He's in London, wouldn't you know. We've reconciled our differences. You don't have to return me home any longer."

He chuckled, the sound grim. "You slipped away from him, too. That explains why he contacted the agency, demanding we double-down on our efforts."

Juliana's jaw dropped. Why, that little... "He's always been a bothersome brother."

"Of that, I have no doubt."

She turned to face him. "How much will it take for you to release me? I can't go home."

"Yet home is where you belong." His fingers tightened. "A single woman roaming the streets of London by herself isn't safe."

She clenched her hands into fists. "I am quite accustomed to being in Town by myself. My father encourages my independence." Except when it contravened her brother's wishes, it seemed. Her father wanted Snow to take on more responsibilities so he'd be prepared for the time when he was master of Bluff Hall. She even agreed that her brother could use the practice.

But her father's allowing Snow to call her home like an errant dog still burned like betrayal.

Mr. Duffy sighed. "I realize you are used to having your own way. Your father has been most...lenient with your upbringing. Perhaps it is right that your brother is stepping in where your father has been lax."

She jerked her elbow from his grip. Heat rose from her chest, up her throat to her face. "It always amazes me," she said coldly, "how the working class so readily adopts the faux morality of the nobility. One would think, with all the injustice levied upon you by the elite, you would be eager to rebel against their silly norms."

He turned in his seat to face her, but she refused to look at him. "And I would think that a woman brought up in privilege and rank would be more sensible of her good fortune. No one gets everything they want in life, and having a titled father, money, and an education seems more than enough compensation for a minor restriction on your liberty. Having family who wish to protect you hardly seems a trade-off at all."

She gaped. That was more than she'd ever heard him speak in one sitting. When he found a topic he liked, apparently, he felt free to expound upon it. And discussing her lack of gratitude was obviously a topic he enjoyed.

"You think me spoiled."

He shrugged.

Her eyes flew wide. *Of all the nerve.* She turned her back on him, planting her shoulder into the seat and staring out her window. How much wealth would he accept in trade for his independence? Men like him took their liberty for granted, thinking nothing of walking to the market alone, of sitting down to a nice bit of pastry in a coffeehouse as they read the paper.

But she was looked upon as spoiled for wanting the same freedoms. "I will only leave again. You might be able to bring me home, but you can't keep me there."

"Delivery is my job. Keeping you there is your brother's."

She spun back to face him. "You would have me held prisoner?"

He winced. "You're as dramatic as that play we just left. It's natural for a brother to want his sister safe at home. How you two arrange your lives is a concern only for your family. I'm not a part of it."

"As you're the means effecting my unwilling return, you are a great part of it."

He remained silent.

Juliana bit make a scream of frustration. There were times she hated being a woman.

Mr. Duffy sighed. "When we arrive at Bluff Hall, I'll speak to your father, make sure your brother is not exceeding his authority."

"How kind of you," she bit out. "And perhaps while you're there you could try to discover who wants my father dead. You are receiving a fine sum of money from my family; it would be nice if you did something useful to earn it."

The coach rolled to a stop. "We're 'ere," the cabbie called down.

Juliana pushed open the door and hopped down, trying to figure out where 'here' was. If she had any chance of escape tonight, she needed to know her environs.

They were in a business district. A block down, the spires of a church rose into the inky night. A church she recognized. "Are we near Bowker Street?"

He jutted his chin west. "A block over." Taking her elbow again, he guided her into the three-story building before them. "We'll spend the night at the Bond Agency's offices. I'll take you home in the morning."

A night in his offices. She glanced at the large hand gently cupping her arm. At the muscled body attached to that hand.

A lot could happen in a night. A lot of ways for her to slip free.

Mr. Brogan Duffy thought her spoiled and entitled. A selfish woman, thinking only of her own pleasures.

She could work with that.

He opened a door, his wide shoulders blocking out the lights from the window. He lit an oil lamp, and those broad shoulders became clearly defined, narrowing into a trim waist, supported by muscled thighs.

She repressed the smile that wanted to curl her lips.

She could work very well with that indeed.

Chapter Six

Brogan fluffed the thin pillow as best he could before tossing it on the cot in the corner of Wil's office. The accommodations were surely not to Lady Juliana's liking, but the woman would have to make do. He couldn't take her to his apartments; his neighbors would speak of nothing else for a month at least.

And he wasn't letting her out of his sight until she was safely back home.

"A blanket's there," he pointed to a chest next to the cot, "and there's a pitcher of water in the main office. 'Night."

Juliana stopped him with a hand on his arm. "Where will you sleep?"

He nodded through the door to the main room. The owners of the agency and Wil had separate rooms as their offices, but Brogan enjoyed sharing the large room with the other investigators. They tossed around ideas and theories on current cases with one another, laughed over absurd clients. For someone used to more solitary work, the brotherhood was a welcome surprise.

"I'll be at my desk," he said. "Good night."

He stepped through the doorway, and she stopped him again. "Can you help me with my gown?" Juliana bit her lip and looked at the floor. "I don't want it wrinkled by sleeping in it."

His abdomen tensed. What she said only made sense, but he didn't trust her new docility.

Nor did he trust his ability to keep his eyes from roaming.

"Or course." He motioned for her to turn around, give him her back. He'd had years of training, of self-discipline. One half-naked woman wasn't enough to make him lose his good sense. He'd make sure of it.

The elegant knot in her hair covered the top button. He brushed it aside, ignoring the silkiness of the strands, trying not to wonder what else on this woman would feel as soft. He pushed the pearl button through its hole. The gown sagged off one shoulder as he worked his way down her back. He kept his gaze off the expanse of skin he was revealing and focused on not tearing any of the buttons from the silly gown. Why did any garment need so many buttons? It was absurd. It was as if it were designed for the sole purpose of teasing a man, delaying his pleasure in seeing his prize, tempting him to follow the trail to its happy conclusion.

The last button rested just above the curve of her arse. A very fine, plump arse.

"Done." He stared at the far wall, willing every muscle in his body to stand down. "Sleep well." He stomped towards his desk.

"My stays..." she called from the doorway.

"Are not my problem." He built a fire, poking at the logs with unnecessary force. Women. Did she actually think she could seduce him into betraying his duty? He glared at the flames.

"It's too cold in there."

Brogan started. In her bare feet, he hadn't heard the dratted woman follow him into the main office.

Juliana stood before him, a blanket wrapped around her shoulders but dipping low enough in front for him to see the curve of her breasts over her chemise. Her long hair hung down her back, looking sexily tousled.

Apparently, she did think she could seduce him.

He sighed. "You can wear my greatcoat."

"But then you'll be cold."

"I'll stay by the fire."

"Can't I be by the fire, as well?" She shivered, her blanket dropping another inch. "Perhaps move the cot out here?"

Brogan pressed his lips tight. Unable to think of a reason to deny her request, he tramped back into Wil's office and hefted the cot over his head. He dropped it down in front of the fire with a growl. "Now will you sleep?"

"Of course." Sliding the blanket off her shoulders, she draped it over the cot.

Leaving her in nothing but her chemise.

The fire flickered behind her, illuminating the thin garment. The curves of her body were on full display behind the gossamer fabric, leaving little to his imagination.

He swallowed.

She didn't have the best body he'd ever seen, her waist a bit too thick to give her the sought-after hourglass shape, her hips a bit too wide for fashion.

But she was soft and feminine and it had been a long time since Brogan had lost himself between a woman's thighs.

He turned, cursing pampered, preening young misses who thought the world owed them whatever their hearts desired.

She pressed against his back, those curves feeling nothing less than perfect. "I'm sorry, Mr. Duffy, do I make you uncomfortable? I'd be happy to spend the night back at Bertie's if that would be easier for you."

He snorted. "Very generous of you. No, we'll both stay right here. You in your cot, me at my desk."

She heaved a deep breath, her breasts sliding against his back. "As you like." Her heat dissipated. "These are lovely. Did you make them?"

He turned. She held his whittled swan. He strode to his desk and took it from her hand, placing it back in its spot. "Yes." He pulled his work in progress from his pocket and added it to the line of figurines. He'd learned his lesson one too many times falling asleep with a hard piece of wood so close to his bollocks.

"What do you do with them?" She picked up the swan again, running her finger along its smooth back.

"I'll paint that one and give it to my sister." He gripped the back of his neck, not liking how she stroked the wood. It gave him inappropriate ideas. "She's ten. She likes that sort of thing."

"Any other siblings?"

"Another sister." The trouble-maker. "She's nineteen." His hands twitched to grab something, so he took the whittling from her again and placed it back down. "Now go to bed."

"If you wish." She clasped her hands behind her back, making her bosom rise. "Though, if this is to be my last night of freedom, I'd have no qualms about making it a memorable one."

He dragged his gaze to her face. He barked out a laugh. "You're that forward with your favors, are you? Do you think I'm stupid? You see a banged-up ex-boxer and think I don't have a brain in my head?"

It was what most people thought when they saw him. The broken nose that hadn't healed straight. The thick shoulders and short neck. He was a bruiser. A brute. Men like him weren't supposed to think, only take orders. It was why he still couldn't believe the Bond Agency had hired him as an investigator. He'd applied, expecting nothing more than an enforcer position. But Wil and the owners had seen past his appearance. And he wasn't going to let them down by tupping what might be the sweetest pussy ever offered to him.

"Do you think I don't see through you as easily as I do this bit of linen?" He fingered the strap of her chemise, the backs of his fingers brushing against her collar bone.

She opened her mouth, shut it. "I...I don't think that."

"'Course not." He huffed. "My size and crooked nose must have reminded you of your men in those philosophical societies."

Juliana tilted her chin. "You're a very handsome man, Brogan Duffy. Surely you're used to a woman's interest."

He rubbed his thumb over her shoulder. How far would she play this game? Not all the way, surely. Not the daughter of an earl.

He stepped close. The scent of lavender teased his nose. He should play along. He lowered his head, their mouths inches apart. See how far she'd go. She obviously thought a man used his smaller head to make decisions, and it would be a great pleasure to have her then disabuse her of that notion.

She stared at his mouth, her breaths growing short.

He closed the distance another inch. He should give this proper young miss something scandalous to write about in her journal. Show her how a working man fucked, what she would be missing with those bloodless toffs.

She leaned into him, her belly nestling against his hardening cock.

It was so tempting. *She* was that tempting. With her soft skin and glistening eyes. Her set shoulders and determined airs. He enjoyed the feel of her body against his for one more moment, then stepped back, putting distance between them.

"Go to bed." He strode to the main exit and pulled a desk in front of the door. There'd be no sneaking off while he got some sleep. He dropped into his chair, crossed his arms over his chest, and gave the vixen one last glare. Dipping his chin, he closed his eyes.

Tomorrow couldn't come soon enough. His first case was at a close. It had a successful resolution. He should be happy.

He slitted his eyes open, watching as Lady Juliana lay down with her back to him, her shoulders hard under the blanket.

Why the hell wasn't he feeling happy?

Chapter Seven

Brogan gave Lady Juliana's elbow a slight tug, drawing her over the threshold of Bluff Hall. The infernal woman hadn't said one word to him all six hours of the drive to her home, although he was becoming quite adept at reading her glares.

The squinty-eyed glare was for when she was particularly irritated with one of his suggestions. The glare with the arched right eyebrow expressed just how inferior the inn he'd taken her to for nuncheon had been. And the glare accompanied by a small huff showed when she clearly thought him an idiot.

As frustrating as all those glares had been, he rather wished she would turn one on him now. The slight shudder that wracked her body as she stood in the entry was most disconcerting. Reasonable or not, Lady Juliana's fear was real.

"Jules!" Her brother hurried forwards, arms outstretched. "Finally, you're here. I'm glad I decided to quit London yesterday so I am able to greet you."

She lifted her cheek for his kiss even as she ground her jaw. "Snow. After yesterday's disagreement, I'm surprised you are happy to see me."

Snowdon flapped his hand. "A trifling soon forgotten. Although I should be angry for all the trouble you put me through. But now that you're back you can have a talk with Mrs. Bailey. I keep telling her I don't want my potatoes creamed. I want them mashed. She doesn't listen to me." The viscount turned to Brogan. "Do you take your payment now? I can draft a bank note."

Brogan removed his hat and finger-combed his hair back. "Yes, now is good. But there is something else I need speak to you about."

"Of course." Looping his arm through his sister's, Snowdon turned and led the way down a corridor.

Bluff Hall was a comfortable home. Far grander than any house Brogan had ever lived in, but nothing to the magnificence of Lord Summerset's or the Duke of Montague's homes. He'd been sent on errands for those owners of the Bond Agency, and their houses had made him near speechless. The furniture here, in comparison, was comfortably worn; the floors scuffed. While far from a pauper, Lord Withington's estate was modest compared to most in the ton.

Snowdon pushed a door open into a sun-filled room. "Have a seat in my office and we can discuss what you will."

Juliana jerked her arm free. "You mean father's office. Where is he?"

"Gone this morning with Rodger Rose up to his home for a month or so." Her brother dropped in the chair behind the cluttered desk. "Rose travelled to Bluff Hall with me yesterday."

"Mr. Rose is a family friend," Juliana explained to Brogan. "He lives in Leeds." She turned to Snow. "I'm glad. Father should be safe there."

"Oh, bother." The viscount rolled his eyes. "Not that nonsense again. No one is trying to harm Father. I for one can't wait for him to return. He's left me with a bothersome amount of business to manage." He poked at a stack of correspondence. "It's dreadfully dull."

Brogan settled in the chair across from Snowdon. "Why don't you think your father could be in danger? His secretary is in prison for attacking your sister."

Snowdon smiled tightly. "Jules, I know cook is baking some of those buns you like as I just stole one myself. Why don't you go get one? It will give you a chance to talk to her about my potatoes."

"Meaning you want me out of the room for this discussion." She shifted her weight between her feet. "Because I'm hungry, I'll allow it."

She wouldn't be hungry if she'd eaten her nuncheon. Apparently, a ploughman's lunch wasn't good enough for her. Still, it was with some regret that he watched her stalk from the room. Even with her quirks, she was the pleasanter of the siblings.

He turned back to face her brother. The man scratched at the soft pouch of skin beneath his chin then examined whatever had come off on his nail.

And far easier to look at.

"Your sister has raised concerns about her safety. What are you doing to address them?"

"Address them?" Snowdon blinked. "Why should I address them? They are naught but flights of fancy on her part. She always was the romantic. Father never should have let her read her gothic novels."

"Have you questioned your servants? Found out if the secretary, Pickens, had any accomplices?"

The viscount sighed. "Pickens was a greedy, little man who got what was coming to him. The rest of our servants were horrified that not only would he steal from us, but then go after Jules to silence her. I can assure you, there are no other traitors here."

Brogan stood. "You won't mind if I ask around." He didn't make it a question. Lord Snowdon was a careless man who did nothing he didn't have to. Before Brogan left, he would be satisfied there was no danger at Bluff Hall.

"Well, I don't—"

"Thanks. I'll be back for that bank note." And ignoring the other man's sputters, Brogan strode from the room. From the cook he discovered that there were only four servants, not counting herself. Two maids, and two men who took care of the animals and acted as footmen. The lord hadn't yet hired a new secretary.

He also discovered that her buns were, in fact, delicious. So good he wondered that Juliana wasn't still down here eating them up.

The maids seemed like good lasses, happy in their employment. One of the men was soon to be married and needed the job. The other just seemed bored, content to do as he was told but taking on no extra work.

All in all, no one who would have a motive to harm their master.

Brogan stood on the front lawn, staring up at the second story windows. Juliana's bedroom was up there. He should probably ask to speak to her, tell her what he'd found. Nothing.

Instead, he turned his feet toward the agency's carriage.

His driver stretched from his spot underneath a willow tree and lumbered over. "Off to London, sir?"

"Yes." Brogan looked back at Bluff Hall. The sun glinted off the front windows. Ivy climbed up the white walls. All in all, a cheerful picture.

A sliver of dread wedged in his gut.

He sniffed. It was Lady Juliana's doing, filling his mind with unfounded suspicions. Yanking open the carriage door, he climbed inside, slamming it behind him.

He pounded on the ceiling, eager to be away. He'd done his job, and kept his promise to the lady. He had nothing to feel badly for.

He stretched his legs out, kicking the blanket-wrapped bundle underneath the seat opposite.

"Ouch!" The bundle shifted.

Brogan's stomach twisted. He bent over and yanked the edge of the blanket toward him.

Dark hair spilled across the floor. Juliana pushed a hank off her face and peered up at him, blinking.

"Good afternoon," she said, with the dignity of a princess instead of the stowaway she was. "I don't suppose I could have a ride back to London?"

* * *

His face went grim, or at least grimmer than usual. He clenched his hand, and for a moment, Juliana thought he would pound the ceiling, order the carriage to turn around.

But Brogan Duffy sat back in his seat and merely said, "Explain," through clenched teeth.

She kicked her way free of the carriage blanket and crawled from her hidey-hole. Truly, her actions should be self-explanatory. Mr. Duffy knew she did not wish to spend even one night at Bluff Hall, and this was her way of escaping. But instead of an explanation, what Duffy needed was a *reason*. A reason he shouldn't turn her out of his carriage this instant.

She settled herself across from him, smoothing hair back away from her face and shaking out the wrinkles in her gown. "You have completed your job." She gave him what she hoped was an encouraging smile. From the way the corners of his mouth drew down further, it didn't have the effect she'd hoped it would. "You safely delivered me home. There was nothing in your contract about ensuring I remained at home, though. Was there?"

After a tense moment, he shook his head.

She spread her hands wide. "There. You have done your duty and received compensation, and now you are free to escort me back to London. A mutually satisfactory outcome. Besides..."

He narrowed his eyes. "Besides what?"

She ran her palm over the carriage seat. The leather was cool and soothing against her skin. "As soon as I stepped through the front doors, the walls of Bluff Hall started to close in upon me. It felt suffocating. Something isn't right in that house. I don't want to be there." And she loved that house. Loved her comfortable rooms, her stacks of books next to her window seat. But the past few months had transformed that love into dread.

She swallowed. "And now that my father has gone, I don't even have to feel guilty about leaving."

Brogan's face softened. "It's not your job to protect your

father. You have nothing to feel guilty for."

She nodded, but inside, she knew. She should have stayed with her father. She'd let fear sway her judgment. Convinced herself she would have a better chance discovering who was behind the attacks when she wasn't under threat herself.

All her hopes and dreams for being a shining light, someone people respected, a notable philosopher her peers looked to for guidance, and she'd failed at her very first trial. Her heart thudded dully in her chest. How could she effect change to help cure society's ills when she couldn't even help her family?

She lifted her chin. All she could do was move forward. Do better. And in order for that to happen, she needed to be free. "My brother most likely feels in his gut that something isn't right, as well. It makes sense that he'd want to have me home. He thinks home equals safety." And she wouldn't be able to convince him he was wrong.

"So when he contacts the agency again to search for you?"

She raised a shoulder. "Tell him you've already performed that investigation and wish to move on to more interesting endeavors. You are under no obligation to take on every enquiry you receive." But perhaps he'd be willing to take on what, in her mind, was an investigation much more compelling. She didn't have a lot of ready money, but when she uncovered the plot against her father, she was certain he would pay the expense that saved his life.

"I don't take the cases." Brogan crossed his arms over his wide chest. "The owners of the agency and the manager make the contracts. I fulfill them."

She nibbled on her bottom lip. Yes, the owners. She, along with the rest of society, had heard when the five noblemen, the Duke of Montague, the Earls of Summerset and Rothchild, the Marquess of Dunkeld, and the Baron of Sutton, had formed their agency for discreet inquiries. Such an enterprise had been quite the *on dit* for a fortnight at least. Matrons had sniffed with disdain at aristocracy sullying themselves in a trade. Gentlemen had laughed at the very idea.

But secretly, they'd all been jealous. Jealous of the nerve and adventure such an undertaking represented. Such men as who would create such an agency would have to be open to hearing her pleas. She should have begged for an interview with them before, shown them that the case they should be taking was hers.

Yes, she would throw herself on the mercy of the owners. Her brother wasn't well-respected in society. She should be able to convince them hers was the better case to accept.

Although it would be a merry-go-round of easy money to work for Snow. She'd run from home; they'd pick her up and deliver her back. Run, catch, get paid. Run, catch, get paid. She grew dizzy at the very thought.

It would also leave her little time to uncover the plot against her father.

She drew her shoulders back. She would just have to be convincing. "When we return to London, we'll go to your office and I'll speak with one of the owners. Ask him to investigate my case instead of my brother's."

Duffy angled his body and kicked a muddy boot onto the seat next to her. "The owners don't spend much time in the office. Only involve themselves in cases they think will be interesting."

Her case was infinitely interesting. Of course, the owners would want—

"You can talk to Wilberforce. The manager. He'll make the decision." Duffy tugged the brim of his hat low over his eyes as he settled into the corner of the carriage. "Don't get your hopes up. Even I can see it would be a conflict of interest taking your case."

And with that, he ignored her for the rest of the journey, napping with the innocence of a babe. As though a man's life, her father's, didn't hang in the balance.

Juliana crossed her own arms, glaring at the man. She tucked the blanket around his boot, making sure his mud didn't dirty her skirts.

She was good at debate, one reason she was so eager to join Rose's debate society. She'd managed to convince this lout not to turn her out of his carriage, after all. She'd convince this manager to take on her case.

She had to.

Because she was running out of ideas. As varied as her education had been, nothing had taught her how to investigate attempted murders. For a woman who prided herself on her ingenuity, she had been running dangerously low on new avenues to explore. Hiring professionals might be her only chance.

Duffy let out a low snore.

Even if said professional was an aggravating, impertinent beast of a man.

Chapter Eight

Her second visit to the offices of the Bond Agency didn't improve her impression of it. Yes, the furniture was all well-made and expensive, and the layout efficient, but the rooms were much too dark, too masculine, to be truly welcoming. The light brown walls did nothing to brighten the aged mahogany floors. Even the light streaming in from the curtainless windows didn't alleviate the office's severity, although that could be because the sun was near to setting.

And the gloomy feeling might be all inside Juliana.

"But don't you see," she explained to the taciturn man who managed the agency. "Your employment with my brother ended when Mr. Duffy returned me home. Now you are quite free to work for me."

Mr. Wilberforce scraped his palm across his jaw. His eyes, a lovely grey-green color, narrowed. "It seems a bit of a conflict of interest, if you ask me."

Yes, one that Juliana hoped to exploit. After all, if she were a client of the Bond Agency then they couldn't very well accept another job from her brother to find her.

"Does accepting an investigation put you under a lifetime commitment to Snowdon?" She glanced at Brogan, but there was no help to be found from that quarter.

After escorting her into the offices, pushing her in the direction of the manager, he'd plopped his rear end on the edge of his desk, picked up a bit of wood, and started whittling. He'd become a spectator to the debate, watching as she pleaded for her father's life with seeming disinterest.

"Well, no—" Wilberforce began.

"And wouldn't you agree that the circumstances surrounding my father's supposed accidents are strange? Deserving of further investigation?"

"His secretary—"

"Might very well be one of the culprits, but who paid him?" Juliana paced to the window and back. "If it was merely about his stealing from my father, then he wouldn't have made attempts on my father's life. Killing my father wouldn't profit him. He'd lose his position and any access to my father's funds."

"But if your father suspected him of the thefts, killing him might keep Pickens out of prison." Wilberforce looked at a longcase clock against the wall and frowned. "That's a strong mot—"

She whirled on him. "But my father didn't suspect! No one thought anything amiss but me. It makes no sense that Mr. Pickens would try to kill him, not if his only crime was robbery. But if someone paid him to hurt my father..." She raised her hands, palms up. "Then it all makes sense."

Wilberforce exhaled noisily. "You and I have differing ideas on what makes sense. Have there— let me finish," he said as she opened her mouth. "Have there been any recent attempts on his life, or accidents that threatened him?"

"No." She chewed on her bottom lip. "But he is not at home now. He's visiting a friend up north."

"He just left this morning," Brogan pointed out. When she glared at him, he rolled his eyes. "But it could make sense for the perpetrator to wait until all suspicions had died down." He cocked his head. "With the fuss Lady Juliana has been kicking up about threats to her father, it would be irrational to strike against him so soon."

She beamed at him gratefully. Finally, some support.

He pressed his lips tight and refocused on his whittling, looking for all the world like he regretted speaking.

But she wouldn't let him take it back. "Exactly. This plot didn't begin with Mr. Pickens. He was merely a tool. There is someone out there who still wishes harm on my father, and I intend to find out who." She clasped her hands in front of her. "I hope you will assist me in discovering the truth."

"What a pretty sentiment." A man dressed all in black stepped from one of the back offices. His nutmeg hair was cropped fashionably close and his bearing was elegant. "Discovering the truth. Some truths, however, don't want to be uncovered. Some truths are ugly and better left buried."

Wilberforce glanced at the clock again. "Lady Juliana, this is the Earl of Rothchild, one of the owners of this agency. Rothchild, the Lady Juliana Wickham. She was the...object of one of our investigations."

Juliana approved of the past tense in the manager's statement. "Yes, and now that that case is over, I was hoping to employ your agency myself."

"So I heard." The earl's gaze drifted to Brogan. "You think her claims merit investigation?"

He stood. "Perhaps."

She gritted her teeth. "I don't know if you've met my father, Lord Withington, but he needs your help," she implored the earl. "I do have my own money. Well, I will have the money to pay you. I receive an inheritance when I turn twenty-five. It isn't large, but it should be enough to pay your fees."

"Payment isn't this agency's main concern." The earl's eyes flicked over her, then back to Brogan. "What do you think? Should we accept her case?"

Brogan shifted. "That's not my decision."

"Nevertheless," the earl said, "I'm asking your opinion. Do you think her father is in danger?"

Juliana clenched her hand. The decision would be left up to this man? Brogan had shown a decided lack of imagination in her encounters with him thus far. Unless there was a handwritten note by the villain confessing his actions, Brogan would never—

"I don't know." Brogan pursed his lips. "But if I wanted the man dead, I'd wait before I struck. I'd wait until Pickens was rotting in prison for some time and everyone had forgotten before I went after him again. Just because there have been no further accidents is proof of nothing."

She blew out a breath. Perhaps not a full-throated endorsement, but more than she'd expected.

Rothchild shared a look with Wilberforce, then shrugged. "Whatever you decide, I'll stand by it. Now, I have somewhere to be." He nodded at another investigator, who hurried over carrying a satchel. "The felt pads for my boots have been replaced?"

"Yes, milord."

Wil frowned. "Wasn't Lord Dunkeld working with you on this investigation?"

The edge of Rothchild's lips quirked up. "His charming wife requested his company at a house party up north, and you know he can never deny her appeals."

Both Brogan and the other investigator stiffened at the mention of Lord Dunkeld, then released matching breaths when Rothchild said he was away.

"Let's go," Rothchild said to the agent. "We have a job to do." He dipped his head towards Juliana as he and the other man strode from the office.

"Please." She clasped her hands together and turned her most desperate look on Wilberforce. "There is very little downside to you taking my case, but you could be saving a life."

"You could be a barrister for how convincing you are," the manager said dryly. He nodded. "Yes, we'll investigate any threats on your father. Do I assume you wish to remain in London during the course of this investigation and not return home?" At her nod, he reached into his desk drawer and pulled out a key. "You can use an apartment we keep available for your stay."

She took the key, squeezing it gratefully. When Mr. Wilberforce chose to be agreeable, he was really quite handsome, not taciturn at all. "Thank you."

"Now to assign an investigator." Wilberforce looked

around the room. "I assum—"

"I'll do it," Brogan grumbled. "I already know the players."

Juliana bobbed on her toes. "I have many ideas. We'll work together splendidly."

His eyebrows slashed downward. "I'll do it.... But there will be rules."

"Then I'll leave you to it." Wilberforce shrugged on a greatcoat. "I have a play to catch. Rest assured, Lady Juliana, the Bond Agency will do everything in its power to find the truth." With one last glance at the clock, he hurried outside.

"Now." Duffy crossed his arms over his chest. "Let's discuss those rules."

Chapter Nine

One bloody hour on the case and she'd already broken rule number one.

"Lady Juliana." Brogan rolled his shoulders, trying to ease the knot tightening his muscles. "You agreed to let me do the speaking."

He should have left her in the agency's apartments. He'd only agreed to let her accompany him this morning while he conducted interviews because he'd thought that a female presence would be a welcome influence on Pickens's sister, the first person on his list to question.

Apparently, Lady Juliana wasn't the welcoming type.

He'd made sure to introduce her without her title. He'd glared at her sternly whenever she'd opened her mouth to ask her own questions. Even so, it hadn't been long before Mrs. Waters had put two and two together and realized that the woman before her was responsible for her brother being in prison.

What had been strange was that Mrs. Waters hadn't seemed angered by Juliana's presence, only defensive. Did she believe her brother's guilt? Was she embarrassed by him? All he knew was that the woman had devolved into one-word answers after she'd ascertained Juliana's identity.

"Did you see the necklace she was wearing?" Juliana took his hand and climbed into the carriage. "She tucked it under her fichu quick enough, but the gold of the chain was close to pure. And I do believe the pendant was an emerald."

Brogan had indeed noticed that bit of flash. He gave the

driver instructions and climbed in after Juliana. But the pendant wasn't large. There were any number of ways a woman in Mrs. Waters's position could have obtained the trinket. The widow of a newspaper editor, she could have come by her comfortable set-up quite honestly.

He grunted. But there were several dishonest means she could have resorted to, as well. "Her carpet in the sitting room was new. Looked expensive, too. Regardless—"

"So, if her brother had been paid to hurt my father, he could have left the money with her."

"Or he could have given her some that he'd stolen." He shifted onto one hip and leaned towards her. "None of that excuses you speaking when you agreed you wouldn't."

She patted his arm, as though having a brute twice her size crowding into her was an everyday occurrence.

Something in his chest shifted. He knew what he looked like. He'd scared more than one opponent out of the ring with a glare and a crack of his knuckles. Something about this high lady seeing him as nothing more dangerous than a child's doll made his temperature rise.

"I agreed *to try* to follow your rules," she said. "Some of them will come more naturally than others."

He narrowed his eyes. He didn't remember her agreeing just to try last night. She'd been so excited that they'd taken her case, she'd readily agreed to everything he'd asked.

Excited.

Or desperate.

He rolled his hat between his hands. "You know we might not find any answers." Optimism was all well and good, but he didn't want her to be disappointed if their investigation came to naught. "There's a good chance that Pickens was just stealing from your father. No grand conspiracy."

"With his sister buying all those pretty new things?" Juliana shook her head. "And with a real, professional's help, I know I'll figure out what is going on."

Her eyes were wide, her face lit with excitement. Her

face looked... well, not quite pretty, but definitely no longer plain.

Brogan shrank back into the corner of the carriage. Her buoyant spirits only served to make him disgruntled. "You still didn't follow my rules. I'm taking you back to the apartments."

She narrowed her eyes. "You will do no such thing. Besides, I only had trouble with that one rule. It's ever so difficult keeping my mouth shut when I want answers. But I wrote my father like you asked. I can follow rules when they're reasonable."

Brogan closed his eyes. "That wasn't a rule, but a request to make sure he made it to his friend's home all right. Let's go over the rules again. One, you let me do the talking. Two, you do what I say—"

"Those two could be combined into one rule. If you tell me not to speak, that would also be doing as you say."

He pinched the bridge of his nose. "Three, if I decide no one is after your father, you go home and leave this nonsense behind."

She sniffed. "That one seems like you are already prejudging the outcome."

He cracked open one eye to see Lady Juliana in a delicious sulk. She sat wedged in the corner of the carriage, arms crossed beneath her bosom, forcing the swells to crest the square neckline of her gown, eyes squinty and lips pursed.

He dragged his gaze from her bosom, irritated with his hardening cock. That one is not for you, he told it. Aside from being too forward, too demanding, she was in a class so far removed from his she might as well have been queen.

"Rules only exist for those who can't think for themselves." She sniffed again, a habit he either found irritating or endearing. He hadn't decided yet.

He grunted. "Regardless, I'm dropping you at the apartment. This next stop isn't a place for women in any case."

"Really?" She scooted forward. "But those are the best kinds of places. Where are we going?"

"I am going to Newgate Prison to speak with Pickens. See if I can't get the information we want straight from the horse's mouth."

She shook her head. "When I went there the guards said only attorneys and magistrates could enter. And family, but I couldn't bring myself to say I was related to him."

Brogan blinked. And he blinked again. "You went to Newgate?"

"Of course." She frowned. "That was one of my first stops. I told you I was investigating. Did you not believe me?"

He didn't know what to believe when it came to Lady Juliana Wickham, except that she was the most foolhardy, falsely confident woman he'd ever had the misfortune of meeting. And he decided to tell her just that. "Newgate is not a place women should visit, especially not gently bred women. The idea was asinine, foolish, and reckless. And to go there unattended, completely—"

"Being born with a bosom and without some dangly bits down yonder," she swept her hand over her lap, "has no bearing on my ability to walk into a building. My feet and my mind work as well as any man's. Well, I wasn't *born* with a bosom, but you take my meaning, I'm sure."

Brogan sagged into the carriage seat. No words came to mind, not after a statement such as that. He stared at the creature across from him as though she were a newly discovered species. Her hair was done up in the way of most woman, with some scattered curls grazing her shoulders in a charming manner. She had the requisite number of eyes and nose as other females, the rounded figure common to her sex. And her lips were averagely formed, with perhaps her bottom lip being more full than typical.

But the words that came out of said mouth didn't belong to those of a lady. If one of those talking birds he'd heard sailors to the East Indies describe had said the same thing to him, he couldn't have been more surprised.

"I've shocked you senseless." She sighed. "How disappointing. My father, bless his heart, found no reason to raise his daughter differently than his son. I was treated to the same education, encouraged to speak my mind just as often. And if you think my speech shocking, I shall never take you to one of my salons. What you hear there could make you faint dead away."

He watched her, making sure this new form of woman didn't make any sudden moves, and slowly reached up to pound on the ceiling. "New direction," he shouted to the driver. "Newgate."

Juliana squealed and clapped her hands together. "There is hope for our investigation yet."

He didn't know about that. Brogan couldn't remember ever feeling an emotion akin to hope. He'd grown up used to the feeling of an empty stomach before bed, of walking around with holes in his shoes. He worked hard, helped feed his family, and kept his head down. With his new employment, he thought perhaps he would be able to save a bit of money. But hope never entered the equation.

He did know Lord Withington deserved a good thrashing for the way he'd raised his daughter. "Nothing of the sort," he told her. He ran his hand up the back of his head. "But with the mouth you have on you, you just might stun Pickens into a full confession."

* * *

Juliana tipped up her chin as she marched past the guard at the front gate of Newgate. Of course, he would accept a bribe to let unauthorized people into the prison. Why hadn't she thought of that before?

Also, why hadn't she thought to wear her worst pair of boots? The soles of her lovely kid leather ones stuck to the floor with each step, some substance she didn't want to identify making the floor tacky. The idea of a visit to a prison had been thrilling; the reality not so much.

She tugged on the hem of her glove. But she was here to save her father. A sticky floor was nothing to that.

"Follow me." The stocky, and unethical, guard grabbed a ring of keys from the wall and led them into a dank hallway. He nodded at another guard, who didn't even raise an eyebrow at their being inside the prison.

Brogan was a warm presence at her back, perhaps walking a bit too close for propriety's sake, but his nearness was comforting. And she was never one to care for propriety.

"You have twenty minutes, no more." The guard unlocked one thick wooden door, leading them down another corridor. "And if I were you, I'd stay back from the door. Some of the prisoners like to throw things, if you get my meaning."

Juliana didn't, but she nodded as Brogan gave his customary grunt of assent. The guard turned down another hall then stopped in front of a door with metal bars forming a window about a foot square. "Pickens," he called. "You have visitors. Twenty minutes," he reminded them before returning back the way they'd come.

"Sister?" Fabric rustled and a shadow crossed the barred window. "You've come back?"

Brogan stepped to the door. "No. It's Brogan Duffy and Lady Juliana."

"Lady Juliana?" The pale face of her father's former secretary pressed to the bars, his jaw and cheeks buried under a mat of a dark beard. "What on earth are you doing here?"

A small shiver worked its way down her spine. The last time she'd seen this man he'd been trying to throttle her to death. It wasn't a happy memory. She pushed out a deep breath. But she was an intrepid investigator now. There was no time for such missish feelings. "I've come to discover the truth. The real reason you tried to kill my father, Mr. Pickens."

He scowled. "I never admitted to trying to harm Lord

Withington. Don't try to get me charged with that, too."

Brogan shifted closer. The smell of soap and man almost beat back the stomach-rolling odor of the prison. "We don't need to. Theft and attempted murder of Lady Juliana is quite enough to see you in prison for life. It's a shame you won't live to enjoy the rewards you earned."

"My attorney thinks I have a shot at getting out in ten years or so." He gripped the metal bars. "I won't die in here."

Brogan inclined his head. "And what will you come out to? Your sister is doing a fine job of spending the blunt you were given to make an attempt on the earl's life. Ten years in prison and you'll have nothing to show for it."

Pickens's knuckles went white. "My sister is a good woman."

Juliana snorted. "She's good at picking jewelry. Her new emerald pendant was lovely."

"She doesn't wear jewels." Pickens's voice had lost some of its assurance. "She wouldn't."

"Every woman would when given the chance." Brogan crossed his arms. "And that's a fact."

Oh, really? Juliana glared at the man. That is what he thought of her sex? She ground her teeth. But his prejudice was of no matter. She was here to learn the truth, not become bosom friends with Mr. Brogan Duffy.

"She wouldn't do that," Pickens said weakly. He dropped his forehead to the bars and closed his eyes.

"I think you know the truth." Brogan rested his hand on the wall above the door, thought better of it, and wiped his palm on his trousers. "Confess now and we'll speak with the judge. Give you a good character."

Pickens shook his head. "I have nothing to say."

Brogan took her elbow. "We'll be back, and perhaps then you'll be ready to talk. Your victim pleading for leniency to the magistrate can make all the difference in your sentencing. Think about it."

He drew her away from the cell, back down the

corridor, and for once she didn't protest. Even she could see that they wouldn't get anything from the man today. He'd looked too beaten. He'd need some time to understand that his grand plans were for naught. That he wasn't coming out of here a rich man.

Her belly fluttered. But he was going to tell them who'd hired him. She could sense he was giving in. Soon, she'd have her answers.

They came to the barred door, and Brogan pounded on it three times.

"I don't know how good I'll be at convincing a magistrate to give him a lighter sentence." She rubbed her arms, the chill of the prison setting in her bones. "He tried to kill my father. I have very little forgiveness for that."

"He tried to kill you, too." Brogan glanced down at her, his eyes curious. "That is the charge he's in here for. Have you forgiven that?"

She stepped back as the door swung open. "It's easier to forgive injuries to yourself."

Brogan's brows drew together. "But—"

"Good." The guard waved them through the door and locked it. "I was about to come back for you two. Have a nice chat?" He chuckled.

"Thrilling," she said dryly. "I'll recommend the tour to all my friends."

The guard laughed some more, the keys in his hand jingling. "You lot are a bit of all right." He opened the outer door, and Juliana had to will herself not to race forward into the sunlight. Just that short bit of time inside a prison had been almost more than she could bear.

Brogan nodded to the guard as they made their way outside. He inhaled deeply once they hit the street.

Juliana's lips quirked. She hadn't been the only one uncomfortable in that place. "Where to now?"

He slanted a glance down at her. "Home." He guided her to their carriage and helped her inside. "You to the apartments. We're done for the day."

"Oh." Her shoulders slumped. Done, and they hadn't learned much at all. She arranged her skirts and settled onto the seat. "Does all detective work go at such a snail's pace?"

He didn't answer.

Juliana tilted her head. "Mr. Duffy?"

"I wouldn't know." He looked off to the side. "You were my first investigation."

"Oh." She flopped back in her seat. Having a new detective on her case wasn't optimal. Her father deserved someone more experienced. But Duffy had discovered her whereabouts. She nodded. And he had her as a partner now. They were sure to succeed.

They rolled to a stop, and Juliana peeped out the window. The three-story stone building the agency's apartments were in stood next to them. "Your woman who keeps the apartments, she said she would have roast duck for dinner tonight. Join me?"

Brogan turned his hat in his hands. "No, thanks."

"Do you have other plans?"

"No."

She sat, waiting for further explanation.

None was forthcoming. "Then why, pray tell, don't you want to eat with me? I may not be a diamond of the first water, but I am not a wholly unappealing dinner companion, I hope." Her heart twisted queerly. It wasn't as though Brogan Duffy's regard mattered. She was his employer, in a manner of thinking, and as long as he performed his duties well, she could have no complaints.

His regard shouldn't matter; but it did.

Something about this large, blunt man was...endearing. She liked him. Was it too much to hope he liked her in return?

"It wouldn't be smart," he said.

Her shoulders relaxed. He was worried about impropriety. He wasn't rejecting her company.

He stepped down and turned for her hand.

She took it and hopped to the ground. "Nonsense. We will discuss the case. Assess where we're at. Besides," she said, laying a hand on his arm, "I don't like to eat alone."

He looked at her hand, looked at his boots. He slapped his hat on his head. "Dinner. But I can't stay for dessert."

She hid her smile of victory. She'd always been prone to making snap decisions, and tonight was no different.

She turned for the front door to the building, leading Brogan to the staircase. Brogan Duffy seemed like a man who had been denied too many desserts.

It was time someone sweetened his life up a bit.

Along with discovering who was after her father, Juliana saw no reason she couldn't also make Brogan's life happier in the process.

And there was no time like the present to start.

Chapter Ten

The agency's apartments were on the third floor. Which meant three floors of watching Lady Juliana's hips sway enticingly in front of him as she climbed. Forty-two steps of watching her arse shift back and forth.

She had a most smackable arse.

Juliana took his hat, removing her own gloves and coat and handing them to the older woman who bustled into the entry as they stepped into the apartments. The agency's rooms took up the entire third floor of the building. Mrs. Forster had her own rooms a floor down, but she came up to cook and clean for whoever might be staying in these.

"Evening, Mr. Duffy." She slapped at the dust on his hat. "Staying with us for dinner?"

He nodded.

Juliana stood in front of a small mirror, adjusting some wayward strands of hair. She arched an eyebrow at him through her reflection. "I told him all about your roast duck, and he begged me to let him join me. Said he hadn't eaten a decent meal in months."

Brogan narrowed his eyes, but allowed Mrs. Forster to pull him into the dining room. "Oh, you poor dear," she said. "You tell all the boys of the agency that anytime they want a good, home-cooked meal to stop on by. Ever since my Harold passed, I've no one to cook for except when someone stays in these apartments."

"That's most kind," he murmured.

"I'll just go check on the soup." Mrs. Forster pointed to the sideboard where bottles of liquor stood. "Be a dear and pour yourself and Lady Juliana some wine, would you? I'll be just a moment."

Wine seemed like a good idea. He strode to the sideboard and poured himself a glass, taking a healthy chug. Something about Lady Juliana was... unsettling, and if he were to spend the evening with her, alcohol would help.

"Are you going to share or is that bottle yours?" She smiled, like eating with the help was a normal occurrence in her life.

Perhaps it was. Perhaps her dotty father invited all the servants into the dining room to eat with the family. Probably thought it made him a man of the people, or some other such shite.

Placing his own glass down, Brogan picked up a clean one and filled it near to the brim. "Here." He shoved it at her. When their fingers brushed, he jerked his hand back like he'd touched a porcupine. She'd removed her gloves, and the feel of that velvety skin wasn't one he wanted to become accustomed to.

"Whoa." She lifted her hand where a few drops of wine had splashed and licked it clean. Her tongue looked soft and pink, and it was all he could do to drag his gaze away.

"Shall we sit?" Without waiting for an answer, he pulled the chair at the end of the table out, holding it for her. After she settled herself, he took his own. At the other end of the long table.

Juliana pressed her lips together before taking her own healthy swallow. She placed her glass down and gave him another bright smile that seemed only partially forced. "I am optimistic that Mr. Pickens will tell us what we want. I think he knows his sister will spend his money. He had been living on false hope before."

"Yes."

She took another sip. "And once we get a name from him—"

"If."

"If we get a name from him, how quickly will the

magistrate have that man arrested?" She leaned forward, placing her elbows on the table, exposing interesting shadows in her bosom. "Could this all be over this week?"

"Depends what name is given." He stood as Mrs. Forster bustled in, a large soup tureen in her hands.

She shooed him back to his seat when he tried to relieve her of the burden.

He cleared his throat and let her ladle the consumé into his bowl. "If a high-ranking person is named, there will be complications. And delays." Her father was an earl, so she did have that going for her. An attempt on the life of a titled person would be prosecuted more strenuously regardless of the status of the perpetrator. But Lord Withington wasn't a wealthy earl, and, more often than not, the wealthier party won the day.

"Thank you, Mrs. Forster." Juliana waited for the woman to leave the room before returning her gaze to him. "You think our judicial system so corrupt? My father will have justice."

She dug her spoon into the broth as if digging someone's grave.

Brogan pursed his lips. She was a determined woman, of that there was no doubt. Even considering her impulsive and naïve nature, he wouldn't want to be on the opposite side of any battle she decided to fight.

"And what would you do if the courts dropped the case?" His tone was part mocking, part curious.

She flushed. "Well, I..."

"Yes?"

"I...I would start a public campaign. Yes, I would lay out the evidence against the scoundrel, stir up public sentiment until the courts had no choice but to give us justice." She nodded stoutly. "I know people at *The Times*. Don't discount public opinion."

"Never." He wanted to laugh at her, but her idea could work. Governments tended to ignore the people until it was no longer possible, and then became most accommodating.

He watched her as Mrs. Forster served the main course. Juliana was so sure of herself, of her own power. She was oblivious to the fact that she enjoyed her style of living only because society allowed it. She was soft. Intelligent, yes, but weak all the same. Without the protections of her family, of the aristocracy, she would be exposed to what the world truly was.

Days of hardship while you waited for death.

He stabbed the duck, tearing a chunk from its breast.

She tilted her head, her dark eyes glittering in the candlelight. "Is there no one cooking for you at home?"

"Are you asking if I'm married?"

Her smile fell. "Are you?"

It would be so much easier if he were. A simple way to keep his distance.

She shifted in her seat, and the silk of her gown rustled.

He ground his jaw. There were many things that kept the distance between him and a woman such as her. "No." He shoved another bite of duck into his mouth.

She loosed a breath. "Good." At his glance, she looked down at her plate, flushing. "I'm glad I'm not keeping you from anyone."

He shoveled in another forkful. Just because there was no one waiting for him didn't mean he didn't want to leave.

She slumped back in her chair. "Is it so awful, spending time with me? To discuss the case, I mean."

He didn't know how to respond to that, so he didn't.

She cradled her glass to her abdomen, like it was a shield. "You've made it clear you wouldn't willingly spend time with someone like me, that you don't find me appealing, but can we not at least enjoy a pleasant conversation together?"

He rubbed the back of his neck. "Lady Juliana," he began.

"I just don't want things to be awkward between us." She pushed a bit of vegetable around her plate with her fork. "We will be working together and—"

"Juliana!"

"Hmm." She kept her gaze fixed on her plate. "Yes?"

He glared at her. "Whatever gave you the foolish idea that I don't find you appealing?" He should keep his mouth shut. He should let her go on having her delusions about his indifference. But he didn't care for how she closed up, went from being a roaring fire to a dim ember. Didn't like the false smile she sent his way, or the way her skin puckered between her eyebrows as though she were in physical pain. And besides, deceptions of any sort never sat right with him.

"Oh, I don't know." She tossed her silverware down. "Perhaps it is the way you flinch away as though I'm diseased when you touch me. Or that you sat yourself as far away from my person as possible." She nodded down the long distance of the table. "Or maybe it's the way you've treated most of my attempts to aid the investigation with contempt. I first thought that was merely because I'm a woman and you have backward ideas about my sex's abilities, but now I see your disdain is saved solely for me."

"Are you done?" A burning sensation started in his stomach and rose to his chest. She truly was a fool.

She held up her hand and pointed to her fingers as she spoke. "Dislikes my touch, physical avoidance, and disgust. Yes, I think that paints a pretty fair picture."

He tossed his napkin to the table. His feet itched to move, but he forced himself to keep his seat. "The Bond Agency for Discreet Inquiries is a somber business. Professionalism and dedication are required of all its agents. I am treating you in the only way I can treat a client."

Although from the stories he'd heard, the founders of the agency hadn't been as dedicated to separating business from pleasure. But they were all toffs. Different rules applied to that lot. He glared at Juliana. Different rules applied to her.

"Are you saying that if I weren't a client—"

"No." He stood. "You're the daughter of an earl. I'm

the son of a woodworker. I'd be run out of town for even looking at you. And I'd deserve it."

She pushed to her feet. "Mr. Duffy. Brogan. I know English society likes to impose nonsense ideas of class structures on to us, but you cannot believe that you are any less worthy because of your parentage."

He huffed. "I don't. I'm a free man, equal to any other. But I'm also a realist. Some things aren't possible. Some people aren't possible." He strode for the entry closet and gathered his coat and hat.

Juliana hurried after him, needing to take two steps for each of his. "I don't understand you. I was raised to believe that it is a person's character that mattered, not their wealth. And..." She bit her lip and looked to the side. "Not to put too fine a point on it, but I also learned that not every affair needs to end in marriage. I was hoping to enjoy your company. No expectations besides pleasure."

He scowled even as his cock thickened. This *education* of hers had a lot to answer for. "Very free with your favors, are you? Or is this a bonus for your investigator?"

The look she gave him was full of disappointment with a hint of anger. "My favors, as you call them, are only bestowed on those I deem worthy. You are looking less and less so. Perhaps it is best if we keep this relationship purely on a business footing."

He slapped his hat on his head. "Now you're talking sense."

"Pick me up at ten tomorrow." She crossed her arms under her bosom. No matter how much she wanted to deny the class system, her voice had perfected the proper tone in which to order a servant about.

The muscles of his body strained, screaming at him to take what had been offered. But his brain pushed his feet a step back.

She stared at a point over his shoulder. "We can continue our questioning then."

"Yes, ma'am." He reached for the door, yanking it

open. "I won't be late. I wouldn't want to delay your entertainment."

Her gaze cut to him. "My entertainment?"

"The intrigue. The excitement of the hunt. You enjoy it."

She went pale. "My father's life is in danger. That's a horrible thing to say."

"But true nevertheless." He wanted to soften his words, but this was good for her. Good for the both of them. "You were bored. The spoiled little aristocrat. And while I don't doubt you care for your father, this was an opportunity you took for yourself, not for him."

She stepped up to him and poked his chest. "How dare you. You know nothing of my life, of who I am."

She went to poke him again, and he grabbed her finger. "I know enough," he growled.

He knew better than to dally with a rich girl who thought it thrilling to have a romance with a bruiser like him. Knew that his career would be over if they were caught. That he'd have to return to the poverty of woodworking, or eke out a few more punishing years in boxing until his body gave up.

And Juliana... She would be shunned from society. She might think she didn't care about such things, but she would when every friend turned their back on her.

She yanked her hand from his, her chest heaving. They were so close her nipples brushed against his chest with every angry inhalation.

So close that her wine-scented breath caressed his own lips.

"Go back to your poets and philosophers." He didn't know when, but his hand had found its way to her hip, and he squeezed it. "Go back to your refined men and stop playing with the commoners."

"Playing?" She pushed his shoulder, her fingers tangling in his coat's lapel. "Playing?" Her next push somehow managed to tug him closer. "I would no sooner play with a man such as yourself than I would a pig in the mud. You,

Mr. Brogan Duffy, are—"

His anger, his lust, it all served to make his brain desert him. He cut off whatever nonsense words she was about to say by kissing her.

His palm flattened on her lower back, holding her close. He gripped the back of her head with his other hand.

At the first touch of his lips, she sighed into his mouth. And pulled his hair, not letting him forget she was still angry.

Well, that made two of them. The kiss was just a continuation of their fight, a battle using teeth, and lips, and tongues as their weapons.

It was the best damn kiss of his life.

Pleasure gathered at the base of his neck and rolled down his spine. Nothing but the taste of Juliana, her scent, the feel of her soft body against his own, registered in his mind. He rocked his hips against her, needing the friction against his aching cock.

When he came up for air, the dazed look on Juliana's face sent a stab of pride through his chest.

Until he remembered it was *Lady* Juliana he had just kissed the starch out of. Lady Juliana who could end his employment with one word.

He shoved away from her. "This was a mistake. It never should have happened. I don't want a woman like you."

And it was definitely Lady Juliana whose chin went up with pride even as her face went red at his rejection.

"Get out." She clenched her hands, her body trembling with rage. Better anger than seductive little glances. Anger he could manage.

She pointed at the door. "Get out of here. I can't stand to look at you a moment longer."

He nodded and pulled the door shut behind him. His shoulders sagged, whether from relief or disappointment he didn't know. He had finally convinced Juliana of their incompatibility, made her so disgusted with him she would never think about an affair between them again. Perhaps now he could focus on his work.

Perhaps now, there would be no danger of him doing the stupidest thing in his life.

Chapter Eleven

His note shouldn't have come as a surprise, not after last night. But still it hurt.

Juliana read the lines again.

It will be better for the investigation if I conduct it myself. I will notify you of any developments.

She pressed her fingers against her lips, ignoring the heat behind her eyes. She could still feel his kiss. Still imagine his taste. Last night had been amazing.

And then he'd run like a scared little boy.

She tossed her spoon into her porridge. If anyone should be angry, it should be her. He had no call to cut ties. He was the one in the wrong.

She pushed from the breakfast table, her knees not quite steady. Well, she was almost entirely certain Brogan was the one in the wrong. He wasn't right about her enjoying this investigation. Her father was in danger, for pity's sake. It would take some kind of monster to enjoy that.

She paced the small but neatly appointed room. Like everything else owned by the Bond Agency, it was tasteful, expensive, and understated. Brogan was the only part of the agency that lacked taste. He was the fly in the ointment. She'd gotten the bad apple in the barrel. Perhaps she should ask for another detective. One who would treat her with respect. One who would appreciate her insights.

One who wouldn't challenge her on her lies.

Her shoulders slumped. She'd tossed and turned all night, not because she was angry at the gall of the man. She'd slept fitfully because he'd been right.

Partially.

She did enjoy the investigation. It was thrilling. A challenge. A bit like a puzzle but with high stakes. If it wasn't someone she cared about in danger, the employment would be just about perfect. It was exciting, important work, something someone in her position had little claim to.

"You finished then?" Mrs. Forster bustled in and began clearing the table. "It's a bit drizzly today. Be sure to bundle up and take your umbrella when Mr. Duffy comes for you."

Her throat went thick, and she cleared it. "Mr. Duffy isn't coming today. He felt his investigation would proceed apace if he did it alone."

Mrs. Forster balanced three bowls along her arm. "Well, I'm sure he knows what he's about. All the boys at the agency do. I'll make a fire in the sitting room, and you and I can enjoy a nice cup of tea. I have some knitting needles if you'd care to keep busy."

Yes, staying in and knitting would be what most would expect of her. The daughter of an earl, she wasn't expected to provide value above that. Even her father, who was generous enough to provide her with the same education as her brother, had never expected her to actually *do* anything of import. Be anything. Nothing but become a more interesting conversationalist for her future husband.

Mrs. Forster was a kind woman, but the idea of a day stuck indoors while someone else investigated her claims was unbearable.

"Thank you, but I'm still going out." She turned and called over her shoulder, "I'll be back for supper. I think."

She made quick work donning her overcoat and gloves, picked an aubergine-colored umbrella from the large vase by the front door, and hurried outside before she could change her mind.

She had no plan, no idea how to conduct an investigation, but what she lacked in knowledge she made up for in determination.

She picked a direction and started walking.

Only to spin about when an idea struck her.

She wasn't completely untaught in how to conduct an investigation. Brogan had shown her just yesterday how he went about questioning suspects. And she knew one other place where she might learn more about Mr. Pickens.

She hailed a hansom cab. "Take me to the Hardmeat Employment Agency, please." She blushed as she said it. The owner had such an unfortunate surname, poor man. Hyacinth hadn't been able to stop laughing after Juliana had explained the innuendo to her.

The driver leaned down. He spit something Juliana didn't want to identify onto the dirt. "What street?"

Her mind blanked. The agency was one her father had used for years to hire his staff, but she'd never actually gone there. She tried to recall the address from her father's letters but nothing came. "I don't know. What street are most employment agencies on?"

He rolled his eyes and heaved a large sigh. "Hold on." Sitting back up, he slapped the reins, urging the horse into a slow walk. He waved down another cab. "Ho. You know where a Hardcock—"

"Hardmeat!" Her cheeks flamed hotter.

"Hardmeat Employment Agency is at?" He jerked a finger in her direction. "This one wants to go but don't know the directions."

"Never heard of it," the new cabbie said. He waved at another. "Mike! You heard of Hardmeat Employment?"

Juliana settled back into her seat, wanting to cover her face in her hands. Two more cabbies were drawn into the discussion, and finally, a location was discovered.

"But if you need a job," one of the cabbies said, a leer on his face, "I've got a position I can put you in. And my meat is more than— Oy!" He rubbed the back of his head where another cabbie had swiped his crop. "What was that for?"

"Keep your filth to yourself." The cabbie with the crop saluted her. "Have a good day, miss."

She nodded her thanks and waved goodbye as her cab pulled into the street. This investigation business wasn't that hard. Her first challenge of the day, and she'd discovered where she wanted to go by... throwing herself on the mercy of kindly cab drivers for an entirely embarrassing discussion.

She slouched down. When she retold the story to Brogan, she would gloss over this part of the investigation.

The cab pulled to a stop in front of a two-story brick building. A large sign on the second floor cheerfully proclaimed she'd reached the agency. She paid and thanked the driver, then stared at the door. Well, there was nothing for it. She pushed inside. She might not know the right questions to ask, but indecision never solved anything.

A young man of not more than twenty sat behind a desk in the center of the room. Two benches lined the walls, three men in various levels of stylish dress occupying them. Three doors led to private offices and a stairwell to the side went to the second floor.

The young man at the desk looked up, a sketch of a welcome smile on his face. "Good morning. Can I help you?"

She dug her fingers into her pocketbook. "Yes. I'm Lady Juliana Wickham. My family uses your agency often, and I was hoping to speak to someone about a former secretary. Is Mr. Hardmeat available?" She ignored the snigger from one of the men on the benches behind her.

"The senior Mr. Hardmeat is not available." The boy raised his voice, directing his words to one of the offices. "The senior Mr. Hardmeat likes to espouse the value of hard work to the younger Mr. Hardmeat, but never seems to actually partake in said hard work on his own."

Muffled cursing erupted inside the office. The door was flung open. "Boy! I'm going to..." He caught sight of Juliana and adjusted his cravat. "Oh." He cleared his throat. "I didn't realize there was a lady present." He glared at his son. "We'll discuss this later."

The younger Mr. Hardmeat rolled his eyes. "Can't wait."

Juliana pressed her lips together, fighting her smile. Young men were the same world over. "My father is Lord Withington. I'd like to speak to you about Mr. Pickens."

Mr. Hardmeat shook his head. "Terrible business that was. Just terrible. But we aren't responsible for what goes on after the man starts work. We ran all the necessary background checks, told your father all the pertinent information. If Mr. Pickens went bad later, it isn't our fault."

She forced her smile to remain on her face. "Of course, we don't hold you responsible. But I would like to know a bit more about the man's background and how he came to us. Do you have any records on him I can read?"

"Well..." He scratched his grizzled jaw. "I can't see a reason why not." Though from his expression it looked as though he had tried hard to find one. "I'll go see what we have in our files."

She started to follow him to his office, but he stopped and pointed at a bench. "Wait here, if you please. Mrs. Hardmeat wouldn't like me having a woman in my office. I'm sure you can understand."

Not really. Juliana didn't understand the point of jealousy. Either you trusted your partner or you didn't. But she settled herself on a bench, keeping a good two feet between her and the other occupant. He smelled of onions, a vegetable she particularly detested, and she didn't want to encourage conversation.

But her space meant nothing to him. He planted a hand on the bench and leaned closer. "Oy. You looking to hire another secretary?"

She examined his work trousers and the dirt underneath his fingernails. He didn't look like the professional sort, but appearances could be deceiving.

"I'm sorry, but we're not looking to replace him at this

time."

The man loosed a deep belly laugh. "Me as a secretary. That's a good one. No, I'm a thief-taker. Looking to get hired by the Bow Street boys, I am."

"A thief-taker?" Those were investigators of a sort. They didn't have the best reputations, however. As likely to extort a fee from the criminal they were after than bring him to justice. But beggars couldn't be choosers, and without Brogan to guide her, she would take what she could get.

"What interesting employment." She gave the man her most charming smile. "When someone hires you to catch a thief, what steps do you take to discover the blackguard?"

He snorted. "Usually, the person who hires me tells me who took their property. It's not much of a mystery."

"Well then, say it is a crime where the victim can't talk. Say it's a murder. How would you go about catching the killer?"

He shot her a wide-eyed look, and she hastily added, "I'll bet that's the type of question Bow Street will ask of you. How would you answer?"

He rubbed his jaw. "Well, in a gruesome case like that, I'd start with the victim, I guess. Figure out what type of man he was. Reasons someone would want to kill him. Work from there."

"Huh." She sat back. She hadn't really considered the *why* of someone trying to kill her father. He was kind and absent-minded and completely harmless. If she'd thought about it at all, she just assumed it had something to do with money.

Although, his earldom was one of the poorest in the land. Why would someone go after him when there were so many richer targets that would be more profitable?

"Here's the file."

Startled, Juliana glanced up to see Mr. Hardmeat holding a folder out to her.

"Thank you." She took it and flipped it open. There wasn't much. The directions to Mr. Pickens past three residences. A list of previous employers. A letter of recommendation. Nothing that would speak to motive. But she wanted to be thorough. "Can I have pen and paper to copy this down?"

Mr. Hardmeat snapped his fingers at his son. "Boy. Earn your keep. Copy this file for the lady, and be quick about it."

With a sigh that would have been more appropriate had he been asked to rebuild Hadrian's Wall rather than write a few pages, the younger Mr. Hardmeat drew paper from his desk and dipped his pen in an inkwell. "Well?" He looked at Juliana expectantly. "I can't read the contents from here, can I?"

"Right." She hurried over and placed the file before him. "I really do apprec—"

"Whatever." He bent his head to his task, but not before his father slapped the back of it.

"How many times have I told you to be polite to the customers?" His father shook his head, despairing, and stomped back into his office, slamming the door.

Juliana rethought her plan to reproduce as the younger Mr. Hardmeat copied the documents. The idea of children seemed all well and good, but the reality of this sullen, petulant being as one's progeny was enough to give anyone second thoughts.

"Done." He handed her the newly-copied papers, the ink still wet on the top page.

"Do you have a folder or envelope I can put them in?" She tried her hardest to make her voice as sweet as possible.

He just looked more irritated. "Fine." He riffled through one of his desk drawers and produced a large envelope. "Good enough for you?"

"Perfect." Now that she had what she wanted, she felt freer to speak. "A bit of advice, young man. If you want to inherit your father's business—"

"I don't."

"Oh." She rocked back on her heels. Well, there went that lecture. "What do you want to do?"

He shrugged. "Nothing, really."

Juliana knew what that sort of indecision felt like. She took his pen and scribbled an address and time on a small piece of paper. She pushed it toward him. "Here. This is a good place to go to help figure out your interests." And if she wasn't thrown out of the salon for inflicting this sullen young man on them, she would consider this good deed worth it. "Remember, your life is what you make of it."

With a nod to the thief-taker, she strode from the building, chin held high.

Life was what she made of it. She'd spent too much time last night crying over Brogan and his ideas on what her life was and should be. She was the one in control of her destiny.

And it was time Mr. Brogan Duffy understood that.

Chapter Twelve

Bertie shifted from foot to foot. "Do you think he'll be here?"

Blowing out a breath, Juliana glared at her friend from the corner of her eye. He'd asked the same question every five minutes of their carriage ride over to the Voltaire Society's meeting. Juliana usually didn't find the conversation of this club as engaging as at the Rose Salon, but this one had meetings every week. Today's was being held at the home of Lady Mary Cavindish, an older woman who was even more untraditional than Juliana.

"You didn't have to attend the meeting with me," she pointed out, shaking her skirts to unwrinkle them from the cab ride. "I know everyone here. There's no danger."

He twisted his hat around his left hand. "At tea, you said you thought one of them might be responsible for the attacks on your father. You're right; no danger here at all," he said sarcastically.

She squeezed his arm as she led him up the steps of the townhouse. He truly was sweet, but she didn't know how much assistance Bertie could provide in a threatening situation. But perhaps she was being unfair. When Mr. Pickens had attacked her, Bertie had done a marvelous job of putting his face in the path of Pickens's fist. It had distracted Pickens from her for a good thirty seconds.

No, Bertie had the heart of a lion but the physical prowess of a mouse. It hadn't been until Brogan had arrived to detain Mr. Pickens that she had felt safe.

She frowned. She hadn't heard from the blasted man all

day. She'd expected a note at the very least, updating her of his progress, when she'd returned to the agency's apartments. Not wanting to spend the afternoon staring at the walls, she'd paid a visit on Bertie.

And wished she'd been having tea with her surly investigator instead.

Pushing away that disconcerting thought, she said, "I don't really believe someone here wants my father dead." She rapped on the door. "But my father introduced Snow and me to this society, too. They were his friends first. And one of them might know a reason my father has made an enemy."

A butler opened the door, looking as much the long-suffering servant as a man could look. From her few visits to this house, Juliana knew he liked to put on the appearance of disapproving of his mistress's radical life-style. The woman had created London's very first gentlewomen's club, for heaven's sake, a wondrous place where the most ungenteel things happened. But the butler's attentiveness to Lady Cavindish, the light in his eyes when he looked upon her, showed his devotion.

"Good afternoon, Lady Juliana. Mr. Huddleson." He stepped back and pointed down the hall. "They are gathered in the morning room."

"Thanks." Bertie handed his hat to the man. "I don't suppose you know... I mean to say..."

Juliana took pity on him. "Is Mr. Smythe here?"

"Yes, my lady." The butler sniffed. "Arrived not ten minutes ago."

Bertie paled.

She secured her arm more firmly through his. "You have nothing to fear from seeing the man." She pulled him down the hall. "The wrong was all on his end."

"I know, but it doesn't make meeting with him any easier." He tugged at the knot of his cravat. "Not when he and I were—" He darted her a quick look. "Uh, such particular friends."

She patted his hand and drew him into the sitting room. Bertie wasn't the only one to face a past lover. She met James Masters's gaze and gave him a smile and nod. But unlike Bertie's relationship, hers had ended amicably.

"Juliana! Bertie!" Lady Mary swept forward and took her hands. "Thank the heavens another woman has arrived." She nodded towards the settees and chairs in the room, most of the spaces filled. "As you can see, the only feminine influence on the conversation has come from me and Miss Lynn. And she, well..."

"I understand, Lady Mary." Miss Bella Lynn was a... challenging conversationalist, to say the least. Never outright rude, yet she seemed to make those around her aware of her disdain all the same. "What is the topic of conversation today?"

The woman sighed and patted her snow-white hair. "We're still up in the heavens, discussing comets and whatnot. I much prefer talking about the going-ons of what happens down here on our planet."

A man peeled himself off his perch on the windowsill and glided their way, his smooth movements impressive considering the height of his heels. The ends of his tawny hair just curled about his collar, and Juliana knew for a fact that he spent a large sum of money on a barber to give him that slightly disheveled look. "The topic has become dreadfully dull, I agree. And since we are guests in your home today, I say we change the subject. Did anyone read the opinion piece in *The Times* about the upcoming demise of Romanticism? They've predicted it every year in the past twenty."

He winked at Bertie, and her friend stiffened next to her.

Juliana burned for Bertie's sake. To act so casually, as though nothing had occurred between the two men, was the deepest of cuts. Mr. Smythe was truly a horrible man. "The Romantics bore me," she said. "All feeling and no reason. They're the toddlers of modern poetry."

Smythe narrowed his eyes. He made his living as a Romantic poet, but had yet to break into the ranks of a Wordsworth or Shelley or Rose. "As the founder of your favorite salon is a Romanticist, I'd say that is a bit hard of you."

"But she may not be wrong," a man wearing a banyan as a coat said. "I've long complained about the maudlin excesses of the movement. Balance is what's needed."

"Balance?" Miss Lynn leaned forward, putting her elbows on her knees. "We've been ruled too long by classical ideals of Rationalism. It's what has led to hundreds of years of domination by the aristocratic class. Romanticism elevates true beauty, spontaneity, the authenticity of the individual. There should be no balance for that."

A loud chorus of boos clashed with applause of support. And any more talk of comets was promptly forgotten.

Pushing Bertie in the opposite direction of Mr. Smythe to mingle, Juliana led Lady Mary back to her chair and settled beside her. "Lady Mary—"

"No such conceits here. Just Mary."

"Mary." Juliana leaned closer, not wanting to be overheard, although with the exuberant ejaculations that accompanied the current discussion, being overheard was unlikely. "You've known my father for some time now."

"If you consider forty years a long time." Mary plucked up a glass from the table in front of her and took a long swallow. "If you consider the entire history of the world, that's hardly any time at all."

"Yes, well, in those forty years, have you ever..." She squinted. How to phrase this?

"Ever what?" Mary smiled, the crepe skin of her cheeks pulling tight. "I can assure you, in my years there is very little I haven't done."

Juliana chuckled. "Yes, but I was wondering more about my father, and what he might have done. Have you ever known him to have enemies?"

Mary sat back. "That, my dear, is a very odd question."

Juliana looked at her hands. "I realize that, but—"

"I adore odd questions." The older woman tapped one of her rings against the rim of her glass. "But I can't think of anyone who doesn't like your father. Henry is, and has always been, a very kind man. After your mother passed, there was quite the flurry of eager young things hoping to become the next Countess of Withington."

"Really?" Juliana pursed her lips. "My father's estate—"

"Was enough to get by on. For a sensible sort of woman, having a kind husband and enough to be comfortable is more than enough. Your father would have been fortunate to wed any one of those women, but he was too heartbroken to consider marrying again."

Her heart squeezed. She didn't remember much of her mother, but she did remember the love. Their family had been happy.

Mary frowned. "There was that odd business with Sir Thomas Miles. Because of your mother's death, it wasn't commented on overmuch. The breach between the two men seemed a trifle compared to your father's loss."

"Sir Thomas..." Juliana chewed her bottom lip. She had a vague memory of sitting on a Sir Thomas's knee, pretending to be riding a horse as he bounced her up and down. He even made neighing sounds, much to her smaller self's delight. "I remember him. He and my father were friends. What happened?"

"I think it was an investment that went bad." Mary tilted her head. "Your father encouraged Sir Thomas to put money in something or other? Perhaps it was the other way about." She shrugged. "No matter. It wasn't a scandal of any sort. No large row, not that I can recollect. They simply ended their friendship."

And it had been seventeen years since her mother died. Holding a grudge for this long seemed improbable, if not impossible.

"Now," Mary said, placing a blue-veined hand on

Juliana's knee, "what's this about?"

"Hmm? About?" Rats. She should have come up with some sort of story why she was asking questions. She didn't want it known she suspected an acquaintance of her father's was trying to murder him. She somehow didn't think people would be as willing to speak to her if that was the case. "Nothing in particular. I did lose my mother so early that I suppose I just want to know everything about my father's life I can."

Mary arched an eyebrow. "And knowing his enemies will fill out the family history, will it?"

Her stomach sank. "Something like that."

"And this has nothing to do with the handsome yet imposing man glaring down at you?"

Juliana looked up and yelped. Brogan stood not three feet away, arms crossed over his chest, looking like he wanted nothing more than to thrash her.

"What are you doing here?" she asked. For such a large man he sure could move softly. How he'd crossed that room without her noticing, she didn't know.

"My job." He held his hand out to her. "I'd like to speak with you. In the hall."

She looked at his hand, looked at the curious glances they were garnering, and hurriedly slipped her own palm over his. "I'd like to speak with you, as well." She had many things to say to this man. Many, many things. First on her list was how unprofessional it was to abandon her simply because they'd had a disagreement.

With a flick of his wrist, he jerked her to standing. "I'm glad we've reached a consensus of opinion on one thing at least.'

As she was pulled from the room, she heard Mary chuckle. "This salon meeting is becoming more interesting by the minute."

* * *

Brogan tried to rein in his temper. The day had started off poorly and only gotten worse. The note from his father had thwarted his investigation that morn, and when he tried to get it back on course, he found Lady Juliana not only not safe in the apartments, but traipsing about with their suspects.

He pulled her through the door and out of hearing from those in the sitting room. "Explain."

She tugged her hand free and shrugged. "Explain what exactly?"

He gritted his teeth. "Why you're here instead of at the apartment letting me investigate."

She shrugged again. "I'm a member of this salon, too."

"You aren't investigating?"

"I didn't say that."

He looked at the ceiling. God give him patience with this woman. "You've hired me to do a job. Let me do it."

"I thought we were to work together." She poked him in the chest, a move of hers that brought up too many memories of intertwined tongues and heated bodies. "You agreed. Then you run off this morning without me. That doesn't mean I'm going to stop investigating."

Damn, why *had* he thought she'd sit meekly at home while he worked? Nothing in their past history should have suggested that. But she'd riled him up last night when he prided himself on staying emotionless at work. Made him so frustrated he hadn't been thinking straight.

"Why are *you* at this meeting?" She cocked her head to the side. "Do you think the perpetrator could be one of my father's acquaintances here, too?"

Brogan scraped his palm across his jaw. All he wanted was to go home, eat enough to make up for the luncheon he'd skipped, and go to bed. Not worry about whether Lady Juliana would interfere with his investigation. Not worry about the trouble his sister was getting into. Not continue down the path of what he was becoming more and more convinced was a wild goose chase. By all accounts, her father was a quiet, gentle sort of man, not someone to target for death.

"Your father's acquaintances in London are few." His friends anywhere were few. The man led a simple life in the country most of the year. "I won't leave any avenue of inquiry unexplored. But is it true he hasn't attended any salon in over a year?"

Juliana nodded. "It does seem unlikely anyone here is the culprit. But like you said, no avenue unexplored."

He eyed her. A request to return to the apartment wouldn't be taken well. Unable to get rid of her, he would have to work with the woman. Besides, these were her friends, too. Her introductions could help.

He waved a hand at the doorway. "Shall we?"

She took her skirts in one hand and turned for the room. "We shall."

Brogan saw one familiar face. Bertie rose with a smile to come greet him, until he saw the other man angling for Brogan and Juliana. Bertie sat back down with a plop.

"Juliana." The other man swaggered up to them in pantaloons tight enough to make Brogan wince in sympathy. The top of his head reached Brogan's jaw, and he had the pale, sickly look that seemed in favor with toffs these days. "Who is this delightfully rough-looking man of yours? I didn't realize your tastes ran to the laborer set."

Juliana went stiff beside him. Before Brogan could correct the implication that they were together, she said, "Mr. Smythe, meet Mr. Duffy, an associate of my brother's and mine. Mr. Duffy, Mr. Smythe. A poet."

The man tutted. "We really must work on your introduction skills, dear." He bowed his head. "I am Jonathon Smythe, poet, philosopher, artist. I'm the type of man who is always looking for a good... associate," he said slyly. "I suffer from gout, high bile, and periodic fits of the vapors."

Brogan looked to Juliana, wondering if this sort of presentation was normal in her circles. When she didn't give him any indication, he turned back to Smythe. "I don't care."

Juliana muffled a laugh before drawing him away. "Mr. Smythe has only been a member of our common salons for eight months or so. He doesn't know my father so no need to question him." She grimaced. "Though I wouldn't mind if you gave him a good whipping."

Brogan stopped. "Why?" Had he hurt Juliana in some way? He looked back at the man and flexed his hand. Weak jaw. Delicate bones. One punch would take him out.

"He and Bertie were... good friends." She glanced at him from the corner of her eye. "It ended badly."

Brogan nodded. That was one suspicion confirmed. But he had neither the time nor the inclination to care about another man's heartache. "Who here does know your father?"

"Almost everyone." She set her shoulders and headed toward the nearest grouping of people. "I'll make the introductions."

And there were many introductions. So many Brogan's head began to hurt. He pinched his temple between his thumb and forefinger as the latest artist Juliana introduced him to, a sculptor this time, told him about the newest method of casting plaster.

"And Lady Juliana's father is a patron of yours?" Keeping his interrogations on track with this lot was as difficult as bailing water with his bare hands. Not that he could let on these were interrogations. His training at the agency had included determining when 'friendly conversation' worked better over direct questioning. Juliana didn't want her acquaintances to know she suspected one of them, and he agreed.

He only wished he were better at friendly conversations. It hadn't been a skill he'd needed in his past career. It wasn't something most people tried to engage in with him. They took one look at his muscles and crooked nose and placed him in a different category from conversationalist.

"Well, he buys a piece here and there." The man, James Masters, gave Juliana a kind smile.

When his funds would allow, was the implication. Just how impoverished was her father's estate? When Brogan had first started looking for Juliana, a cursory examination had shown that Lord Withington, while not wealthy, was far from wanting. But perhaps his finances deserved a closer look. Money was the strongest motive for murder.

"I can't wait to see your latest piece." Juliana squeezed Masters's arm. "You will let me know when it's finished?"

"Of course."

"Mr. Duffy is also an artist," Juliana said.

Brogan looked around. There had to be another Mr. Duffy here. She couldn't be referring to him.

"Do you have one of your sculptures with you?" She pointed at his coat pocket. "I know you keep your work in there at times."

Mr. Smythe sidled up. He'd been circling them like a shark for the past half hour. The man didn't seem to know how to take an insult and move on. "Oh, do show us. I'm always on the lookout for new talent."

"No." Juliana should know how absurd this was. That artists and poets wouldn't esteem a bit of whittling. But she nodded to him, encouraging, as though in her mind a man who scratched away on stray bits of wood was in the same league as a professional sculptor.

He sighed, and dug his hand into his pocket. He held up the miniature stallion, its hind legs still hidden in the wood.

Mr. Smythe didn't try overly hard to hide his snort of laughter behind his hand. "You whittle? That's your great artform?"

"I never claimed it was art." He rubbed his thumb over the horse's mane. It was coming along nicely, however.

"It is art." Juliana turned to Masters. "Sculpture takes many forms, isn't that right, James?"

Brogan's shoulders rolled back. James? Juliana was awfully familiar with the man. He glared at the sculptor. What exactly was their history?

Masters took a wary step back. He held up his empty glass. "Anyone else need a refill? I'm going to get another drink."

Without waiting for a response, Masters hurried towards the makeshift bar on an end table.

Brogan swiveled his head to stare Smythe down. "You go too."

Having some sense, the man turned on his high heel and joined another group.

Juliana frowned. "Whittling is art. And you are talented at it, no matter what these Philistines say."

Brogan cracked his neck. "It doesn't matter." Though her insistence on the matter was surprisingly... sweet. "Everyone here seems to like your father."

"My father is a very likeable man." Juliana eyed the room, picking her next target it seemed.

"If you're right, someone doesn't like him." A shout of laughter drew his attention to three men and a woman gathered together in the corner. "So, either someone is lying, or no one here is responsible."

Juliana tucked her hand in his elbow and headed for that corner. "I'm beginning to think my idea of investigating my father was in error. Sometimes criminals are just mad, right? The motive might make sense to him, but not to anyone else."

"Not usually." He plastered a polite smile on his face as Juliana drew him before the group. His cheek muscles felt stiff, unused. "Good afternoon," he told them all.

Juliana made introductions. "Miss Lynn," she addressed the woman of the group, "I heard that your brother was injured, and that you were up in Stanhope to tend to him. I do hope he's recovered."

Miss Lynn drew her narrow shoulders back. "How does one ever recover from being beaten to within an inch of his life by men who'd rather kill than share the game rights to land that should belong to everyone?"

Juliana flushed. "I'm sorry. I'd heard he was injured. I

hadn't realized he was involved in the lead miners riots last year."

Brogan had heard about those. The riots had reached even the London news, with the papers alternatively taking the side of the Bishop of Durham enforcing his property rights then sympathizing with the miners. It was like the editors wanted to cause strife.

"Your brother is a miner?" the man next to Miss Lynn asked. "How delightfully proletarian. However did you manage to rise from the miasma of the commoners and become the charming woman you are?"

Miss Lynn scowled. "You have such pretenses to thinking freely, Harry, but man's natural prejudices always reveal themselves in the end."

Brogan muffled a groan. He did not need his investigation deflected by politics. Especially when he could feel Juliana coiling beside him, readying to strike at Harry's condescending words. "I heard Lady Juliana's father has gone to visit a friend in Leeds. That is near Stanhope, is it not?"

"Not particularly." Miss Lynn adjusted a purple turban over her cap of dark curls. "The weather is dreadful up there this time of year. You should tell your father to return home," she told Juliana.

"If only I had the power to tell my father what to do." Juliana frowned. "If I did, perhaps he wouldn't have gotten into that jumble with... well, you all know who I'm talking about."

Brogan had to give her credit. She was a clever one, and much better at the friendly interrogation than he was. Juliana had laid out the bait very prettily; it only stood to wait to see if anyone would bite.

The men looked at each other, eyebrows drawing together. Miss Lynn merely looked bored.

"I didn't know your father was having problems with someone," a man who had been introduced as a historian said. "I'm sorry to hear it."

The other men nodded.

Harry leaned forward. "Who is he having a dispute with?" He nearly licked his lips, eager for that piece of gossip.

"Ah." Juliana tugged at the wrist of her gown. "It is of no consequence."

Harry deflated.

Miss Lynn elbowed his side. "You have another chance to feast on the misery of others." She nodded to the door. "Snowdon is here. Perhaps he will tell you something."

Juliana stiffened, shifting closer to Brogan.

Lord Snowdon wended his way through the sitting room to where they stood, his eyes narrowing as they caught on his sister's face. "Jules, what a treat seeing you here. I thought you had an aversion to my company and gone into hiding again."

"It's almost like you didn't have to pay someone to hunt me down," she said sweetly. "You could have just written to see me."

Harry and the other men looked between Juliana and her brother like their words were a ball in a tennis match.

Snowdon's cheeks went brick-red. "We'll discuss this later." He greeted the group and positioned himself next to Miss Lynn. "What did I miss?"

"The usual. Comets, the Romantics, the natural state of man." Miss Lynn rolled her head. "I thought you said this salon was interesting, but it's the same ideas all the time."

"You could introduce a new topic of conversation," Juliana said. "Something more to your liking. What topics do interest you, Miss Lynn? Where do your passions lie?"

The barest hint of a smirk crossed Snowdon's face. His hand went behind Miss Lynn's back, and if Brogan wasn't very much mistaken, gave the woman a small squeeze.

"I can't tolerate inequality," she replied. "Watching as some are born to privilege while the rest of us struggle." She ran her gaze up and down Juliana's body, pausing on her neat slippers and the lace trim of her gown. "If I am subject to these passions you accuse me of, that would be where they lie."

"A noble calling, to be sure." Juliana stepped forward eagerly. "Have you heard of Rose's idea to form a debate society to try to address this problem? I've sent him some essays with my thoughts—"

Snowdon snorted. "You and your little scribblings. Perhaps you should leave the big ideas to those more qualified, Jules."

Juliana's face went scarlet.

Brogan cracked the knuckles on his right hand.

"Writings and debates are all very well and good," Miss Lynn said, "but it is action that is needed. And don't mock your sister, Snowdon, not when she is at least trying."

Snowdon cleared his throat. "We all must do our part. Make sure the tenants have food, and all that. Now, I need a drink. The ride over here was damned dusty. Miss Lynn, can I get you anything?"

"Alcohol can only make this meeting more interesting." She placed her hand on Snowdon's arm. "I'll come with you."

Harry scratched his chest. "We let her in here, didn't we? I wonder what she thinks is so unfair."

And Brogan wondered what Miss Lynn saw in Snowdon, given he was one of the aristocrats born to privilege she seemed to disdain. But you never could tell what attracted some people to others.

The heat from Juliana's body warmed his side, and he stepped away. "Ready to go?" The salon had been useless. The only hope he had to solve this investigation was with Pickens telling them what they needed to know. Brogan didn't want to tell his employers he was hanging his hopes on such a thin thread. How soon would they regret their decision to give an ex-boxer a chance?

"All right, let me go see if Bertie is ready to leave, too."

Brogan trailed behind her, picking up snippets of conversation here about human nature and there about the darkness in Renaissance painting. These were Juliana's people. Her peers. And he felt as out of place as a fish in a meadow.

"We're leaving," she told Bertie. "Want a ride back with us?"

"I have to go to work, and the theatre is in the opposite direction." He shook Brogan's hand. "I'll get my own cab."

Smythe slunk up beside him. "Can you afford a cab on your salary?" He tutted. "If you need a friendly loan—"

"And now seems like the perfect time to leave." Bertie's Adam's apple bobbed up and down. He gestured to the door. "After you, Jules."

Brogan followed after them to where the butler waited. He handed them coats and hats.

Brogan looked down the hall. Smythe stood just inside the sitting room doors, talking with an unseen person and gesticulating wildly. Brogan looked back at Juliana's friend, who had stood beside her when the chips were down.

As Brogan passed Bertie on the front steps, he said, "You're better off."

He handed Juliana up into his carriage. He settled across from her and turned his hat in his hands. "Your acquaintances are quite varied."

"You thought I'd only be friends with members of the peerage?" She scooted to the side and tugged down one of the windows.

"That is what most members of the aristocracy do." Although the men who'd started the Bond Agency weren't like that. Brogan had felt nothing but respect from them in their treatment of him and the other investigators.

"When will you learn that I am not like most daughters of earls?"

He caught her gaze. Her eyes were a lovely shade of brown, coffee mixed with cream, like his morning drink.

"I think I figured that out the moment I found you hiding in Mr. Huddleson's apartments."

"Mr. Duffy. Brogan. About last night—"

"Last night didn't happen as far as you and I are concerned." He shifted, parts of his body remembering quite well that the kiss had happened. And those parts wanted more.

She turned to look out the window. "People of my station tend to believe the working class are immoral when it comes to relations, but you're actually the prudes, aren't you?"

"There is nothing prudish about keeping things professional. About understanding one's place in the world." He arched an eyebrow. "And there is certainly nothing wrong with not debasing members of the fairer sex, of any station."

She laughed. Out and out laughed at him. "Oh, how simple it must be in a man's mind, placing women into neat little boxes. Purity, innocence, motherhood, all those ideals we're wrapped in." She leaned forward and whispered. "I have news for you. I'm no longer pure. And I have very little innocence left to protect."

He blinked. Swallowed. Blinked again. After that kiss last night, he'd had his suspicions that she'd had at least *some* experience. But experience or not, whether he'd be ruining her or not, it made no matter.

He stared at the hat on her head. At the slight crack in the wood at the back of the carriage. Anything but at her. His body might be eager to explore with this new knowledge, but the circumstances hadn't changed.

She was a client. He was a new investigator who needed to earn his place.

She was the daughter of an earl. He was one step up from the streets.

Nothing could come of their attraction.

"I don't pretend to be an experienced woman. I've only had one lover," she said casually. "The affair lasted all of three months. But it was enough to show me that there is a whole world outside of society's expectations that I want to explore."

Brogan dug his fingers into his thigh. It was that damned education her father had given her, treating her just like her brother. Taking her to salons and who knew what else. Most women didn't talk like this.

Most women didn't make him want to shut them up with his tongue down their throat.

"You actually met him," she continued. "James Masters, the sculptor. He was very kind. And instructive."

His fingers had to be leaving bruises the way they dug into his flesh. Had he thought Masters one of the more normal people at the salon? The man deserved to be shitting out his teeth.

"We're here." Thank God. He couldn't take more of this conversation. He'd see her settled in the apartments and get the hell out of there.

He didn't wait for the driver to open the door but hopped down himself. Twilight had fallen, and the boy lighting the gas lamps was making his rounds. Brogan cracked his neck then lowered the steps for Juliana.

She took his hand and descended with more sway in her hips than he thought the occasion called for. She was trying to provoke him, and damn it, it was working.

"Tomorrow I'm going back to Newgate." He gritted his teeth. "Would you like to come?" Did he want her to come? No. But with Juliana he was learning that keeping her within eyesight was preferable to letting her loose on London.

A slight whirring sounded, and he flapped his hand in front of his face. He couldn't see any insects, but they weren't shy about making noise.

"Yes." She shook out her skirts. "I also wish to speak with Sir Thomas Miles. Lady Mary said he and my father had a falling out. It was some time ago, but leave no stone unturned and all that, right?"

The whirring grew louder.

Brogan frowned. "Let's get you inside before you get eaten alive."

Juliana took a step then paused. "One moment. I have a pebble...," she said as she bent at the waist to adjust her slipper.

Something crashed into the stone building above Juliana's shoulder.

Brogan didn't think. He rushed forwards, wrapped an arm around Juliana's waist and took her down. He twisted, trying to take the impact, but from her cry of pain he knew she had hit the pavement, too. He rolled, putting her body beneath his, and squinted up the street, looking for any movement.

The driver jumped down, pulling a pistol from his greatcoat. "A horse just went racing back up the street. What happened?"

Brogan waited for his heart to calm. For all his senses to assure him the danger had left before he picked himself off of Juliana. He pulled her to her feet then dropped to a squat, searching.

"This." He picked up a stone the size of his fist. "That whirring. It wasn't insects. It was a sling."

"A sling?" Juliana rubbed her ribcage. "Who uses a sling nowadays?"

The driver put his pistol away. "Medieval, but effective."

Brogan nodded agreement. He turned to Juliana. "It looks like you were right. Someone is trying to kill your father. And now they're after you."

Chapter Thirteen

"I think I was injured more by the rescue than I would have been by the rock." Juliana rubbed her side as she gently stretched out her leg. Her knee hurt like the devil, and she knew she would be sporting several bruises the next day.

They were in the sitting area of Brogan's apartments, he deeming the agency's rooms no longer safe as the assailant knew their location. After grabbing her few things, he'd bundled her back in the carriage and directed the driver to go to his home taking as many twists and turns as possible to avoid being followed. It had worked so well even Juliana had no idea what part of London she was in.

Brogan held up the rock that had nearly taken her head off. It was the size of his palm.

All right, maybe her minor aches and pains were little compared to what she would be feeling had she been struck with that boulder.

She dug the pebble that had been harassing her for an hour from her slipper. She placed it on the side table. "The rock that saved me from a rock that would have killed me." She sagged back onto the sofa. It was hard and the fabric worn, but she liked it. It reminded her a bit of Brogan. Rough on the outside but supportive. Safe.

A tremor rolled through her. Someone had tried to kill her. And unless Pickens had escaped Newgate, it was someone new. Unknown. And that was the scariest bit of all.

"I've never seen anyone use a sling before," she said. "Is

it difficult?"

Brogan strode to a cabinet and pulled out a small box. He came back to kneel before her. "Swinging a rock around your head isn't hard. Directing the rock to fly where you aim it is the part that requires skill. Your assailant was very skilled."

He gently took her hand and peeled down her torn glove. He blew on the reddened skin on the heel of her palm.

A quivery, fluttering sort of feeling started in her belly and worked outward. His head was bent to his task, and she had the strangest urge to run her fingers through his dark tousle of hair. He obviously didn't spend his money on a barber. Or his lodgings. She glanced around the nearly bare room again. But she preferred him this way. Blunt. Direct. No pretensions.

"Perhaps you were the target." Her voice came out a bit breathy, and she cleared her throat. He'd made it clear he didn't want an affair. No use letting herself yearn for things she couldn't have. "Perhaps the assailant wasn't so skilled and the rock came toward me by mistake."

Brogan wet a rag with a bottle of alcohol he pulled from the box and dabbed at her scraped skin. "Perhaps. But the simpler explanation is usually the right one. You thought your family was targeted; this appears to be proof."

She winced at his ministrations. "I never thought I'd say this, but I wish I weren't right. We need to get Pickens to talk to us. He's our only lead."

Brogan moved to her other hand. "He'll talk. To me. Tomorrow, I'm taking you to the agency's offices. You will remain under the guard of one of my associates at all time."

"What?" She jerked upright, sucking in a hiss as her ribs protested. Pressing a hand to her side, she glared down at the infuriating man. "After all this, I thought we'd come to an understanding that we would work together. I don't want to be hidden away." She had never been one to be cossetted. Didn't want to become only something Brogan needed to protect.

Didn't want to become useless.

She had been given so many more opportunities than most women. It felt like a betrayal to her sex to sit back and allow someone else to resolve her problems.

He frowned at her and pushed her back on the sofa. He pressed his hands to her side and felt along her ribs. "I remember no such understanding. My job is to protect you. You'll stay in the office."

"Your job is to find the person responsible for the attacks against my father," she reminded him. "And I'm the one who hired you. I get to dictate the terms of our relationship. Our professional relationship at least," she muttered. He seemed to be the one in full control of their personal relationship, or their lack thereof.

"And I can quit anytime I want." He pulled back, seemingly satisfied she had no broken bones. "I will if you don't act responsibly and stay in the office."

She bit the inside of her cheek. They would just see about that. He wouldn't find it so easy to walk away from her case. As much as she annoyed him, he wasn't the type of man who would leave her to her own devices, not when she was in danger. But as she'd learned, it was better to beg forgiveness than ask permission. She'd go to the office with him tomorrow... then leave after him and follow him to the prison.

"Where else do you hurt?" he asked.

"I'm fine."

He arched an eyebrow and waited. And waited. He truly was devilishly good at outlasting her patience.

She sighed. "Fine. My hip is a bit sore, and I scraped my knee when I fell. But nothing serious."

"Your knee." He looked at the body part in question as though he could see it through her skirts. He swallowed. "I'll, uh, raise your gown just enough to have a look, shall I? Or I could call for a doctor?" He sounded much too hopeful for her liking.

There was nothing wrong with her knees that should make him leery of seeing them. Any man would be lucky to see her knees. And, damn it, she'd make him realize that.

"No doctor." She dug the tips of her fingers into the material on her thighs and pulled it up an inch. He'd have to work for the rest. "You seem more than competent at treating minor wounds. I believe you said you used to box? Did you have to patch yourself up often?"

He didn't answer, not unless one considered a grunt as a response, which Juliana didn't. So, he didn't want to talk about his past life. Didn't want to have an affair, and she didn't think it was because he wasn't attracted to her. There were a whole host of 'didn'ts' when it came to this man. He had walls thicker than a fortress.

And Juliana wanted nothing more than to tear them down.

Steeling himself like he would be uncovering something ghastly between her legs, Brogan eased her skirts up over her knees. He kept his gaze focused on the scraped and swollen skin, as though if he let himself look anywhere else, he'd turn into a pillar of salt.

She didn't know if it was anger at his attitude, the high emotions resulting from a near-death experience, or just her natural perverseness, but Juliana let her thighs fall open. Just a little. Just enough to relax her muscles. And set Brogan to grinding his jaws together.

He pulled out the alcohol again and slapped the cloth on her skin with a bit more vigor than needed.

She narrowed her eyes. "Do you have somewhere else you need to be? Another woman to tend to?"

He looked up, startled. "No."

"Then perhaps you could slow down with that cloth. You're rubbing more skin right off."

"Sorry." He pulled the cloth away then blew on her knee. "I'll wrap a bandage around it to help with the swelling. You should rest it for the next couple of days."

"It's only some scrapes and bruises. I know you must

have had much worse and still somehow managed to get on with your life." She eyed the spread of his shoulders, the meatiness of his hands. Perhaps he hadn't had to deal with much pain. He looked like he would have been the one inflicting it in the ring. But still, it was the principle of the matter. "How delicate do you think women are?"

"Your kind are especially fragile." He took a roll of linen from his box and shook it out.

Juliana sat forward, putting her face in his. "My kind? Unlike the women in your social circle?"

He didn't answer.

She threw out her hands. "I'm not a separate species just because I'm an earl's daughter. I'm like any other woman of your acquaintance."

He snorted and began winding the cloth around her knee.

Heat raced up the back of her neck. "Truly, your ignorance is impressive. People think class bigotry only resides in the aristocracy, but they've obviously never met you. Why should you treat me differently than any other woman?"

He knotted the linen and placed both his hands on her knees as he glared at her. "Why do you insist on pretending to be like one of the commoners? People are different according to their status. The rules are different. What do you think would happen if your father and brother found out I had dallied with you? They would rightfully come for my head, and I'd have to kill them defending myself. Do you want that?"

She rolled her eyes. "Obviously not. But don't you think you're exaggerating just a bit? As I've said, I've had an affair before—"

His fingers tightened on her legs.

"—and it was nothing but a lovely experience. We didn't announce it to the world. Such relationships are quite common among the Ton, and I'll bet in the working class, too."

He rubbed his thumbs along her skin. The motion seemed unconscious. Natural. And sent a delicious curl of heat through her core. She instinctively widened her thighs a bit more.

"Perhaps among widows, not unmarried women." He inhaled, and a low sound rumbled through his chest. "It wouldn't be right."

She reached out and smoothed a lick of hair behind his ear. She cupped his cheek, enjoying the bristle so unlike her own smooth skin. "Why live how others wish? Why not live by your own rules? Unless you believe I'm a fallen woman. Impure." The word was bitter on her tongue. Among her friends, social conventions were paid little mind. It would hurt if this man thought less of her because she hadn't remained chaste. If he thought she was a harrid—

"No." He grabbed her hand and kept it pressed to his cheek, turning his face into it to kiss her palm. He rolled down to his knees and closed his eyes. "Don't ever think that."

She bent over and framed his face with her hands. "Then live by your own rules. By the ones we make together." She brushed her mouth over his, gently taking his lower lip and sucking on it. "Please, Brogan. I want you so much."

More than she ever had James. Her want was so deep it shocked her.

He opened his eyes. She saw the conflict. The desire. Needing to make the decision easier for him, she winked and said, "You still need to check my hip." With one last kiss, she leaned back and hooked her fingers under the edge of her skirts. She slowly, seductively, slid the fabric up her thighs, giving Brogan a view of her pantalets.

He groaned. Resignation lined his face. Surging forward, he claimed her in a deep kiss, cupping her breast with one hand as he explored her mouth. His teeth scraped along her tongue, sending shivers down her spine and making her body arch into his touch.

She fumbled with the ties to her undergarments. She felt empty, needy.

He pulled back, out of breath, and stilled her hands. He placed one of her palms on the seat next to her thigh, the other on the other side. He squeezed her wrists, telling her silently to keep them there, and kissed her again.

Well, if he wanted to do all the work, that was fine with her. For now.

He trailed kisses down her neck. Grabbing the back of her thighs, he pulled her to lie flat on the sofa.

The twinge in her side was easily ignored. His mouth had a way of making all pain disappear.

Brogan slid a hand behind her, arching her back. Without lowering her gown, he laved at her breast. He suckled her nipple through the silk, using his teeth to scrape across the sensitive nub. He slid his other hand up her pantalets to the slit at her crotch.

She whimpered at the first brush of his fingers against her lower lips. Moisture pooled, and Brogan growled as he spread her desire up to her clit.

She clutched his head. "You feel so good."

He pulled back from her body, ignoring her protest, only to circle her wrists and plant her hands back on the sofa. "Stay."

Her chest heaved. It took more energy to not reach for him than it did running upstairs. But when Brogan raised the hand that had been petting her, inhaled deeply and licked his finger, she forgot all about her discomfort.

Giving her a wicked smile, he slid down her body, shouldering her knees wider, and stared at the slit in the fabric. And what lay behind. He placed his hands on her hips and peeled the opening wider with his thumbs. And to her disbelieving eyes, he lowered his head and put his mouth on her.

"Oh, Lord!" Needing something to hold onto, she reached over her head and grabbed the back of the sofa. James had never shown her this. She wanted to protest.

Wanted to take a bath, perhaps, before letting Brogan know her so intimately. But her body refused to say any words to stop it.

Brogan traced a path between her lips, lapped at her essence before sliding that marvelous tongue into her core. His nose brushed her clit with each bob of his head, sending streaks of pleasure through her body.

She pleaded. Begged. Urged him not to stop. To never stop. Her life would be perfect if Brogan could live between her thighs. She'd care for nothing else, not even food or shelter.

He gripped her bum, pulling her closer as though he couldn't get enough of her taste. And just when she thought she couldn't take another minute of his delightful torture, Brogan wrapped his lips around her clit and sucked.

She exploded into a thousand vibrating bits of pleasure. She bucked into his mouth, writhed with ecstasy until it all became too much. She collapsed back, sucking down air and blinking at vague shapes her eyes refused to focus on.

The fabric of her gown was smoothed back down her legs.

She held out her hand, not able to do much more than that. "Give me a moment. That was... spectacular." She shook her head clear and gave Brogan a big smile.

Which quickly dropped at his closed-off expression. "What's wrong?" He didn't answer. Her stomach clenched, and dread withered the last, lingering feelings from her crisis. She swallowed. Keeping her voice light, she said, "Is it the sofa? I know it isn't big enough for the both of us. We can go to your bedroom to finish."

She glanced down at his trousers. The bulge, the *large* bulge, behind the falls proved he wanted her. Perhaps he just went quiet during intimate times. Any moment, he would throw her over his shoulder and take her—

"This was a mistake." The clench of his hand was his only display of emotion. "If you want a different investigator, I'll understand. You can interview the other agents tomorrow."

Juliana pushed a hank of hair off her face. "I don't want another investigator. I want you." In her bed. In her life. And maybe, if they were both lucky, in her heart.

"Then we'll forget this ever happened." He took a step back. Away from her.

Her insides twisted. He might have been able to discard a kiss, but he couldn't ignore what had just happened between them. "Brogan..."

"I'll get some blankets for you. You can sleep on the sofa tonight."

And as fast as his long legs could carry him, he fled the room.

Juliana bent her head, fighting the tears that threatened. Perhaps she *was* different than the women he was used to. Perhaps she was too different from him.

Because apparently he could ignore what had happened between them.

And she knew she would never be able to forget it.

Chapter Fourteen

He should have offered her the bed. Brogan frowned as Juliana rubbed the small of her back again. The sofa had been no place to let a woman sleep. But if she'd taken his bed, he'd never be able to sleep in it again. Not knowing her body had lain on it. Rolled about on it. Perhaps touched hers—

"And you say the assailant used a sling?" Wilberforce sat on the edge of Brogan's desk, turning the rock that had almost brained Juliana over in his hand. He stared at it as though the stone would reveal the secret of who had wielded it.

"Yes," he said. Juliana arched her back in her seat behind his desk, and Brogan wanted nothing more than to rub her aches away. He truly was an arsehole. Last night never should have happened. Now that he knew what she tasted like, how she sounded when in the throes of passion, he would never be able to rid her from his mind.

Brogan forced his gaze back to his boss. "One of my friends used to hunt with a sling when we were growing up. I'd go with him some times. The sound is distinctive." But unusual enough that he hadn't placed it until it was too late. He clenched his hand. If Juliana hadn't bent over at that precise moment...

Wil looked at Juliana like she was an abused puppy. "Are you certain you're all right, that we shouldn't call a doctor?"

"I'm certain." She gave him a firm smile. "I only want to find this blackguard so my life can return to normal."

Brogan winced. A normal that didn't include him, no doubt. She'd hardly said two words to him this morning, and why should she? He'd led her to believe something that wasn't possible. That their class differences didn't have to come between them. But in the back of his mind, he'd known the truth.

She was an aristocrat, a noble, someone not to be touched by the likes of him. It was better this way, for the both of them.

Wil stood and tossed the rock to Brogan. "What's your plan?"

"I'm returning to Newgate. I think Pickens is ready to talk, he just needs some prodding." He jerked his head at Juliana. "I want Lady Juliana to stay here while I'm out. She should be guarded at all times."

Wil nodded. "Of course. Lord Summerset's office is quite comfortable. He spared no expense in furnishing it. Lady Juliana can rest there."

The woman in question remained suspiciously quiet.

"No objection on your part?" Brogan asked.

"Would it do any good?"

"No." Brogan narrowed his gaze. Submitting to reality wasn't a trait he had credited her with.

She pulled a timepiece from her pocketbook. "Then why object? I will be fed, won't I?" She raised an eyebrow at Wil. "I become awfully grumpy if I haven't eaten by eleven."

"Of course." Wil's lips twitched. "There is a fine bake house around the corner which delivers. I do believe it was the reason the owners of this agency fixed on this location for their offices." He tilted his head towards the window. "A word, Brogan, before you go?"

Brogan followed the manager across the room. "Yes?"

Wil rested against the window sill and crossed his arms over his chest. "Do you need a reminder of your professional responsibilities?"

Brogan blinked. "What?"

Wil gave him a look, glanced at Juliana, then turned his gaze back to Brogan. "She is a client, and one under threat. She needs our protection and help. She doesn't need to have her emotions toyed with."

The back of his neck heated. "I have said nothing to make you suspect—"

"There is much that can be said without words." Wil ran a hand through his hair. "I don't want to involve myself in the affairs of my investigators, but if it involves a client, it becomes my business. Take care."

Brogan swallowed, the back of his throat aching. "You don't need to worry. I have made it clear to the lady that nothing can happen between us. Besides, she is more worldly than you give her credit for. *She* would not be hurt emotionally by an affair."

She would walk away from him as easily as she had her past lover. With a smile and a wish to remain friends, a wish that would never happen. He felt nothing *friendly* towards Juliana.

Wil smiled sadly. Rubbing his thigh, he rose to standing. "Take care," he said again.

Brogan nodded. He strode for the door, gathering his coat and hat from the pegs on the wall. Without a backwards glance, he fled the offices and headed toward Newgate.

Solving this case had become more imperative than ever. Not only because the threat against Juliana had become apparent, but so had the threat to him.

He needed Juliana out of his life, happily settled back with her family, with her odd friends and untraditional lifestyle.

Perhaps then thoughts of her wouldn't consume his mind every waking moment.

"Sorry." The guard he'd spoken with before remained stone-faced in front of the prison's door. "No visitors today."

Brogan sighed. He moved to take his billfold from his

pocket. "How much to change your mind?" It was good the owners of the agency had deep pockets. With the way his expense account was adding up, he wasn't sure the fee Juliana agreed to pay would cover it.

The guard looked longingly at the banknotes. "The prison is closed. No exceptions. But I do have something you might want."

Brogan's brow furrowed. "The entire prison? No one is getting in to visit at all?"

"The place is in lock-down." He shrugged. "It happens sometimes. Probably an inspection was scheduled by the magistrate. But the man you saw last time. The thief."

Pickens was more than that, but Brogan merely nodded. "What about him?"

"He wanted a message sent to you. I told him I might be able to help. You know, depending?"

"How much?"

The guard licked his lip. "What you paid me last time to get in should do."

Brogan provided the funds, the guard provided a crumpled letter from his coat pocket, and the exchange was made.

Brogan scanned the note. Pickens wanted to talk. Useless information as Brogan was intending to speak to the man whether he wanted to or not. He shoved the letter in his pocket and turned to go, frustrated. Even waiting one day to speak with Pickens seemed too long.

That left another night with Juliana.

Unless he got another agent to watch over her.

His gut churned. No. No one else would be watching over her at night but him. He didn't trust any of the other investigators to have the restraint he did. He stalked back to his carriage. All right, so he hadn't been all that restrained when he'd kissed her like a man dying of thirst and she was a tall drink of water. Nor when he'd put his lips on her quim and taken her to climax.

But, he reminded himself, he had stopped there. Hadn't

satisfied himself. He climbed into the carriage and slammed the door shut. And that had taken a Herculean amount of restraint.

A knock rattled the carriage door.

Frowning, he pushed it open.

And just like that, all his vaunted restraint went up in smoke.

Juliana smiled up at him. "Why aren't we going into the prison? I have ever so much more I'd like to say to Mr. Pickens."

* * *

The scowl Brogan shot her would have made a timid woman flee.

Luckily, Juliana wasn't a timid woman.

"What are you doing here?" Brogan leapt from the carriage, forcing her back a step. "How did you leave the office?"

She dipped her chin and shook her head sadly. "You didn't truly think I was resigned to remaining in the office all day, did you?"

Brogan's scowl deepened.

Her smile remained firmly affixed, but inside, her chest ached. He didn't want to spend time in her company. He rejected her again and again and yet still she hoped.

She was an idiot.

"Wil wouldn't have let you traipse out on your own." He peered down the street as if expecting the agency's manager to come sprinting up at any moment.

"I asked to use the necessary as soon as you had left." She adjusted the hem of her gloves. "As a gentleman, he wasn't going to stand outside waiting for me. It was a trifle to slip outside from there and hail a cab."

She did feel a bit badly about tricking Wilberforce. He seemed a kind man. Too kind, however. He wouldn't want a woman to involve herself in danger, so the subterfuge had been necessary.

"Now, you couldn't have spoken with Pickens so

quickly," she said. "Why are you leaving?"

"The prison is closed to visitors today."

She eyed the gray monstrosity. It squatted like a toad over the London streets. "Closed?" They would have to return on the morrow, when Brogan would be prepared for her stratagems. Her shoulders rounded.

Brogan ran a hand up the back of his neck. "Pickens sent a note. He's ready to talk."

She bounced on her toes. "That's wonderful. Can I see it?" She held out her hand.

He sighed. "It says nothing but he wants to talk." But still, he handed over the letter so she could read it with her own eyes.

"I was right. Someone paid him to attack my father. He's going to tell us who is behind the plot." By tomorrow, the threat to her father's life, and hers, would be over.

By tomorrow, she might never have a reason to see Mr. Brogan Duffy ever again.

Her excitement drained away.

"Perhaps," Brogan said. "Or he might tell us to jump in the Thames. We'll see."

She nodded. "Shall we visit my father's former friend, Sir Thomas, in the meantime? I'll only have to send a note to Hyacinth. She'll know where he lives."

"I'll go." He cupped her elbow and lifted her into the carriage. "You'll return to the offices."

Juliana settled on the seat opposite him. "Hmm." She tapped her bottom lip. "I don't believe a Mr. Brogan Duffy will gain admittance into the home of a baronet, not without me." She kept her voice light, but his words had been like a lash to her skin.

He couldn't wait to be rid of her. Well, tomorrow, his wish would most likely come true. Good for him.

"Besides." She crossed her arms over her chest. "When did you decide to make prisoners of your clients?"

Hands on his knees, he leant forwards. "Since I met you."

They stared at each other, neither speaking. She tried her best to ignore the scent of sandalwood soap wafting off his skin. The way his blue eyes darkened to navy when filled with emotion. The crooked ridge of his nose that begged her fingertip to trace its curve.

He slouched back. "Fine. We'll do it your way. For now."

The victory didn't elate her as it should.

After receiving the direction to Sir Thomas Miles's townhouse, along with an invitation to a musical evening at Hy's home the next night, they set off. The baronet lived in a smart section of town, one occupied by nouveau rich merchants and the fashionable set. Whatever investment had gone poorly with her father, it couldn't have affected Sir Thomas's wealth overmuch.

The townhouse was three stories high, made of a gleaming dark stone, and had an entrance even Prinny would have been proud of.

Unfortunately, it didn't hold Sir Thomas. He was at his offices off Bond Street, the butler told them. Another silent carriage ride, and finally they were in the baronet's presence.

"Little Lady Juliana." Sir Thomas took both her hands and held them wide, looking her up and down. "Is it truly you?"

She laughed. Something about the man's rosy cheeks and sparkling eyes allowed her to do nothing else. "Not so little any longer, but yes, it's me." She made the necessary introductions.

Sir Thomas pointed to the chairs in front of his desk. "Sit, sit, and tell me what this lovely visit is all about."

"Did you hear about Lord Withington's troubles with his secretary?" Brogan asked.

The older man's face clouded. "Yes. Nasty business. And what the scoundrel did to you?" He nodded at Juliana. "Attacking a woman? He should hang. I thought about writing to your father..."

Juliana scooted to the edge of her chair. "You and my father were good friends."

"The best." A smile curved Sir Thomas's lips. "You and your brother used to call me Uncle Thomas."

"What happened between you and my father? Why did you have a falling out?"

Sir Thomas shifted in his seat. "That, perhaps, is a question best asked of Withington."

"He wouldn't answer a question like that." Her lips twisted. She'd prided herself on having an adult relationship with her father, one where he treated her as he did his son, as an equal. But there was no depth to it. Her father, her brother, and her were like three acquaintances who happened to live together. No confidences were shared. No advice sought. Her father had cultivated his children's minds with his unorthodox educations, but there was much work to be done with their hearts.

She swallowed. "Please. I hope you won't divulge this confidence, but I believe my father in some danger. If I can understand what brought about a breach between the two of you, perhaps I can understand why someone else would want to hurt him. All I know is the kindness of my father. Is there something about him that has garnered him enemies?"

Sir Thomas started. "Enemies? Good heavens no, child. I hope you don't think I am his enemy. We had a falling out, yes, but your father isn't the kind of man to truly anger anyone."

"And your falling out was about...?" Brogan tapped his fingers on his knee.

Sir Thomas sighed. "Money, like so many fights. Your father had started an investment circle, and I was one of the members."

"And your investment was wiped out," Brogan said.

Sir Thomas nodded. "I, and the other two investors, lost a lot of money. We'd told your father that we thought his contact in the Bahamas wasn't trustworthy, but he refused to listen. We were all robbed." He scrubbed a hand across his jaw. "I should have made more of an allowance for his grief. What man could have been expected to concern himself with finance when he'd just lost his wife? But I was scared I'd lost it all, that I'd never recover. I haven't spoken to Withington since."

Brogan waved his hand at his office. "Obviously you did recover."

"Yes." Sir Thomas smiled, but it held a hint of sadness. "I learned to be more actively involved in all my investments. I've done well over the years."

"And the other investors?" Sir Thomas might have done well, but if one of the other men had remained impoverished, his resentment festering for seventeen years...

"Sanders died two years ago." Sir Thomas pursed his lips. "And Hatherford moved to the Continent. Venice, I believe."

Brogan looked to her, but she had no more questions. She shrugged.

"Thank you for your time." Brogan rose and held his hand out for Juliana.

She took it and stood, as well. "Yes, it was lovely seeing you again."

Sir Thomas circled the desk. "And you, too, my dear. You don't suppose, if I reached out to your father, that he..."

Juliana rose onto her toes and kissed his wrinkled cheek. "I think that is a splendid idea."

The carriage ride back to the agency's office was quiet. Juliana was lost in her own thoughts, about former friendships and relationships that were never allowed to begin. She didn't know what occupied Brogan's thoughts.

Wil had gone by the time they returned, but another agent was there manning the office, with a message for Brogan. "It came from your father."

Brogan took the slip of paper and turned his back to

read it. His shoulders went hard as rocks beneath his jacket.

Juliana placed her hand on his arm. "What is it? What's wrong?"

He crumpled up the note. "It's my sister. She's run off again."

Chapter Fifteen

"He's no good for 'er. I told 'er, but did she listen?"

Brogan clapped a hand on his father's shoulder. "It's all right. I'll get her back."

Juliana sat next to his mother on the sofa in his parents' small sitting room. She had an arm around his mother's curved shoulders and had handed over her handkerchief after his mother had soaked hers through.

His little sister had been told to remain in her room.

"When you find that man, you teach 'im a lesson, you hear?" His father shook his fist but there was no power behind it. Apoplexy had depleted the man of his strength two years previous.

Leaving Brogan responsible for his family. It was a responsibility he took most seriously. He took a determined step towards the door.

Juliana rose. "Should I...?" She nodded at the door then towards his mother, her indecision showing.

"Come with me." He hadn't particularly wanted to introduce Juliana to his family, but he hoped that another woman, one of Juliana's breeding and who was plainspoken, could convince his sister of her folly. Lord knew she didn't listen to him.

He ignored the carriage that idled in front of his parents' home. He strode down the street, knowing he was making Juliana trot to keep up but unable to slow his pace. Anger controlled his steps. How could his sister be so stupid? The man didn't care for her. When Brogan had spoken to him before, he'd found that out only too easily.

But Sally thought she was *in love*. Sentimental tripe. That's all this was.

Juliana gasped as they reached the next corner, pressing her hand to her side. "Being with you does put me through my paces."

"Sorry." His voice was gruff, but he made a concerted effort to slow his feet. They crossed the street and turned at the next corner.

"How do you know where your sister is?"

He glanced at her from the side of his eye. "Unlike you, Sally makes no attempt to hide where she goes." He stopped at a squat block of apartments. "She has been very open about the man she stupidly believes she will marry. She thought we would like him just as well as she does."

Juliana clasped her hat as she tipped her head back to look where he did. "And you didn't, I take it."

"No," he said grimly. "There's nothing in that man to like."

"There must be something." She sniffed. "After all, your sister likes him. She cannot be completely without sense, not if she's related to you."

He grunted. His sister was eight years his junior. She'd grown up when he'd already started making some money in boxing. Her life had been easier, and perhaps she had been indulged too much.

He pushed open the building's door. "Let's get this over with. The man lives on the second floor." He and Juliana climbed the sagging steps, and he pounded on the door.

The neighbor next door poked his head out, then scurried back inside his home at Brogan's glare.

Juliana laughed. "You have picked the perfect profession. Intimidation comes easily to you. If a person didn't know you better, he'd think you were capable of ripping their heads right off."

He glanced down at her. Was it Juliana who didn't know him better? Because at this moment he felt capable of tearing off some heads.

The door opened to his sister's smiling face. "Brogan! You came. I was going to send a note as soon as the wedding date was set—"

He pushed open the door and brushed past her. His eyes immediately found the man responsible for this mess.

Charles Barbour sat at a small table, a cup of tea in front of him and an ironic expression raising one of his eyebrows. "A family visit. How nice."

"Sally, this is Lady Juliana." Brogan cleared his throat. "A friend. Go downstairs with her and wait for me."

Sally protested. "This is my home now."

Brogan eyed the stack of dirty dishes in the sink. The clothing piled on a chair. This was nobody's home. This was a hovel not fit for his sister. The arsehole only wanted a mistress to tidy for him. And warm his bed.

"I'm going to speak with your intended," he told his sister. "If the man still wishes to marry you when we're done, I'll leave you be and object to the match no more."

She crossed her arms. "Of all the nerve. Of course, he'll still want me."

Brogan nodded to the door. "Then you have nothing to worry about."

Juliana, for once silent, opened the apartment's door and gave his sister a reassuring smile.

"Give me just five minutes," Brogan asked his sister.

She narrowed her eyes. Glancing between Brogan and Juliana, she shifted her weight. With a nod, she finally relented. Brogan thought it was more curiosity about Juliana than his persuasive talents that got her out of the apartments.

He waited until the door was shut and their footsteps had faded.

"So, you've come to collect your sister again." Barbour smirked. "When are you going to learn she has her own mind? She's a determined lass. You can't stop her from taking what she wants."

Brogan smiled, all teeth. "I can stop her. The only

question is whether you'll be happy with my manner in which I do so or not." He cracked each knuckle in his hand. His fist longed to strike flesh. It had been too long since he'd had a real fight, even as an agent for an inquiry agency. There was too much talking in this job, not enough bruising.

His body had been swirling with unmet need for days now. Juliana had been an aggravating temptation he'd barely refrained from succumbing to. If he couldn't pound out his frustration in a more pleasurable way, he'd take a fight over nothing.

Barbour's smile faded. "Come now. You're not going to use violence— gah!" He stumbled from his chair, just avoiding Brogan's hands. "It's the nineteenth century," he yelled. "Men don't resolve disputes through beatings."

Brogan's fist put proof positive to the opposite of that sentiment. Perhaps other men didn't. Finer men. Noble men. He landed another blow, reveling in the solid crack of bone meeting bone. But this was his way. When a man deserved a good thrashing, he was more than happy to deliver it.

It didn't take long to receive Barbour's promises. He had taken Sally into his home on a lark, and the situation had ceased to amuse him. Brogan hopped down the stairs to the street in a much better temper than when he'd ascended.

Sally hurried to him when he emerged, casting a worried glance behind her at Juliana. "Are you satisfied? Charles and I are going to marry as soon—"

The window above them screeched open. Brogan pulled Sally aside as a tumble of clothing was shoved out. Two ladies' boots, one after the other, followed.

"What...?" Sally picked up one of the boots. "My things."

"And good riddance to the lot of you." Barbour leaned out the window. "You've been nothing but trouble, and I'll be glad to have some peace."

Hurt flashed across his sister's face before being replaced by a scowl. "You bounder!" She threw the boot up at the window.

It came nowhere near close to hitting its mark, but Barbour jerked inside all the same.

"The nerve of that man," Sally fumed. "Coward." She caught Brogan's satisfied smile and narrowed her eyes. "And you! You're no better. Interfering, meddlesome brother. It will be a cold day in hell before I speak to you again." She gathered up her belongings, refusing his attempt to help with a lift of her chin. Wrapping the bundle up in one of her gowns, she held it to her belly and stamped to Juliana's side.

"You're better off than with a man who won't fight for you," Juliana said as they made their way down the street, Brogan following. "Now, as I was telling you, the commonly expected moralities of women have been fairly dissected by Mrs. Jones's latest monograph. Her works—"

Sally gave her a tight smile then drifted back to join her brother. "You brought a missionary to save my soul? And an odd one at that. She has yet to mention God."

Brogan didn't comment on the brevity of his sister's silent treatment. "She's not a missionary." He pointed out the next turn for Juliana, slowing his steps to stay behind her. His gaze dropped to her bum. Her gown and pelisse did a decent job of hiding it, but he remembered how it felt in his hands. If feel was anything to go by, she had a superior arse.

Regret swirled through him that he hadn't taken the opportunity to look upon it.

"Then who is this Mrs. Jones she keeps talking about? And Mr. and Mrs. Percy? She said their marriage was a bit uncertain and an example for why women shouldn't be so eager to join themselves in wedded matrimony, not without a true meeting of minds."

Brogan took her bundle of clothes and dropped his other arm around her shoulders. The clenching in his chest

eased with each step closer to home he took his sister.
"Those are her high saints. Don't worry, Sally, she won't
convert you."

Chapter Sixteen

Juliana folded one of her shawls into a triangle and laid it on the back of Brogan's sofa. There. That bit of color quite spruced up his sitting room. "I'm happy to loan your sister some of my books about sex and women's role in society," she called. "She might learn not to value her worth by a man's affections. She seemed interested when I spoke of them."

Brogan minced into the room, balancing trays and dishes on his arms. "I think she'll be too busy with whatever punishment my father will devise for her to read."

"Oh!" She hurried forward and took the plate of mutton and the dish of green beans from him. "I do hope he won't treat her too harshly. She was young and in love." An emotion she wasn't certain she had ever felt. She had certainly felt tenderly toward James, but when they had agreed to part, her heart hadn't been injured. What would it be like to fall in love?

She cast a glance at Brogan as she set the plates at the small table in the corner of the room. His apartments didn't have a separate dining room, consisting only of a bedroom, a small kitchen, and this sitting room. A bachelor's rooms.

Had he ever been in love? Ever thought about ending his unmarried state? She couldn't quite picture him professing words of love to a woman, either. Perhaps they were alike in that regard. Perhaps neither of them were destined to feel such deep emotion.

She swallowed, the back of her throat thick. But he would marry eventually. Of course, a man like him would marry. And he would be devoted and steady and everything a husband ought. And she would be...

She cleared her throat. "Tomorrow we speak with Mr. Pickens. This should be a celebratory dinner. Tomorrow we learn all, and you'll be rid of me." She tried to make it sound like a jest, but the truth in it made her chest ache.

Seeing Brogan with his family hadn't helped. He was such a caring son and brother. What would it feel like to be someone this man cared for? Her brother had paid people to find her, true, but she couldn't imagine him ever coming to fisticuffs over her honor.

"Yes," he agreed. He set a plate down then nudged it a couple inches over then back to its original location. For once, Brogan seemed uncomfortable.

"I like your family." She took a seat and started serving. "There is true affection between all of you."

She would have preferred if Brogan's father had discussed Sally's behavior with her instead of a gruff, 'go to your room,' when they'd returned, but she could tell he loved his daughter.

And the way his mother had held Juliana so tightly before she'd left...

Juliana knew it had been misplaced gratitude, thinking she might have played a larger role in recovering her daughter than she had, but having the woman's arms wrapped about her had felt wonderful. It had been a mother's hug, and that was something she hadn't felt for a long time.

His parents didn't seem to have issues with class distinctions like Brogan did. They'd treated her like a friend, without regard to her title. She wondered where he'd learnt it.

"Of course." He looked at her strangely as he settled himself. "As your father and brother feel for you."

She nodded, but inside, she wondered. There was affection between the three of them, she didn't doubt that. But as enlightened as the Wickhams were when it came to education and philosophy, she feared that when it came to family relations, they hadn't yet learned the finer art of familial affinity.

Love, but quietly. Feel affection, but in a constrained, elevated sort of way. Anything else was just too mortifying in their set.

"I promised to write your mother." She poured a glass of wine and took a sip. It was a bottle that would never be allowed in her father's cellars, but the flavor was bold and tasty if not complex. "Will that bother you?"

He started. "My mother's correspondents are her own."

"Yes." But he didn't sound happy about it. She pushed a bit of meat around on her plate. "Is my association so distasteful that you want to sever all contact after this case ends?"

"You know it isn't distasteful," he said in a low voice.

"Do I?" She tossed back more wine. "I know men can make mistakes, such as the one you feel you made last night, without engaging their emotions. That you could... kiss me... the way you did and still dislike me. That—"

He covered her hand with his own. "Stop." He brushed his thumb over her skin. "You know that isn't true."

She stared at his thumb. At the new scrapes on his knuckles. Anywhere but at his face. "Then why are you stopping what's between us? What could be between us?" Because his rejection hurt more than anything she could remember in a long time. Hurt her in a way that said that what she wanted from him wasn't a purely physical affair.

She wanted more.

"What do you think could be between us?" He placed a finger under her chin and lifted her face. "Truly? The son of a woodworker and an earl's daughter."

"There could be joy."

He glanced at the fire, looking torn. His shoulders firmed. He opened his mouth, and she rushed to interrupt him. A resolute Brogan wasn't in her favor.

"I wished I had seen how you convinced your sister's

beau to let her go." She traced the mark on one of his knuckles.

He shifted. "I only had a conversation with him."

"With your fists?"

"People understand fists better than words most times."

Yes, she could well imagine. Fists were direct, honest. Words could be twisted so as to become meaningless.

Her belly fluttered. Perhaps she had been approaching Brogan in the wrong manner. She lived in the world of words. He, in touch.

And with everything she was feeling, her touch could be very expressive.

She stood and circled the table.

Brogan pushed his chair back, looking wary, like he expected some sort of assault. He didn't look prepared when she dropped down into his lap, however.

Circling her hands around his neck, she leaned against his chest. Never had she felt one so broad, so strong.

"What are you doing?" His voice was a hoarse whisper. His hands flexed into fists by her sides, never touching her.

"Having a conversation with you." She leaned forward, kissing his jaw, speaking without words.

He groaned. "I'm not as strong a man as I should be."

"You're as strong a man as you need to be." She slid her palm across his jaw. "You're exactly as strong as I need you to be. Please," she whispered in his ear. Then licked the lobe. "Please don't deny me. Don't deny us."

He muttered an oath. But that was the last resistance he gave.

He fisted his hands in her hair, drawing her face to his. He took her mouth in a long, deep kiss.

She sank into him, loving the feel of his arms around her, grasping her waist as though he were scared to let go.

Loved the feel of his tongue, sliding into her mouth, sparring with hers.

There wasn't much about this man that she didn't love.

"This can work," she said, more to herself than to him.

"We can make this work."

He stood abruptly, gathering her in his arms. His chair clattered behind them. He strode from the sitting room into his bedroom.

He didn't give her time to look her fill, but she had the impression of sparsity, of heavy wood furniture, the room like the man himself. His masculine scent filled her senses.

He laid her on a firm mattress, following her down, settling himself over her.

His weight was a comfort against her body, his heat warming her straight through.

"Why can't I stop myself?" He trailed his kisses down her throat, pulling the bodice of her gown down to expose her decolletage. "Why can't I help myself around you?"

She had no answer. He had the same effect on her.

He was a man. She was a woman. What more needed to be explained?

She slid her hand up the back of his coat. Ran it along the lines of his muscled back then down, down to grip the firm mounds of his arse.

He ground into her, and she widened her thighs in welcome. His length settled just where she needed when she wrapped her legs around his.

He pulled back, breathing heavily. "Turn over." Without waiting for her to acquiesce, he gripped her waist and flipped her to her belly. He made short work of the laces of her gown and dragged the fabric down her body and off her feet.

In moments she was bare before him. Bare, and uncharacteristically shy.

She forced herself not to cover her nudity. Her body was different than the current standards of beauty. Her stomach was a bit rounder. Her shoulders too broad.

But she saw nothing in his eyes that reflected disappointment. Only heat could be found in their depths.

Gently, as though she were fine porcelain, he ran the tip of his index finger along the curve of her breast, down her side, over her hip. "You're beautiful." His voice was rough sandpaper. His touch as soft as a kitten's fur.

"So are you."

The edge of his mouth twisted. He obviously wasn't used to such compliments.

But he was beautiful to her. All strength, honor, forthrightness. Those were the things that made a man handsome. Those were the things that mattered.

His well-formed body didn't hurt, either.

He shucked his coat.

She tore the cravat from his neck. She ran her hands under his shirt, feeling every inch of him until he groaned, impatient. He pulled her hands away and yanked the shirt over his head.

She sucked in a breath. He truly was magnificent. His past profession had done his body a world of good. And she was the fortunate woman to take advantage of it.

His chest had a generous amount of hair. She ran her fingers through it, loving the feel of the springy curls. Loving his growl as she stroked across the flats of his nipples.

She ran her hand across his abdomen, tracing the faint line of hair that delved beneath his falls. Loosening one button, she reached inside and rubbed the hard length of him.

He pushed his trousers and small clothes down his hips.

Juliana sucked in a breath as his erect length rose to greet her. She rubbed her palm over the head of him, amazed by how soft this part of him was, and yet at the same time, how very hard. Hard for her.

He took her hand and pinned her wrist above her head. Leaning down, he took her mouth again, making this kiss slow and intimate. He lowered his body, his shaft resting in the cleft of her legs. Slowly, with each plunge of his tongue he rolled his hips in time, sliding his length between her lower lips.

He did this until she was gasping with need and she felt her slickness cover every inch of him.

"Christ, Juliana." His eyes burned down into hers. "You make a man want things he shouldn't."

"There's nothing wrong with wanting things," she said. "There's nothing wrong with getting what you want, either." She tilted her hips so that his next movement brought the tip of him to her core.

He hesitated only a second before steadily pressing in. He slid into her in one smooth, long push, stretching her walls, filling her completely.

She couldn't stop the gasp that escaped her mouth. The feeling was exquisite.

Everything about this man was.

With one hand on her wrist, the other cupping her breast, he began to move. His thrusts were long, even. He adjusted her legs, changed the angle, and went even deeper. He circled her nipple with his thumb as his length massaged her inner walls.

Their eyes locked on each other. She'd never felt more connected to a person in her life.

They could make this work. They would make this work. There was no other option.

She locked her ankles behind his hips, rising into his thrusts and clamping down her inner walls.

Brogan groaned. His movements became harder, uneven, and his bed knocked against the wall.

She gave a thought to his neighbors, about whether she should be embarrassed, but the notion slipped from her mind when he hit a place deep inside that made her shudder.

He trailed his hand down from her breast to rest on her hip. His thumb searched through her nest of curls, and found her clitoris. With each thrust he circled. With each thrust her body coiled tighter.

She squirmed beneath him, aching for release. Seeing it in sight but not quite able to reach it. "Brogan," she whispered. "I need..."

He nibbled at her lower lip. "I know what you need."

He thrust faster, the banging on the wall increasing to thunderous proportions.

Heat flushed through her body, and with one more circle of his thumb, she burst.

Her body tightened around him, making his strokes falter, making him groan.

He grabbed both her hips, chasing his own pleasure as he pounded into her.

The delicious ripples cascading through her body were just starting to ease when he pulled out of her, gripped the base of his cock with one hand, and spent on her belly.

He fell forward, catching himself with his hands on either side of her head. His chest just brushed hers. He stayed there as they both caught their breath.

As the air cooled their skin.

He gazed into her eyes. She saw a hint of confusion, and a lot of satisfaction.

"Juliana, this..."

"I know." She raked her fingers through his hair, brushing a lock off his forehead. "It's going to be interesting." Difficult, more like. Brogan would make it difficult with his prejudices. "But we'll make it work."

He dropped his head and climbed off the bed. He found a soft square of flannel and wiped her clean. He climbed in behind her and pulled her back flush to his front, kissing the top of her head.

"Interesting." He sighed. There was a lot that went unsaid in that sigh. "I can handle interesting."

Chapter Seventeen

Brogan sat in the bustling coffeehouse, tapping his thumbs on his third cup of the dark brew. He felt tense. Twitchy.

He didn't like it.

And his restlessness had nothing to do with the coffee. Juliana sat across from him, looking as calm and collected as no woman had the right to look after the night they had spent.

The things he had done to her.

His groin tightened at the memories.

There had been nothing in his apartments that morning to feed her, so Brogan had taken Juliana to the coffeehouse near his office. A half-eaten jam tart rested in front of her along with a steaming cup of chocolate.

Juliana slid her finger through a bit of jelly that streaked her plate and brought it to her mouth.

Brogan pulled at the leg of his trousers, hoping to give his poor, teased cock some breathing room as she sucked at the tip of her finger. The little minx must know what effect she had on him.

He knew how his body felt about the woman seated across from him; he didn't know quite how to feel about what they'd done last night, however.

She was the most enticing woman he'd ever met. She knew what she wanted, and she put all her efforts into getting it. Unfortunately, what she seemed to want was him. And he had doubts about the intelligence of that.

"Are you expecting an attack from some quarter?" she

asked. "Some dangerous criminal to draw down on you?"

He started. "What? What are you talking about?"

She shrugged. "You've been tense all morning. As though you're expecting something bad to happen at any moment."

He blew out a long breath and rolled his shoulders. She was right. She just didn't realize that she was the threat he was wary of. "I'm fine."

She dabbed her lips with her napkin. A rousing chorus of jeers and laughter at the table next to theirs made those lips curve upwards.

Juliana was a strange woman. She even joined in other people's joy, and he had a hard time seeking his own. It was a realization that didn't sit well. He didn't want to live a cheerless life.

He didn't want to live an immoral one, either.

"Look," she said, "things don't have to be awkward between us. I think you're making too much of last night. I know you think there can be nothing between us. But we aren't even at the point of seeing if we would want to make each other promises. Can't we just enjoy each other and see where it goes? It might end in a month. We might become sick of the sight of each other."

He snorted. "I sincerely doubt that." His gaze dropped to her bosom, her hips. Even covered in a thick, scarlet silk, her body was a tempting sight. He finally had an accurate image of her every inch, no imagination needed. And it wasn't something he'd ever tire of seeing.

She leaned forward. "This doesn't have to be complicated. We'll make it whatever works best for us."

Brogan ground his back teeth. She made it sound simple, something easily had... and easily broken off. He should be grateful she felt the way she did. Grateful she wouldn't cling or cry when their affair came to its inevitable end.

But would a few tears be too much to ask for? Her nonchalant attitude grated on his nerves. "An affair between you, an unmarried daughter of an earl, and me, a Cit, is not only complicated, but scandalous if it ever comes to light."

"We'll be discreet." She picked up her cup. "Such things are not as uncommon for my set as you might think."

He gripped the edge of the table. How casual she was. How careless. The sentiments she'd developed from her unusual education had made their affair possible, but it also made her blind to its dangers.

In civilized circles, their liaison was unthinkable.

Letting her go was equally so.

He slapped his hand on the table. She made it sound simple, and perhaps it could be. Perhaps he was thinking too far ahead. It was better to enjoy the moment, sweet as it was, and not worry about the future.

"All right," he said. "One day at a time."

The door to the coffeehouse swung open and two familiar figures strolled inside.

Brogan nodded at Wil and Lord Summerset, one of the owners of the agency.

Wil caught his eye and changed direction, heading toward their table, the earl a step behind.

"Good morning," Lord Summerset said. He tipped his hat to Juliana, a monstrously tall, purple job that matched his waistcoat. He flicked the rim of it with his thumb, looking for all the world like he was proud of the eyesore. "I see you share my affection for this coffeehouse, Mr. Duffy. And who might this charming companion of yours be?"

Wil gripped his hips. "Lady Juliana Wickham is a client of the agency. Mr. Duffy has been assigned her case."

"And you breakfast with our clients to show them the full array of services our agency provides." Summerset arched an eyebrow. "I applaud your dedication."

Wil cleared his throat. "There was an attempt on Lady Juliana's life. She is staying with Mr. Duffy until we know she is safe."

"I see." Summerset smirked at Brogan before turning

his charm on Juliana. "I do hope our agency is providing everything you might desire, Lady Juliana."

"Quite," she said. Brogan had to give her credit. Her voice was unruffled, but the faintest hint of a blush stained her cheeks. Perhaps she wasn't as worldly as she pretended. "In fact, just this day we might come to a resolution of the case."

Wil looked to Brogan.

He told his employers of Pickens sending a note asking to speak to them.

"Good," Wil said. "The sooner this business is over, the better it will be for Lady Juliana. For all involved." The look he gave Brogan carried significance, and Brogan flushed.

"You look familiar, Lady Juliana." Summerset placed his hand on the back of her chair and leaned forwards, much too close for Brogan's liking. Much too smirking and simpering. The earl was married, and by all accounts happily so, but marriage hadn't taken the flirtation out of him. "Did we dance together at Lady Mary's fête last autumn?"

Juliana favored him with a smile the earl didn't deserve. "I was there, but didn't dance. Though we weren't formally introduced, I believe we were in the same circle of conversation at one point. Lady Mary does have the most interesting evenings. She is one of my favorites."

Summerset smiled. "Mine too. Are you planning on attending—"

Brogan stood. "Well, we must get going." He rounded the table and pulled Juliana's chair back. "The day is getting on."

Juliana looked to her half-eaten tart to him, and sighed. She stood. "Yes, we have an appointment with Mr. Pickens, one I don't want to be late for."

They made their farewells and left the coffeehouse. They climbed into an agency carriage and rolled away.

"Do you not care for your employer?" Juliana asked.

Brogan looked out the window. "He's fine."

"Is it a problem with nobility in general that you object to then?"

Brogan narrowed his eyes. "I object to nothing in general. I look to specifics. The earl is as fine a man as any."

"Do you ever socialize with him?"

Brogan shot her a sharp look. "Of course not."

She lifted her hands, palms up. "Why? He's not a different species. You have interests in common. Would he snub you?"

Brogan shook his head. "I, and all the other agents, were invited to his home for a holiday party. The earl, all the owners of the Bond Agency, have extremely varied acquaintances. I was unable to attend." Rather, he'd chosen not to go. He worked with the men. He didn't need to be friends with them.

"Then it is you," she said. "You seem to think you have a place in this world, a box you should remain within." She looked at her skirts. "A box I might not fit into."

She didn't fit into his life. And yet they fit together so very, very well in other respects.

They passed the remainder of the journey in silence. Brogan could feel her hopes as though they were a tangible thing.

He wanted to share them, but commonsense prevailed.

He flipped back and forth between believing that they could just enjoy each other day to day, to knowing they would come to an end soon.

At the prison, he helped Juliana down and led her through the streets to reach the front gates. He pounded on the door, sliding his other hand into his pocket for his billfold. How much would this visit cost the agency?

Whatever it was, it would be worth it if it brought the threat to Juliana to an end.

A guard he didn't recognize opened the door. "What?"

"We're here to see Mr. Pickens." Brogan held up a banknote as encouragement.

The guard's face hardened. "Pickens won't be seeing nobody today."

Brogan's shoulders went back. The prison couldn't still be closed for inspection. Was this an extortion attempt for more blunt?

The guard glanced at Juliana then at the space over Brogan's shoulder, saying nothing. He looked as immovable as a gargoyle.

There was shuffling behind him, and the door swung wide. A familiar face poked his head out. The guard he'd dealt with previously looked longingly at the banknote Brogan held.

"Forgive my friend," he said. "He doesn't mean to be rude. He doesn't know any other way."

That garnered a glare from his fellow guard.

The second guard wrinkled his nose. "What he meant to say is that Pickens won't be seeing anybody at any time. He was killed yesterday."

Chapter Eighteen

Juliana paced the wooden floors of the agency's office, making sharp turns at either end of the room. She bit back oath after oath. Her frustration should have boiled her blood.

Dead.

She couldn't believe it. Right when Pickens was ready to talk. The timing of it seemed too coincidental to be believed. Could someone have set it in motion?

Brogan sat on the corner of his desk, arms crossed, speaking to Wilberforce. "The guard said a fight broke out yesterday in the common area during afternoon exercise. Two other people are receiving care for knife wounds, but Pickens was dead when the doctor arrived."

"And the man wielding the knife?" Wil absently rubbed his thigh.

"No one seems to know who it was. No one saw, or at least no one's talking." Brogan ran his hand up the back of his hair. "There was a mass of bodies rolling about and the guards couldn't see who was doing what."

"And your one lead is dead." Wil's voice showed as much disbelief as Juliana felt.

Brogan nodded.

"It can't be coincidence," she said. "It would be too providential for the person responsible for the attacks against my father to have the one person who could name him die before he spoke."

She leaned against the windowsill. "How hard would it be to pay someone to kill Pickens inside the prison?"

Wil pursed his lips. "Not hard at all."

She slapped the wall and started pacing again.

Their one lead gone.

"My brother must see the truth in my suspicions now," she said. "Once I tell him Pickens was killed, he'll have to believe me. Do more to protect our father. Question all the servants, investigate his friends. Something. Anything."

"Our questions and investigations have discovered nothing." Brogan flexed his hand. "I don't see how you brother's would do any better," he grumbled.

She frowned. Men and their egos. "I just mean it will be nice not to have to work against my brother in this matter." She nodded. "I must talk to him."

"If you wish," Brogan said. "But for men predisposed not to believe any danger exists, this will easily be brushed away. Prisons are full of violent people. A violent act occurred. Pickens getting killed isn't all that unlikely."

"Even my brother," she began then paused. No, her brother probably wouldn't see the truth of this. He would believe it was naught but coincidence because that was what he wanted to believe. It didn't mean she didn't have to try.

She checked the clock in the office. "I'd still like to talk to him."

Brogan stood and gathered his coat. He paused when Wil grabbed his arm and whispered something in his ear.

Brogan tensed, but nodded. Keeping his gaze averted, he led Juliana from the office.

She fiddled with the hem of her glove on the ride to her family's rented townhouse. Last night had been amazing. Today, not so much. She knew Brogan had regrets. She wasn't used to being someone's regret. She didn't like the feeling. And she didn't know how to allay his concerns.

She wasn't looking to trap Brogan. And they were obviously compatible. Why couldn't the blasted man just enjoy what they had? Why did he have to see a barrier where none existed? It was like he intentionally looked for an excuse for them to fail.

He was a pessimist. Like he didn't expect his life to go the way he wished it. She chewed on the inside of her cheek. Perhaps his life never had gone the way he wanted.

She'd had it easy. When she wanted something, she almost always got it. Brogan had to work for everything he had. He faced struggle after struggle.

Would he work to have her? Was she worth the struggle?

They rolled to a stop in front of a three-story townhouse. Juliana got out of the carriage and stared at up at her family's London residence. She lived there almost as much as she lived in Bluff Hall. She knew every inch of every hall and still, standing there before it, she felt like a stranger.

She trudged up the steps and knocked at the door like a guest.

Mr. Johnson, the butler, gave her a smile and a nod when he opened the door. "Lady Juliana. It's very good to see you."

"Thank you. Mr. Johnson." She and Brogan stepped into the entry. "Is my brother at home?"

"No, my lady."

"Did he go to his club?" She looked up the steps. Everything was quiet. Solemn almost. She couldn't remember much laughter in the house, but today it seemed excessively glum. The oppressiveness of Bluff Hall had extended here.

"I don't believe so, my lady. The carriage went in the opposite direction." Seeing as they weren't removing their coats and hats, Johnson folded his hands.

Juliana sucked on her lower lip. She didn't think any of their societies or salons had meetings today, but Snow had a busy social life. He could be anywhere.

The butler cleared his throat. "The driver has told me that my lord frequents an apartment above a tea house on Butler Street of late. He seems to meet there a couple times a week."

Juliana gripped the man's forearm and squeezed.

"Thank you, Mr. Johnson." It was improper for a butler to speak of his master's whereabouts, but the servants had always favored Juliana over her brother. A fact for which she was becoming increasingly grateful.

With one last squeeze of his arm. Juliana turned and skipped down the steps back to the carriage.

Brogan handed her in and gave the driver directions.

"Should we send a note ahead?" Brogan asked.

Juliana tipped her head. "Why?"

"In case..." Brogan paused. "Well, if he's in an apartment... Your brother could be..." He shifted.

"*In flagrante delicto?*" Juliana supplied. She shook her head. "It's the afternoon. Broad daylight."

Brogan dipped his chin and gave her a look. "Desire doesn't account for the time of day." He proved his point by giving her a very lascivious look up and down her body.

She pulled at her fichu, suddenly warm. "Be that as it may, we're talking about my brother. He's not like that. Too... cold-blooded. He's probably just with a friend."

Brogan arched an eyebrow. "You brother is in a relationship with Miss Lynn, the woman from your salon. Does that sound cold-blooded?"

"What?" She fell back against the carriage seat. "Why do you think that?"

"I saw the way they looked at each other, the subtle touches." He ran his finger over her knee. "Something only lovers would do."

She thought about that. She also thought about climbing onto Brogan's lap here in the carriage and having her way with him. But Butler Street wasn't far so she turned her mind back to her brother.

Snow did seem fond of the woman, more than Miss Lynn's abrasive personality would warrant. She was attractive, no doubt, but Snow needed something more than just obvious charms. Perhaps Juliana had misjudged the woman. Perhaps hidden depths lay within.

She smoothed her skirt. "Still, I'm sure wherever he is

now, it'll be fine for us to call. He is my brother and I have something urgent to speak with him about."

Brogan shrugged. "As you say."

They found the tea shop and, ignoring the delightful smells of fresh bread, they climbed the steps to the apartments above.

Brogan knocked.

Expecting a maid servant to answer the door, Juliana's eyes popped wide when it was her brother's face that appeared instead. "Snow?"

His posture stiffened. "What are you doing here?"

"I've come to speak with you." She peered over his shoulder. "I don't want to interrupt your... meeting? But it is most important."

He pressed his lips together. "It's a small gathering from the Rising Sun Society."

Her brother had taken her to one of that society's meetings. There had been a lot of shouting and anger over the inequalities in England, but no productive ideas. Juliana had only attended once. She'd forgotten Snow was a member.

"Snowdon, who's there?" a woman's voice called.

Juliana had also forgotten that the Rising Sun was where Snow had met Miss Lynn, and then brought her into Voltaire and the Rose Salon.

"My sister and her..." Snowdon narrowed his eyes at Brogan.

"Her friend." Brogan folded his arms across his chest.

"Well, let them in," Miss Lynn said.

Her brother sighed, but did as he was told.

Juliana stepped into a small room, made even more confining by the abundance of furniture, knickknacks, and rugs piled everywhere. At the far wall, a striking cerulean blue settee drew the eye. Arranged on top was Miss Bella Lynn, wearing nothing but a silk robe. Her calves were bare, along with one shoulder as she lay on her belly, posing.

A man sat across from her, an easel before him, painting the image.

Another man sat scowling in the corner.

"Lady Juliana, Mr. Duffy," Miss Lynn said, "how lovely of you to join us."

Brogan stiffened beside her. He studiously kept his gaze everywhere but on Miss Lynn and her partial nudity.

Juliana's heart melted. He was a dear man.

"We don't mean to intrude," she said. "I came to speak to my brother about some important news."

"By all means." Miss Lynn waved her arm. "We were merely discussing the constitutional rumblings being heard in Spain, and how such an uprising might sweep across England, as well. Nothing too important we can't spare Snowdon."

Juliana bit the inside of her cheek. Insolent woman. How did Snow stand her company?

"Well?" Snowdon said. "What is it?" He tapped his foot and looked longingly over his shoulder, back at Miss Lynn.

Juliana shook her head. Brogan had been right. He had seen something that she had not. Her brother was most definitely infatuated.

She drew him into a corner of the room and used Brogan's large body to block them from view. And hopefully from hearing.

"It's about Mr. Pickens," she whispered.

"Pickens," he exclaimed, loud enough for the patrons of the tea shop below to hear. "Why would I care about that man?"

Juliana sighed. "He's dead. Killed. He said he wanted to speak with me and Bro— Mr. Duffy, and then was murdered the next day. Do you not find that suspicious?"

Snowdon scratched his ear "Should I?"

"Yes." Juliana flapped her hands. Sometimes, her brother was impossible. "He wanted to talk to me, he was going to tell us who had hired him to go after father. And then he gets killed. The timing of it is too—"

"Improbable," Snow said. He shook his head. "Your whole story is improbable. The man was a criminal. He was killed by another criminal. That's the way life goes. Truly, Jules, I begin to worry for you."

She planted her hands on her hips. "That is not—"

Brogan nudged her. He shook his head.

She took a deep breath, trying to calm her ire. Her brother probably needed time to fully assess the situation. It was shocking news. He would come around. "Well, I thought you ought to know."

"And now I do." He stepped around Brogan and picked up a platter, heavy with grapes and orange wedges. He brought it to the model on the settee. "You've been posing for hours. You must be hungry."

She plucked a fat grape from its stem. "So, was the news your sister imparted as interesting as she made it sound?"

He scoffed. "Hardly. Just my father's former secretary, apparently dead, killed in prison. Saves the Crown the expense of a trial. Good riddance, I say."

Miss Lynn sat up, readjusting her robe as it threatened to expose more than just a shoulder. "The Crown can spare the blunt in order to provide a fair trial to one of its citizens. Truly, Snowdon. Sometimes I do despair of you."

The man in the corner snorted. "What did you expect from the son of an earl? A humanitarian?"

Miss Lynn's lip curled. "Lady Juliana, have you met my brother?"

"I haven't had the pleasure." Juliana stepped forward and inclined her head. Upon closer examination, she could see this must be the brother who had been in the riots last year. He showed signs of serious injury. One eye was discolored, milky, as though covered in a thin layer of egg white. He held his left arm close to his side, protectively, and a wooden brace covered the lower portion of his leg.

"How do you do?" she asked.

He said nothing, just looked at her with contempt.

"Jacob, play nice," his sister reproached him.

But it was only when Brogan stepped up beside her and glowered at the man that he deigned to nod.

"And this is Philippe LaConte." Miss Lynn pointed to the artist. "A name you, and everyone else, shall soon recognize."

He waved his paintbrush in the air, but kept his focus on the canvas.

"I seem to have become one of his favorite models," Miss Lynn said.

The artist glared at her. "You'd be even more favored if you'd stay in position."

Miss Lynn sighed dramatically but rolled back to her belly. She gave the painter a wink. "Have you heard of the pressure being brought on King Ferdinand? How the people are demanding he restore the constitution?" she asked, Juliana. "If your father has any influence in the House of Lords, don't you think it would be good for him to propose such reforms here as well?"

"I have heard of Spain's troubles." Some saw them as an opportunity to bring freedom to more of the world. Others worried it would be a repeat of France. Juliana was of both minds. She wanted more opportunity and rights for the lower classes, but after hearing Madame Tussaud speak to the Rose Salon of her time casting death masks on all the severed heads in Paris, well... She shivered. That wasn't something she ever wanted to see happen in England.

"I'm not sure how my father feels about such reforms," she said. "I do know he would do much to prevent seeing our streets run red with blood like they did in France."

Miss Lynn flapped her hand. "It was a noble attempt on the French citizens' part. And if it inspires other countries to revolt, it was all for the good."

"Can that amount of blood spilled ever be good?" Juliana asked. Although America seemed to be making a go of it, and much blood had been spilled in that war.

Miss Lynn fluttered her fingers. "That business was over years ago."

"Over for some," Brogan said, his voice low. "Many still live with the consequences of what the French revolutionaries did. Those left without mothers or fathers, sons or daughters."

"So, he does talk." Miss Lynn rolled to her hip. "I thought you were just here to look pretty."

Snow handed her another grape. "That's your job, my dear."

Miss Lynn rolled her eyes.

"Not that you don't have many other fine attributes," Snow quickly added. "Your mind is as sharp as a razor."

"No need to go overboard," Miss Lynn said. She turned her attention back to Juliana. "Well, what do you say? Will you at least broach the subject with your father? This one," she gave Snowdon a look, "seems to have no influence with the man."

Most likely because their father knew Snow had never had an interest in politics before, and a suggestion now would be curious, to say the least.

She watched as her brother fed Miss Lynn another grape. A small shiver worked its way down Juliana's spine. Juliana wondered that her brother seemed happy to act the acolyte. He was much different with this woman than he was at home.

Brogan's arm brushed against hers, and she leaned into him.

She supposed she acted differently with her lovers, as well.

Jacob chuckled. "The impotent viscount. You sure do know how to pick 'em, sister."

Snowdon straightened. "My father and I no longer see eye to eye on a great many things, but I will try again. That's what's best for the people of England, of course."

Juliana barely bit back her response. *When have you ever cared about what was best for the people of England?* His new friends might be having a benevolent effect on her brother. She might not agree with the policies he wanted, but caring about the hardships of those in the world around him was a solid first step in becoming the man she wanted him to be.

And one day, he would be earl. Be a member of Parliament, be able to effect change. Make a difference. While she...

Her stomach twisted.

While she attended lectures, salons, discussions. She learned as much as she could, but what did she actually accomplish? What good was she to the world? She swallowed. It wasn't Snow's fault he had been born the son. That he had a path to be of service. It was only to the good that he finally became serious about his responsibilities.

But jealousy gnawed at her. Along with the fear that she would remain useless throughout her life.

"Have you heard from our father lately?" Juliana asked, proud that her swirling emotions weren't revealed in her steady voice. "Is he still at Rose's house?"

"Yes." Snowdon sat on the edge of the settee, swinging his leg. "You know how he loves the plum puddings Rose's cook makes. I swear, he'll come back a stone heavier."

Juliana's lips curled up. She remember that cook, as well, and hoped her father enjoyed every bite.

"Plum pudding?" Miss Lynn sat up. "That does sound good. Anyone else want Snowdon to pop down to the tea room for a little snack? Get us some pastries and breads, will you?"

The artist put in an order for currant cake. Her brother demanded a sandwich.

Snowdon nodded. "I'll just show you out as I go down, shall I, Jules?"

Nodding, she and Brogan followed her brother down the steps and out onto the street.

She adjusted the brim of her hat to block the sun's rays. "Think about what I said, will you Snow? Tell Father to stay where he is for a while more until this gets sorted out. With Mr. Pickens dying—"

"Pickens tried to steal from father. He tried to hurt you. Now he's dead. I see nothing bad in this."

Juliana's shoulders slumped. Unless something was staring him right in the face, her brother would never see it. "All right, Snow. Take care." She rose up on her toes and kissed his cheek.

He hurried inside the shop without a backward glance.

Juliana blew out a breath. "My brother..."

"Is an idiot." Brogan cupped her elbow and led her to the carriage.

She settled her skirts on the bench and sat. "He's not an idiot. And his new friends seem to have an improving effect upon him. He never used to care about the working man."

Brogan leaned into the corner of his carriage and stretched out his leg so his boot rested next to her hip. "You think that was him caring about the little man? He only cares about acceptance from his peer group."

Juliana frowned. "That is too harsh. And even if true, why does he want to be accepted by that particular group? He could seek acceptance with his stuffy club members at White's. No, his befriending such reform-minded people can only be for the good."

Brogan snorted but said nothing.

"Surely you cannot disagree with the ideals of reform." She prodded his leg. "It is aimed to help men such as yourself."

He stared at her flatly. "It is men like me who are the ones to fight and die in revolutions. The world can change without such *reforms*. It is changing now. Fifty years ago, a man born to a woodworker would never have had the chance to sit at a desk working as an investigator."

"But still, our society doesn't treat you as equal." She swallowed. She hated that he could be looked down upon by anyone, especially by those she considered friends. But he would be. And it wasn't fair. He was a good man, honorable, hard-working. That was all that should matter.

"No." He clenched and released his fist. "In society's

eyes, we will never be equal." He looked out the window.

The silence was a heavy, oppressive thing. A vise wrapped its tentacles around Juliana's chest and squeezed. Brogan already saw the end for them. He'd seen the end before they'd even begun.

She inhaled deeply, let it out. Again and again until her mind had calmed along with her breathing. She'd already known his objections. She'd broken through many of them. Against his better judgment, they were having a relationship. She couldn't hope to alleviate all his misgivings at once, but she would keep working on him. And she was determined to succeed.

She changed the subject. "After seeing your relationship with your sister, you must think mine with Snow awfully superficial." And perverse. For what else could her jealousy of her brother be called?

Brogan nudged her hip with the toe of his boot. "You can't make people listen. Or see the truth. Your brother is no different than many people."

"Yes." She chewed on her bottom lip. Her brother was as obstinate and foolhardy as most other people.

The threat against their father wasn't like what most other people had to face, however. "But an inability to see the truth doesn't usually risk someone getting killed."

Chapter Nineteen

"No, absolutely not." Brogan widened his stance and crossed his arms over his chest. Of all the foolish ideas Juliana had, this might top them all.

"Brogan, it's an evening of music and conversation. What are you concerned about?" The light from the window caught Juliana's hair, lighting her head up like a halo. Thankfully, the woman was far from angelic, though in this instance Brogan could wish her more tractable. They were back in the agency's offices, ostensibly to make plans for the future of the investigation, but more because he wanted a safe place to stow Juliana.

He grimaced. Even if the event hadn't had the potential to pose a threat to her life, an evening of music and conversation sounded interminable. Luckily, her safety was a good excuse.

"Someone tried to take your head off with a stone, not two days ago," he said. "Need I remind you that putting yourself in a room full of people is not the smart way to stay unharmed."

"But these are my friends," she argued. "It's at Hyacinth's house. You've been there before. It's safe."

"You suspect one of your father's friends might want him dead. This event at Miss Butters's home will be full of his contemporaries. You might be walking into a pool of suspects. You don't know it's safe."

She sighed, her bosom rising and falling most becomingly.

He leaned closer. "If we skip the musicale, I promise

you much more enjoyable entertainments this evening."

She drew her fingertip down his sleeve. "Or, we could go to the musicale and then enjoy those entertainments on our return to your apartments. The best of both worlds."

He ran his hand up the back of his head. He didn't know if he was more annoyed that she didn't go calf-eyed at the idea of an evening spent in his bed or that she could so easily out argue him. His talents had never lain in debate. He usually settled arguments nonverbally.

For instance, if Brogan ran his own investigative agency, he would have taken Juliana's brother outside and learned everything he'd known quite quickly. The conversation this afternoon at Miss Lynn's sat uneasily in his gut.

Juliana seemed to think nothing of it, but something had struck him as amiss. That lot seemed too fond of bloodshed. Or at least too indifferent. Among the intellectual class, that romanticism of The Terror seemed more and more common.

For people with such revolutionary leanings, what lengths might one go to in order to affect change? Murder an earl? He couldn't believe Snowdon would kill his father. He was too disinterested in becoming earl. His father provided for all his needs so there was no gain for him.

But he had shown himself to be a weak man. Easily manipulated. His associates could use such a man as a pawn, be scheming right under his very nose. And with Miss Lynn ready to step in as the next countess...

Unfortunately for his theory, Lord Withington had little power in the House of Lords. Less influence among his peers. If the son stepped into his place, not much could change. Surely Snowdon's friends knew this.

Still, something about that lot unsettled him.

"I understand Mrs. Joanna Bergen is going to be playing the harp this evening," she said. "She's supposed to be marvelously talented. Please, Brogan. I do so want to hear her."

Juliana gave him a most bewitching look, all big eyes and

pouting lips.

His resolve began to crumble, just the tiniest bit. "Even if I were fool enough to agree to this," he grumbled, "I still cannot go. I have nothing to wear to such an event."

She arched an eyebrow. "That is your excuse?" She looked him up and down, shaking her head. "What you're wearing now is fine. You might not be in the highest fashion, but that matters naught."

Highest fashion? Brogan wasn't in *any* fashion. A fact that mattered to him less than the latest needlepoint stitch. Unless he was seen by Juliana's side. He didn't wish to embarrass her.

"What would we tell people?" he argued. "I'm not a family member to chaperone you. An unmarried woman cannot show up with a *friend*." He put emphasis on the last word. He had been so quick to describe Juliana as such before, but it now left a bitter taste in his mouth. "I suppose I can accompany you as a bodyguard." His lack of fashion sense would hardly matter in that case.

But the whispers that would erupt from such an announcement, that Lady Juliana needed a protector, well, he didn't suppose that was something she wanted to face.

"Splendid." She clapped her hands together. "Then that's what we'll do."

His shoulders sagged. When would he learn? She never gave him the expected answer. It was one of her best features, and one of her most irritating.

She eyed him critically. "But if you don't want to stand out, perhaps we could improve your wardrobe, just a bit. I don't suppose you have a top hat?"

He snorted. "Never been needed."

"Your coat and trousers are fine." She tapped her lip with her finger. "Perhaps a jauntier cravat. Something in silk."

He fingered his cotton neckcloth and leveled her with a withering stare.

Juliana called out to Cyrus Verity, the agent at the next

desk. "Do you have a top hat and cravat Brogan could borrow?"

The investigator burst out laughing. "Brogan Duffy, spruced up? This I have to see. Oy, Hurst," he called to another agent, "do you have a top hat for Duffy? The taller the better."

Brogan groaned. He would not live this down.

Wil stepped out of the back office. Catching Brogan's attention, he waved him over.

Brogan was only too happy to escape to speak to the manager.

He left Juliana discussing waistcoats and men's shoes with his fellow investigators.

"I don't have new information about the investigation," Brogan began. He leaned his shoulder against the door jamb to Wil's office. He kept watch over Juliana, not liking how every male eye seemed fixed in her direction. He didn't blame the arseholes. When she laughed, she seemed lit up from within.

He trusted the other men, but only to a point. Juliana was a very alluring woman.

Another burst of merriment had Brogan narrowing his eyes. Hurst was telling the story of Lord Dunkeld tossing a former agent onto the street...via a window. It had happened before Brogan's employment at the agency, but Brogan had oft heard this account. It was spoken as a warning not to try the patience of that one particular owner. But he'd never heard it told with the exaggerated gestures and playacting that Hurst was putting into it now.

He cracked the knuckles of his right hand. He'd have to watch that one. Too familiar by half with Juliana.

Keeping his eyes on the scene across the room, he said, "I want to look into her brother again. His acquaintances give me cause for concern. But in case I'm wrong, a visit back to Bluff Hall might be in order. I might get more out of the servants without Snowdon in residence."

"Good," Wil said. "But that's not why I wanted to talk to

you."

"Oh?" Brogan turned to face him.

"What's going on with her?" Wil jerked his head towards Juliana.

Brogan slowly straightened. "What do you mean?"

"You know what I mean." Wil dipped his chin. "I have eyes. Anyone can see that there's something going on between you two."

Brogan's chest burned. *Anyone* should mind their own damn business.

But the hell of it was, his relationship with Juliana was Wil's business. Brogan had crossed every professional boundary there was. He knew it. He hated himself for it.

And he'd do it again.

"It won't be a problem," he told Wil.

"It might already be a problem." Wil scraped his hand across his jaw. "When you become involved with a woman, develop feelings—"

Brogan grumbled at that accusation. Not because there wasn't some truth in it, who couldn't like Juliana, but at the fact that his emotions were so easily discerned. When the affair ended, his associates might pity him if they suspected he had been hurt. An unbearable thought.

"—your judgment becomes compromised. I think I should assign a new investigator to her case."

"Like hell." Brogan took a step into the man. Physically intimidating his boss probably wasn't the smartest idea, but there was no way he was going to let someone else stand by Juliana's side. He was going to be the one to protect her. He was the only person he trusted to take her safety as seriously as needed.

"My judgment is fine," he said. "This is my case. She's my responsibility. Even if you took me off it, I'd be sticking by her side."

Wil looked heavenward. "I knew I shouldn't have accepted this job. When Summerset asked me to manage the agency, I should have said no. The whole lot of you are ungovernable. I was better off as his servant. Good food to eat, a nice roof over my head. And I only had to manage one oversized ego."

Brogan huffed. Wilberforce might have worked for Lord Summerset, but there was nothing subservient in his manners towards the man. They were friends, it was clear. Otherwise, the earl would never have put up with Wil's impertinence.

"Look." Wil glanced at Juliana, then turned his back to her, facing Brogan and blocking out the others. "I'm saying this for your sake. Lady Juliana seems like a very nice woman."

Brogan rubbed his chest. Nice wasn't the word for her. She got under his skin too deep to be considered *nice*.

"But sometimes..." Wil swallowed, his Adam's apple bobbing. "Sometimes, as men, we don't get the women we want. Sometimes, life doesn't work out the way we hope. If you can withdraw now, you'll save yourself a future of misery. Trust me on this. I know."

Brogan slumped back against the wall. It was good advice. He eyed the man's drawn face. And apparently learned from personal experience. And it mirrored Brogan's own judgment on the matter.

But every time he told himself to back off, he only craved Juliana more.

Wil was right. Brogan knew his future. It didn't include the daughter of an earl.

But if his future was going to be missing her smile, her quick wit, her unconventional manners, he'd best soak in as much of Juliana in the present as he could.

His memories would have to last him.

And he wanted Juliana to have fond memories of him, as well. So, if she wanted a boring evening, full of insipid harp music and stilted conversation, by damn, he'd give it to her.

Even if he hated every moment.

"Thank you for your interest," he said. "I know it is

kindly meant."

"But?" Wil asked.

"But I'll handle my affairs as I see fit."

Wil nodded. "I understand." He shrugged. "That's the most that any man can do."

Brogan started across the office, but Wil placed his hand on his arm. "If you're going to this musicale, you do know we have a closet full of clothes to suit any occasion. Our agents use them for disguises. I think this qualifies."

Brogan's shoulders drooped. It looked like he would be playing dress-up this evening. He trudged over to Juliana.

She smiled up at him, her face full of joy.

His spirits couldn't help but lift. He shouldn't grumble so much about dressing up for the evening.

Because when it came time to undress, she would be there. Having her in his bed was worth any sacrifice.

"What time does this evening of torture begin?" he asked.

Chapter Twenty

Juliana sighed in delight. Mrs. Joanna Bergen's nimble fingers dancing on the harp were more than she had hoped for. "Isn't she a talent?"

Brogan grunted an assent. He'd sat next to her for the whole performance, arms crossed and gaze sweeping over the guests in Hyacinth's sitting room with a regularity that had so disconcerted the couple on his left, that they had found other seats halfway through the second song.

Juliana and Brogan had decided that he was to be a cousin of hers for this evening, sent by her father to chaperone her about the city. If anyone disbelieved them, they were too polite to raise an eyebrow. And the clothing he'd borrowed from the agency fit the ruse. His cravat was a lovely camel color, with a waistcoat with matching stitching. He still wore trousers, but they were finely sewn, and hugged his thighs in a way that made her belly quiver. Tall, leather boots, a tailored jacket, and he was as well-dressed as any man there.

What he didn't look was comfortable in those clothes.

Fortunately, Juliana was of little consequence. No eyes were turned their way to see the odd couple they made. As the daughter of a poorer earl, there was no dowry for suitors to fight over. She offered no great beauty or charm for those who didn't require a wealthy bride. Her decided manners and conversation turned many men off. All in all, she was in the perfect position to enjoy evenings out among society without having to worry about the demands of said society.

Even discounting their lie of his familial relationship to her, surely Brogan could see how inconsequential it was for her to be seen out with someone who wasn't a peer. How easily he could integrate into her world if he chose.

Hyacinth's sister went to the pianoforte at the front of the room and joined Mrs. Bergen in the next set.

Brogan grumbled. "I thought it was over."

"It has only been twenty minutes," she whispered. "It will go for at least an hour and a half."

Brogan blew out a long breath, then resumed his statue-like posture, the only thing moving was his head as it swiveled to keep an eye on the guests.

For a man who spoke little of his feelings, he said much in just the way he held his shoulders. There was his 'you're boring me with your stupidity' posture. The 'I sense trouble and am ready to leap into action' stance. The 'I'm patient and can wait until you finally agree with me' set of his shoulders. That one was by far her least favorite.

But tonight was different. Tonight Brogan sat, his shoulders slightly raised towards his ears, his posture all but screaming, 'I'm uncomfortable and can't wait to leave.'

At Brogan's insistence, they had taken seats at the back of the room. It was easily done to take Brogan's hand and slip from the musicale unnoticed.

"We're leaving." He sighed. "Thank God. I'll ask for the carr—"

"We're not leaving." She peered down the hall, searching for an appropriate room. Dragging Brogan behind her, she opened the first door on the right. Large, uncurtained windows let in light from the street. She opened another door, and another, until she found a room suitable for her purpose.

"What..." he began.

She dragged him inside and closed the door behind them, turning the key in the lock. The music from the main room could still be faintly heard, the cheerful melody from the harp urging her to recklessness.

"I think we both need to learn the fine art of compromise," she said. She placed her hands on his chest and pushed him backwards until the backs of his thighs hit a high desk.

He plopped down. "What are we compromising on?" His eyes scanned the room before settling back on her face.

"On us both getting what we want. Me, a night of lovely music." She paused, listening as the harpist's efforts danced about the room. "And you..." She plucked at the corner of her fichu and dragged it off her neck. She drew her finger along the edge of her bodice. "And you get me."

She didn't mention that she would enjoy having him as much as he would her. This compromise gave her two things she wanted to his one. But no one said compromises had to be completely even.

He wrapped his hands around her hips, squeezing. "Juliana." His voice was a low rumble. "This is the home of your friend."

"Yes." She ran her hands up and down his arms. "And if Hyacinth knew how much pleasure I expect, she wouldn't begrudge me a moment. Do you not think these rooms have been used for such before?" She pressed her lips to his jaw. "Many men get bored at these events and escape to side rooms with their wives to be better entertained."

The fine muscles around his eyes winced, so quickly, she almost missed it. It was the word 'wives,' she knew. At some level, he still thought their affair immoral. But that wasn't anything she had control over.

She slid her hands under the lapels of his jacket and pushed the fabric over his broad shoulders. She widened his legs with her own, and stepped into the space between his thighs. He might think their actions immoral, that a man in his position shouldn't be with a woman in hers, but he didn't stop her from removing his jacket. Didn't stop her from untying his cravat and tugging it loose.

He cupped the back of her neck and drew her face to his. This kiss held none of the frenzy of their first joining, nor the sweet tenderness of initial exploration. But this kiss held expertise, an awareness that couldn't exist without some practice between two partners.

He rolled his tongue along hers, and she moaned. He dug his teeth into her bottom lip, nipping with just the right amount of pressure to make her gasp.

She wrapped her arms around his neck and leaned against his chest. This kiss was perfect.

He slid his hands to her back. His fingers tangled in the laces to her gown.

She pulled back. "Leave it on." She licked her bottom lip, still tasting him. "It's harder to redress a woman than it is a man."

"Agreed." In a movement so quick she barely had time to blink, Brogan gripped her waist and spun them around so she faced the desk and he stood behind her.

A bit dizzy, she rested her palms on the cool wood surface. "Oh my."

He pressed his palm between her shoulder blades and urged her down until she lay flat against the desk.

Her breath grew choppy as Brogan flipped her skirts up over her hips.

He ran his thumb along her bare flesh. "No pantalets?"

"Not with this dress," she said cheekily.

The sound of flesh smacking flesh rang in her ear a moment before the sting from his palm registered in her brain.

She blinked, shocked more than anything else. "Did you just spank me?"

"Do you regularly go about London not wearing underthings?"

"It isn't my typical mode of dress, no." Sarcasm dripped from her voice.

He smacked her bottom again, the bloom of heat from the spank merging with a different heat. She rubbed her legs together, trying to ease the ache between her thighs.

"Make it a never mode of dress," he replied.

Fabric rustled. She looked over her shoulder in time to see Brogan drop to his knees.

He gripped her arse with both hands, spreading her cheeks apart, exposing everything.

She squirmed. She was more liberated than most women of her acquaintance, but still, some things should remain private. "Brogan, I don't think—"

Her throat squeezed shut, her eyes rolling to the back of her head at the first touch of his tongue. "Dear Lord," she whispered when she caught her breath.

He sucked at her swollen folds, switching between nipping at her with his teeth and lapping at her with his tongue. He plunged that organ into her opening, mimicking the motion of tupping. His fingers moved dangerously close to her other hole, and her modesty deserted her.

What he was doing felt so good, she didn't care where his touch, his gaze, might land. He felt heavenly inside of her, even though his tongue wasn't nearly large enough to fully satisfy.

Brogan dragged his lips down to her clit and latched on.

She moaned, loud and long. This was her best compromise ever. She dug her nails into the desk as Brogan brought her higher and higher. As her body coiled tighter. The sounds that left her mouth were barely human. She felt barely human. More animal, wanting without thought, needing without worry of consequence.

Before she could crash over the edge. Brogan pulled back. "No," she wailed.

"You're going to bring the whole damn house to us with the noise you're making." He grabbed her hair, and pulled her head back. "Open up."

Her forehead furrowed. "What—"

Brogan shoved the balled-up cravat into her mouth, cutting off her question.

She gurgled in protest, shooting him a baleful glare.

He smoothed his hand down her flanks, looking much too pleased with himself. "Even with your known eccentric upbringing, your reputation wouldn't withstand someone finding us alone in this room together." He flicked open his falls, pushing his smallclothes out of the way. "Especially not with my cock buried in your quim."

He notched his crown at her wet channel and entered her in one smooth stroke.

The silk cravat felt awful on her tongue, but she could moan and squeal to her heart's delight, a definite benefit.

And when Brogan gripped her hip with one hand, and the back of her neck with his other, her heart delighted. A lot.

He plunged into her with long even strokes, stretching her walls, hitting all the places inside that made her quiver.

His power, his control, were all intoxicating. She was a modern woman, educated equally with her brother. She shouldn't love being putty in a man's hands. Being molded for his pleasure. Powerless before his dominance.

Claimed.

Her body melted into the desk.

But she did.

She could do nothing more than roll her hips with each thrust, take the pleasure Brogan gave. Her breath caught. He claimed her so thoroughly in the bedroom, it was almost enough to make her forget he didn't want her outside of it. Almost.

He drove into her faster. The smack of flesh against flesh, the wet sucking sound of his cock tunneling into her body, were a companion to her muffled screams. His hips battered the patch of skin that he had spanked, increasing the sting, making her question everything she thought she'd known about lovemaking.

Brogan Duffy fucked like the man he was.

Elemental.

Hard.

Determined.

Brogan fucked like he owned her. Like it was his right to pin her in place, take what he wanted. And a small part of her heart answered that he did. As long as he gave as much as he took, he could own her body in any manner he wanted.

She didn't think she could ever go back to the soft caresses of an artist, the polite respects of a nobleman. She reached back, needing to touch him, and gripped the waist of his trousers hanging from his hips. She dug her fingernails into the cloth as he pounded her harder.

Her muscles seized, everything inside her going tight. Her ribs wouldn't expand to give her air. Dark spots danced before her eyes.

Brogan slid his hand around her hip, the tip of his finger butterflying over her clit.

She shattered. Wave after wave of ecstasy pulsed through her body, arching her back and curling her toes.

Brogan's fingers dug into her skin. He groaned, pulling from her. Liquid heat splashed her lower lips before he spent on her bottom. "God damn." He released his hold and planted both palms on the desk. "God damn, you feel good." He brushed hair off her cheek before pulling the cravat from her mouth.

"Brogan?"

"Hmm?"

"I didn't wear pantalets tonight for you."

His lips curved against the skin of her neck. He gave her one last kiss. "Stay here."

That was a demand Juliana had no problem following. She rested on the desk as her heart calmed and her breath slowed. The desk was actually quite comfortable. Her eyes slid shut. She could stay here for the rest of the night.

Brogan wiped something soft across her bum, cleaning her. "The music is still going. Do you want to slip back in to the musicale?"

With a sigh, she pushed herself to standing and shook her skirts out. She moved in front of the mirror above the mantel and tried to fix her hair. "We'd better not. Even fully dressed, I still don't look quite respectable. I'll send a note to Hy tomorrow telling her that I had a headache."

He plucked her fichu from the floor and shoved one end down her bodice. "I can't say that I regret mussing you up."

Juliana smoothed the lump he'd made with the fichu and tucked the other end of it in her gown. "I don't regret anything about our time together."

Their eyes met in the mirror. His gaze dropped away. "We should go."

"Brogan," she said, turning. She hooked her finger between the buttons of his waistcoat. "You don't regret our affair, do you?" She knew he enjoyed it. But even the most pleasurable things could lead to remorse. To Brogan's strict mind, probably the more pleasurable, the more remorse he felt.

"I regret acting foolishly." He held her wrist, brushing his thumb back and forth over her skin before removing her finger from his clothing. "I regret not doing more to protect both of us from the inevitable disappointment to come."

"You don't know there will be disappointment." If she was a foot-stamping kind of lady, she would have dented the Butters's parquet floor by now. The man was too cynical. Too constrained. And much too frustrating to give her peace of mind.

He made a simple knot in his cravat and smoothed down the ends. "We should go," he repeated.

She pressed her lips together. It was a strange tug o' war they were engaged in. A woman shouldn't have to work so hard to make a man want such a liaison. And the sick feeling in the pit of her stomach warned her she might not win this contest. He could end their relationship at any moment.

The smile she pasted on her face wavered only the littlest bit. "I'm ready." She hurried to the door and poked her head out.

A maid lounged against the far wall, holding their coats.

"Maisey?" Juliana peered down the hall. "What are you doing here?"

"I saw you sneaking into this room." The girl's eyes twinkled. "The butler has positioned himself at the front door. You won't slip past him unnoticed, and he notices *everything*." She ran her gaze down Juliana's rumpled gown, her smile widening.

Brogan followed Juliana into the hall. "Is there another exit we should take?"

Maisey tossed them their coats and pulled a dented top hat from behind her back. She popped out the crease and handed it to Brogan. "Down this hall and to the right. It will take you to the west garden. There's a gate to the street from there."

"You are a jewel, Maisey." Juliana squeezed the girl's hands. "I won't forget this."

The maid shrugged. "You've been good to me."

With a last farewell, Juliana and Brogan followed her direction and escaped into the brisk night air.

She stepped next to Brogan, seeking his warmth. But though his body was inches from hers, he felt farther away than ever. She breathed deeply. "Maisey deserves a gift for that rescue."

"Why?" Brogan trudged toward the wooden gate, poking his head above the slats. When a pedestrian had passed, he opened the gate.

She slipped through, frowning. "Because she went out of her way to help us. Because if the butler had suspected something and told Mr. Butters, he most likely would have forbidden Hy from seeing me." Something she should have considered before dragging Brogan into the room. But all was well that ended well. "Because she acted as a friend."

Brogan hailed his carriage which was waiting down the street. "She's not your friend. She makes her living assisting your kind. She provided you a service, which was her job. Nothing more."

Juliana scowled. She had half a mind to walk back to his

apartments. She didn't think she wanted to spend the next twenty minutes in a confined space with him, not when he was in this mood.

But she was a rational person, and she didn't see why she should suffer blisters when Brogan was the one who was being a right pain.

She ignored the hand he offered to assist her into the coach. She settled herself into the far corner of the bench. Yes, Maisey worked for Mr. Butters, but that didn't mean she had to help anyone who came through the doors of the house. The girl had a mind of her own, and she'd used it to help Juliana, without any expectation of payment, only because she liked her.

It had been a compromise of sorts across class and rank. Why was it so difficult for Brogan to attempt the same?

Chapter Twenty-One

Brogan gripped his pen. His gaze drifted to where Juliana sat across from him at the agency's offices.

Her expression was placid, but he knew she felt the same frustrations swirling under her skin that he did.

It had been a week. A week of Brogan going out to question people while leaving her here in the offices under the watch of his fellow agents. He'd made sure everyone knew not to be fooled by her 'wanting to use the necessary' excuse.

She had been furious with him for investigating without her at the beginning of the week, but that fury had dwindled into intermittent irritation. She was at heart a sensible creature. She wouldn't stay in high temper just for spite's sake.

"You done with that report yet?" Wil called from his office.

Brogan turned back to the paper before him. "Not yet." Reports. No one had told him becoming an agent of inquiry would require so much paperwork. He could have written the same damn thing each afternoon after he came back from questioning his suspects. The name at the top of the report for the person he'd interviewed would change, but since he had learned shit all from each questioning session, the rest he could write by rote.

No one suspected Pickens of anything beyond petty theft. Everyone thought Lord Withington a decent man with no enemies.

With a neat motion, Juliana slit open the seal of her

letter. They'd set up a forwarding system for her correspondence to be sent here.

He hoped reading and replying to her acquaintances would alleviate some of her boredom at her confinement. Guilt gnawed at Brogan. It was for her own good. No one would be throwing rocks at her head if he could help it.

But it was for his own good, too. And that's what made his guts twist. He was depriving her of her right to investigate in order to keep himself sane.

Wil had brought in a couple of books for Juliana to entertain herself with while Brogan was away, something Brogan should have thought of himself. He didn't know if Juliana actually read them. Every time she picked up a book, it looked like she wanted to chuck it at his head instead of dive into the pages.

Brogan needed this investigation to end to preserve his own sanity. He put the finishing touches on his day's report and shoved the paper into the corner of his desk. He laced his fingers together and placed them behind his head. "Anything the matter?" he asked when Juliana's lips pursed.

"Nothing." She put down that letter and went for another. "Just a ball I was invited to. I didn't want to go in any case."

He remembered Juliana dancing by herself in her friend's room when he'd found her. She enjoyed such frolics. She deserved to have fun, deserved to get her life back.

Even though it wouldn't include him.

He sat up straight and put his pen and inkwell away.

It shouldn't include him. Juliana might think she wanted him now. After all, she'd made herself quite comfortable in his little apartments, taken to cooking them dinners, even darned a pair of his socks.

He'd pretended he didn't see the unevenness of her stitching, eaten everything she'd served even as he breathed through his mouth so he couldn't actually taste the food. She was trying everything in her power to show him they weren't as unsuited as he believed. And he loved her for it, even knowing how futile her efforts were.

They were too different. She would have to sacrifice too much to be with him. He was resolved to let her go as soon as the investigation ended.

It didn't help his resolve that they fucked like animals every night. The way she shuddered when he slid deep was like a blow from a chisel to his willpower. The jokes she told to make him smile when they lay sweat-slicked in bed after their crises were another blow. She was like a damned sculptor, chipping away at him all day long.

It was enough to make a man want to believe that their lives could suit, that she could content herself to live in relative squalor.

But he knew better. The lack of her usual comforts would gnaw on her, dimming her spark day by day until she looked at him with resentment. If Juliana didn't marry a nobleman, she should at least partner with a man who was her intellectual equal. Someone who enjoyed going to those damn salons. Who could match her fact for fact in talking about the planets, about philosophy.

Brogan wasn't that man. He rubbed at the ache in his chest. He needed their affair to end, and soon, if he wanted to remain whole at the end of it.

Juliana's eyes flew wide. She quickly sliced open the next letter. "This is from my father."

Her eyes flicked over the lines. "He says he's returning to London in a month's time." She bit her lip. "We will have found our suspect by then, right? We must."

Brogan stood, his legs twitching with the need for motion. He walked back and forth. "At the rate I'm going, I don't think I'll ever find the perpetrator," he admitted. "I've learned nothing new this past week. Nothing to indicate who paid Pickens. Nothing at Bluff Hall to think something is amiss." He blew out a breath. "I believe that someone is after your father, but I'm damned if I can prove it."

She sagged back in her chair, draping her arms over the

sides. "We must do something."

Agent Verity at the next desk over snickered. "It's tough using your head instead of your fists, eh, Duffy?"

Brogan flexed his hands. The agents all teased each other. He knew it was meant in good fun, but still he wanted to throttle the man. Mainly because he was right.

Brogan was more comfortable beating answers from someone instead of investigating. He thought about his fights, thought about the broken ribs, the blows to the head he'd taken. Boxing might have been where he'd excelled, but he didn't want to return to that life. He needed to start using his head, for Juliana's sake, if not for his.

He dug a bit of wood from his pocket and tossed it from hand to hand. The kernel of an idea formed. Even in the boxing ring, he had needed to employ some strategy. One didn't win purely from brute force. One of his tactics had been to lure his opponent in, make him think Brogan was tired so he would draw in close.

Then Brogan would snap the trap around him.

"Your father will be here in a month?" he asked.

Juliana nodded. "Only a month left." She sighed.

A vise wrapped around his ribs. A month. It seemed like forever when he needed her out of his home, out of his life, in order to find peace again.

The fading sun caught her dark hair, making it glint auburn.

And a month also seemed like no time at all. Not when he knew he would no longer see her again at the end of it.

He hardened his shoulders. "I have an idea. It will require your father's cooperation, but if we can get him to go about on errands alone, to places that would tempt our assailant to strike, then I think we can lure his enemy out into the open."

Juliana jerked up straight. "You want to use my father as bait?"

He nodded.

"No." She narrowed her eyes. "The risk is too great."

He cocked his hip on the edge of his desk, his leg inches from her knee. "We can make it safe. It won't just be me protecting him. There will be other agents there, watching. We'll only make it look like he's alone, unprotected, and when the assailant strikes, we'll catch him."

It was a good plan. It was his *only* plan, and he knew Wil and the others would back him up.

But that left him with Juliana. For a month. With her close enough to touch. To taste. To worship.

He didn't know if that month would kill him, or be something he remembered for the rest of his life.

Juliana popped to her feet and paced about her chair, her skirts swishing angrily. "Why wait?" she asked. "We already have bait you can use."

He cocked his head. "What are you talking about?"

She spread her hands wide. "Me. That same person wants to kill me, as well. We can lay a trap for him to try and kill me again."

"No." His voice brooked no dissent. There was no way in hell he was going to let Juliana risk her neck.

"You said it was perfectly safe." She smiled sweetly. "That there would be no risk to my father. Then there should be no risk to me, either."

His palm itched to spank the smug right out of her. She thought she'd caught him in a neat trap. What she didn't know was that he didn't care if he was hypocritical, not when her safety was at stake. He wasn't going to let her do it.

"We would all be there for her." Verity and the other three agents in the room nodded.

Brogan glared. They all were much too friendly with Juliana, but he understood it. They were the ones spending their days with her. Watching her, talking with her, enjoying her. Of course, she'd crawl her way into their hearts.

"I said no." He slammed the half-formed badger on his desk. The bang was loud enough to bring Wil out of his office again.

"Problems?" he asked.

Brogan squeezed the wood piece until he felt the badger's claws imprint into his skin. "No problems."

"No, there isn't a problem," Juliana agreed. "Brogan came up with a plan to catch the man after my father, and we're just deciding how best to implement it. If I'm to be used as bait, how will we make it look realistic that I'm off on my own without Brogan following me around?" She tapped her fingers to her lips.

"It's not happening," Brogan said.

Wil stepped further into the main office. "It's not unheard of for you to sneak off without a chaperone." He gave her a wry grin. "If any woman were to go about alone without it causing suspicion, it would be you."

Agent Hurst planted his elbows on his desk. "No, I think she's right. We need a better pretext."

"She doesn't need a pretext," Brogan said, "because she's not doing it."

They all ignored him.

"A fight?" Juliana said. "A public break with this agency?"

Wil limped closer, rubbing his thigh. "Where could this fight happen?"

Juliana hurried to Brogan's desk and picked up one of her discarded correspondence. "This ball. It's in two night's time. I can have the fight with Brogan there. If we make it loud enough, word of my separation from this agency should reach whoever's behind this."

Heat rose up Brogan's neck. "I said—"

"That is a good idea." Wil nodded. "But if you severed ties with our agency, you would naturally return to live at your London home. That'll be a hard place for us to protect you."

"I'll stay with Hyacinth again." Juliana shrugged. "There won't be a problem."

Brogan threw the wood piece across the room. "I said no," he roared. He was the lead investigator, damn it. He was the only one who truly cared about Juliana's well-being. They *would* listen to him.

Silence descended. Every eye was on him, some pitying, some confused.

"Brogan," Juliana began.

"No." He planted his hands on his hips. "Not happening. It isn't your place."

"My place." Her voice was flat. "And you think you have the authority to tell me what my place is?"

There was a loud shuffling as the other agents stepped out from behind their desks and hurried towards the back. "We're just..." "This seems private..." "Good luck." This last was directed at Brogan and said with a snort.

Wil followed them into his office. "Let us know what you decide." He closed the door.

Juliana waited for his answer, eyebrow raised, hip cocked to the side.

Brogan rubbed the back of his neck. "I'm only thinking of your safety. You're the daughter of an earl. You should be enjoying your teas and balls and salons. Leave the work to me."

She swallowed. "You still think I'm spoiled."

He huffed. She had everything and didn't even see it. "Only someone who has every comfort provided for would risk them so easily. You think life is a grand adventure. You don't know how easily everything can be taken." Someone in her position couldn't know that, and for that he was glad. He didn't want her cynical. He didn't want her exposed to the harsh realities.

She turned her back on him. Her shoulders were rigid blocks, and he fought the urge to rub the tension out of them.

"I..." She cleared her throat. "I want to help. Be useful for once. I've never felt more alive than I have during this investigation." She laughed bitterly. "Which must prove to you just how horrible I am, enjoying myself when my father's life is at risk."

He did move to her then, resting his palms on her shoulders and drawing her back to lean against his chest. "It's natural to feel a thrill at life and death situations." He rested his chin on top of her head. "That doesn't mean you should seek them. You can be useful in many other ways."

"Are you certain about that? The daughter of an earl is expected to look pretty and keep her mouth shut. Be an adornment instead of a partner." She rested her head against his shoulder. "You think you're protecting me, but it feels like you're taking away my one chance to live a life with value."

His resolve wavered. Men could choose to go into war, duel over their honor, even become investigators. They could seek glory or execute their duty without anyone trying to cosset them away, protect them from harm. He didn't want to deny Juliana the same opportunity.

But he didn't want to see her body knocked senseless by a rock. Or pierced by a bullet. Or hurt in any manner of ways that his imagination provided.

"Besides," Juliana said softly. She turned and rested her hands on his hips. "We can't wait a month for my father." She huffed. "I don't know if I have the funds to pay for another month of your agency's time. This is a good plan, and I'm not scared, because you're going to be there, and you'll protect me."

Her eyes were as rich as chocolate. Soft, intelligent, and full of an emotion Brogan didn't want to identify.

"Please." She ran her hand up his abdomen and rested it over his heart. "Please Brogan, let me be a part of this. I need to be a part of this."

He closed his eyes. His muscles loosened as resignation took hold. He was a fool. But when she looked at him like that, he couldn't refuse her.

And she was right.

He would protect her. He would keep her safe. Anything else was unacceptable.

"Fine." He opened his eyes and pinned her with his

glare. "But you're going to do everything I say."

Chapter Twenty-Two

Juliana hummed along with the music, twisting and turning her way down the dance floor. She did so love to dance. She had yet to entice Brogan onto the floor as her partner, but there were plenty of other men who did her the service. The glower on Brogan's face every time one of them placed his hand on hers was enough to warm her heart.

He was a conflicted man, but she finally felt that she was making progress. Her presence here, to take part in his plan, was proof of that. Most men would have dismissed her arguments, patronized then ignored her. He thought her spoiled, and to a degree, perhaps she was. But she knew how fortunate she was to be involved with a man like Brogan. To have his respect. She would show him they were compatible in all regards. She didn't want their affair to end.

She wanted more.

She dipped into a curtsy, her chest heaving with exertion, and thanked her partner. He led her back to the corner where Brogan stood, scowling. "Your cousin is a fine dancer," Mr. Chancey said.

Brogan nudged her behind him, blocking most of her with his body. "And now the dance is over." He crossed his arms and stared the man down.

Mr. Chancey shifted on his feet. "Yes. Quite. Well... I'll just be going now, shall I?" He nodded to Juliana and slunk off.

She slapped Brogan's arm. "Why are you being so

difficult? He was a nice man, and a good dancer."

"I can dance." Brogan sniffed. "I choose not to."

She rolled her eyes. That hardly sounded likely. But men did so need to protect their egos.

"Is your brother here?" he asked.

"Uh..." She rolled onto her toes and scanned the room. "I don't see him. Why?"

"Nothing."

Juliana cocked her head. "Did you need to speak to him?" Perhaps it would be good to talk to Snow again. He'd had some time to digest the news of Pickens murder. He might think differently now.

"No." Brogan held himself stiffly, not looking at her.

Her stomach turned. "You don't suspect him, do you?" She laughed, but it sounded distorted, as though she was standing in water. "That would be absurd."

He said nothing.

"Brogan." She turned to stand in front of him. "You don't suspect him?"

He scraped his palm over his jaw. "I think your brother is too eager to be admired by his crowd. That makes him easy to manipulate. His *friends* could be trying to install him as earl without his knowledge and hope to profit from the connection."

Juliana blinked. He was serious. "Is this because they spoke of revolutions and equality? Some revolutions are needed in order to progress. Not all of them devolve into bloodshed."

"Most of them do."

She pressed her lips together. Was he so determined to maintain the boundaries between classes that he would condemn those who would fight against them? "To be honest, I'm a bit envious of Miss Lynn. She is passionate about changing the world. She's someone who will actually work towards that end. I only discuss it as philosophical theory." She traced a seam in the wood plank floor with the toe of her slipper. "I do hope becoming a member of

Rose's debate society will change that for me."

"You don't have to change the world to live a life of value." He placed his finger under her chin and tipped her face up. "You're worth a hundred Miss Lynns."

Her shoulders sank. The words were sweet, but what she read behind them left her cold. Of course, he'd think she didn't have to actually *do* anything. He'd put her on a pedestal, someone he could enjoy but not hold.

But she'd show him her actual worth. "We came here to cause a stir." She held out her hand as the first notes of a waltz filled the room. "There seems no better place for a public disagreement than the dance floor."

Brogan squared his shoulders, looking like he was facing a firing squad rather than a dance. "Very well." He gripped her hand, striding to the dance floor, making Juliana hurry to keep up. He took her in his arms, holding himself stiffly, keeping the proper amount of space between their bodies.

Juliana could almost see him counting the steps in his mind as they moved across the floor. But though he held himself rigidly, his steps didn't falter. He moved with the sort of grace that came with being an athlete.

"You dance well," she said.

"I dance. The quality of it is irrelevant."

She sighed. "Is it so hard to you to come to a ball, or a musicale, like the other night?" The couple next to them swung in a dizzying circle, the woman's skirts brushing Juliana's legs, her laugh lighting up the room. Juliana stared at them wistfully. "Is my life so distasteful to you?"

He started. "Nothing about you is distasteful."

Well, that was something. Something to build upon, perhaps. "Do you think you could ever see yourself living a life like this?" She held her breath. His next words were important. His answer could determine her future.

Sometime during their affair, she'd realized she didn't want it to come to an end. Aside from their attraction, which only seemed to grow, she'd discovered how much she liked him. She'd realized she wanted to keep him.

Their lives could merge together, she knew they could. It only remained to convince Brogan.

His nostrils flared. "That's a foolish question. This isn't my life, unless it is as part of an investigation. It can't be my life."

"You use the word 'can't' very easily." Her chest heaved. "You're here now. No one has given you a second look." Well, that wasn't quite true. A man as intimidating looking as Brogan garnered plenty of looks, but nothing to call the magistrate over. "My life isn't all parties and salons, you know. It's quiet evenings by the fire, reading a book curled up next to someone I care about."

She swallowed, the back of her throat burning. "I could be quite content living a quiet sort of life, with only the occasional appearance in society. Don't you think, that is, could you not meet me half way?" Her heart beat a rapid tattoo. She was used to speaking boldly, but that might have been the most courageous words she'd ever said.

She'd laid it bare, her desires to be with him. There was no artifice, no double-speak to hide behind if he didn't want her.

Her stomach twisted, and she thought she might cast up her accounts. What if he didn't want her?

His Adam's apple bobbed. "Juliana," he said, his voice low, "you do not know what you ask. You think life is something from a novel, or like one of your salons where an eclectic group can mix and meet. But that's not real." His feet slowed, until they were hardly moving to the music. "Real life is judgmental. It's hard for a man like me, and for any woman I would take as a wife, it would be doubly so."

"Shouldn't that be a choice made by the woman?" she asked, her voice tart.

His eyes darkened to a stormy sea. "You might think you would be happy, but you wouldn't be. You'd grow tired and bitter." He jerked his gaze away. "That is something I couldn't bear to see."

She stared at the glint from his gold cravat pin. His

agency spared no expense when it came to its agents' disguises. Her skin flushed hot, whether from anger, humiliation, or despair, she didn't know. "I would make a man, any man, a good wife. I'm not as demanding as you seem to think. My happiness isn't bought with houses and jewels."

He inhaled sharply. "That is because you think the only difference in your circumstances would be between wearing a ruby or a garnet, between wearing silk or cotton. You don't know how the other half live in London. How they struggle not to walk upon the streets with holes in their shoes, the effort needed to get food on the table."

"That's absurd." She frowned at the couple who nearly bumped into them, and forced her feet back into motion. "I've seen your apartments. You might not be wealthy, but you are hardly the pauper you are describing. That caricature isn't how you live."

"Not now. But my parents didn't always live in the apartments I took you to. My sister did not always have gowns enough to throw out of windows." Brogan's boot kicked her slipper, and he frowned. "And I'm always just one job loss away from finding myself right back in that place."

She shook her head. "You delight in being a pessimist."

"You delight in ignoring the problems we would face." His hand at her waist tightened. "I will not have you lower yourself to be with me. I don't want a wife I'd have to struggle to keep happy."

She pushed on his shoulder, putting even more space between them. "You don't get to tell me what makes me happy and what does not," she hissed.

Another couple swirling next to them glanced over, and Juliana forced a grin between gritted teeth. Their pretend fight was turning all too real.

"In this matter, I do," he said, much too calmly for her taste. If she was getting riled up, he damn well should be as well. "I, also, get to decide what best suits my happiness, and having a wife who was raised getting whatever she wanted would suit me ill."

"We're back to my being spoiled, is that it?" Pins and needles stabbed her chest. "I might be the daughter of an earl, but I wasn't raised in this great wealth that you seem to think I was. I had a budget. There were trips I couldn't take, things I couldn't buy."

Brogan snorted, and her face grew hotter. "My father is not wealthy," she insisted.

"Your father is a nobleman. He has land, a large home. He has the kind of money most people in England could only dream of seeing."

Another pair of dancers looked at them with interest.

They were curious, and her life was falling apart. She'd never felt such anger before. So mad she wanted to spit or yell or stomp on Brogan's foot.

She did none of those things. "That's it then? You have it all figured out. I will marry some soft nobleman who will keep me content with chocolates and books and bore me out of my senses. You think that will protect my happiness. And you will marry..."

She didn't want to think about the kind of woman Brogan would end up marrying. It wouldn't be some creepmouse. Brogan needed someone strong to stand up to him, and he was smart enough to know it. His wife would be tough, used to a bit of hardship.

She'd be someone Juliana would probably like, if she didn't feel obliged to hate her on sight.

"You know what I think?" she said. "You're a snob, Brogan Duffy. A reverse snob. You pretend that my place is higher than yours, that you would never deign to dirty me with your lifestyle. But you actually think the working class are better than my kind. Nobler somehow, through their suffering. Smarter. Tougher."

Her lungs shuddered. She wasn't what Brogan wanted. All her education, her modern ideas about society, and where had they got her? The man she loved didn't want her.

His wife would be useful, she could see that now. Someone who wouldn't waste her time talking about the world's problems, but just dig her hands in and get to work.

She raised her chin. He might be right. She might be of no use to a man like him. But she had her pride. "You've made a pretense of saying that you're not good enough for me, when in actuality, you don't think I'm good enough for you."

"Right." He stopped dancing and glared down at her. Turning on his heel, he stalked off the dance floor.

And since he was holding her hand, she was dragged along behind him, sputtering and calling him every creative oath she could think of.

Oh yes, they were garnering plenty of attention. Her plan was a stunning success. Everyone in her peer group and beyond would hear of this fight.

"Where are we going?" she snarled, tugging at her hand in vain.

"Going?" He pulled her out of the house, ignoring the gaping footmen. He sighted their carriage and headed towards it. "It's time Lady Juliana learned just how the other half lives."

He threw open the carriage door, gripped her waist, and practically threw her inside. "It's time you realize just how different we truly are."

* * *

Brogan fisted the bit of wood in his pocket. Its smooth curves did nothing to ease his anger. He should have whittled a star, something spiky. He needed to feel the bite of pain. Or the satisfaction of split knuckles, bruised bones, something, anything to remind himself that the drivel Juliana had spewed couldn't be true.

She was wrong. They couldn't be together.

He rapped on the ceiling of the carriage. "Stop here," he shouted to the driver. Plucking Juliana up from the seat across from him, he plopped her on his thigh and faced her toward the window.

She gripped his arm for balance. "Much as this tour of London has been interesting," she began.

"Quiet." His hand curved around her hip against his better judgment. She was warm and soft and everything he couldn't have. "This isn't a tour. It's a lesson." He pointed. "See that man there? The one lying in the gutter."

Juliana sucked in a breath. "What's wrong with him? Should we send for a doctor?"

"We could," Brogan agreed. "If you could find a doctor who would come out here. Besides, there are ten more just like him all down this block."

She leaned forwards, her cunny pressed against his leg as she peered out the window.

He could feel her heat through their clothes, though that didn't surprise him. Juliana exuded warmth. She made everyone feel welcome, as though they could belong with her. The muscles of his thigh jumped under his skin.

"Where are we?" she asked.

"Shoreditch. And there." He pointed again. "That woman with her skirt ruched up around her hips and weaving down the street."

Juliana drew back, her cheeks flushing. "I don't—"

He gripped the back of her neck and pushed her forward. "I know you don't want to see this. See how people who aren't earls and viscounts and famous poets live." He swallowed. "Don't want to see where I come from. But you need to."

She needed to understand how far apart they truly were. How foolish her notions were.

She swiveled her head to stare at him. "This isn't you. Brogan. This isn't your life."

"I'm closer to these people than I am to you." Something twinged hollowly in his chest. Damn her. Damn her for making him want something he couldn't have. For making him be the responsible one who had to end it.

A wail rose from the street, and Juliana popped her

head out the window. "It's a girl. A child." She frowned. "That man is shaking her."

Brogan looked, checking to see if the child was in danger. His shoulders relaxed. "Yes. Her father. Probably angry she didn't earn enough coin begging today." He waited until he saw the father relent, wrap his arm around the girl's shoulders and rest his forehead against hers.

It was a common enough scene in his old neighborhood. If the child were fortunate, the parents would only scold. The unlucky ones received beatings for not contributing enough to the family finances.

"She's dirty. She's hungry." He shook his head. "No matter how much you speak of equality, her life will never change."

"You don't know that. You can't know that."

"There is much I don't know," he agreed. "What I do know is that a man like me can never marry into nobility."

He paused. Hadn't his employers married unconventionally? Married much beneath them, according to society's standards? Was it really so unreasonable to dream?

Hope drained out of him until he felt nothing but numb. It was different when a man married a woman of lower standing. The consequences were fewer. A wealthy and consequential man could protect his wife from the barbs society would throw her way.

Brogan had nothing but his fist to protect Juliana, a weapon unsuited to guard against the humiliations and snubs from her peers.

Damn her to hell and back for wanting to throw her life away on a man like him.

She pushed the carriage door open.

Brogan grabbed her arm. "What are you doing?"

She pulled the pearl bobs from her ears. "I'm going to give the girl my jewelry. And the ribbon trim on this gown should fetch enough money for a couple of meals." She tugged at the edge of lace on her bodice as she moved toward the door.

Brogan pulled her back inside and closed them in. He pounded on the carriage ceiling. "Roll on," he called.

"What are you doing?" She wriggled on his lap. "I can help her."

"You can get yourself killed. Even I don't want to step outside in this neighborhood after dark." He snorted. "No, this lesson will be conducted safely from within the confines of this carriage."

With one last wiggle, she slid from his lap and plopped down across from him. She sat back and crossed her arms over her chest. "This feels less like a lesson and more like a lecture. You're showing me problems, but not allowing me to help. My father might not be the richest earl in England, but as you're overly fond of pointing out, I'm not going hungry. I can help. Stop the carriage."

"We'll stop again." They rounded a corner, and Brogan pounded on the ceiling. The next thing he pointed out to her was the front door of a brothel. Two scantily clad women lounged against the entrance, calling out to men as they passed by.

"There are probably twenty such girls in that whorehouse," he said. "Do you have ribbon enough to help them all? Will you dissect your gown until you're down to your skin trying to feed the world's hungry?" He scraped his palm across his jaw. "There's so much misery here, you could drown in it."

"But..." She peered out the window until one of the working girls caught her eye and gestured lewdly. Juliana drew back. "There must be something we can do."

"You want to help?" He set his shoulders. "You have to use your head, not your heart. You can start a charity or a foundling home. It's something a woman in your position sometimes does. And it does help. But you can't help everyone." He glanced away. "If you married me, you wouldn't even be in a position to do that."

His guts squeezed. If she married him, she would be

nothing. A small footnote in history. The Earl of Withington's idiot daughter who let her heart overcome her good sense.

Brogan couldn't do that to her. He wouldn't, even if he spent the rest of his life regretting letting her go.

She was but a shadow in the darkened carriage, but his gaze traced every dark line and curve of her form.

And he would regret it, he knew. He'd have moments when he lay in bed alone and kicked himself for rejecting everything she had to offer. Before he remembered the kind of life he'd saved her from.

But he would be full to bursting with regrets.

He regretted meeting Lady Juliana Wickham.

He regretted taking her case.

He regretted starting this affair.

He regretted ending it this night.

Juliana wasn't a woman a man could just walk away from unscathed. She left scars.

"I want to go back to your apartments, please." She laced her fingers together on her lap.

"Not yet." He pounded on the roof once more. They had a final stop. One more piece of evidence to prove to her that he... He swallowed.

"Please, you've made your point," she said.

"One more stop." Two more turns and they were there. "Halt," he called to the driver. This time he opened the door. He didn't let her climb down, of course, but he wanted her to have a full view of where the man she claimed to want to attach herself to came from.

They leant forward together to look out the opening.

"What am I looking at?" she asked.

It was a squat, three-story building. The roof slanted, giving the building the appearance of listing to one side. Who knew? Perhaps the structure actually did lean. If there had ever been paint on it, it had long since worn away. The windows were boarded up, even on the upper floors. There was nothing on the streets that a resident could possibly want to see.

"That building." He jerked his head at it. "That's where I grew up, where my family and I lived until I had some success in the boxing ring." He fingered the wood piece in his pocket. "This was my home."

A man stumbled from the alley next to it and vomited upon the street. They were twenty feet away, but Brogan imagined he could smell the acrid scent. He probably could. The same man had probably cast up his accounts every night this week.

The man looked up from his hands and knees. Brogan could see the moment when his look became calculating. Whether he would come begging or attempting to steal, Brogan didn't care to find out. He shut the door and told the driver to move on.

Juliana worried the fabric of her gown, rubbing her skirts between her thumb and forefinger. "That's it, then? You rub my face in poverty, a poverty I was fully aware of by the way, and think I'll go running?"

Being aware of poverty and seeing it right under one's nose were two very different things. Brogan knew it. Juliana knew it. Her words may have been defiant, but the tone was already becoming more uncertain. His previous life had shocked her.

Which was what he wanted. He dug his knuckle into his breastbone. So why did he feel like a right bounder?

"That's it," he said.

She laughed, the sound high, unsteady, and false. "So, we'll carry on as before, having a diverting liaison until the case ends."

"No." He was done dying by a thousand cuts, one small lash a day. It was time to cut this off, once and for all. "We will only have a professional relationship from now on."

"What?" She clasped a hand to her stomach, her voice rising. "We don't need to do that. We can go back to the way we were before."

"In life, you can't go back." Something else her

privileged upbringing hadn't taught her. In this instance, he didn't relish being her instructor. He sighed. "You'll thank me for this later."

She curled against the wall of the carriage. "I'll thank you to take me to Hyacinth's now. Don't expect thanks for anything else."

"As you wish." He called the directions to the driver.

He stared out the window, watching as the dark streets of London rolled past. He would have to get used to this darkness. With Juliana out of his bed, his days, any light that had brightened his life was gone.

Chapter Twenty-Three

Juliana tossed the volume of poetry on the seat beside her. Even Rodger Rose's melodic words weren't enough to soothe her depressed spirits.

"Is something the matter?" Hyacinth asked, looking up from her needle work. "You've been as fidgety as a cat all day."

"I'm fine." Juliana slouched back on the settee.

Hyacinth 'hmmed' and cast her gaze back to her work.

Juliana was thankful her friend didn't press further. She knew she was being a poor companion to Hy, knew that ever since her fight with Brogan she hadn't been able to muster up the will to be pleasant or interesting.

Hy thought it her public fight with Brogan that caused her ennui. Even though Juliana trusted her with the truth, she couldn't bring herself to expose her deepest feelings, even to her closest friend.

She stared out the window, wondering which agent had been assigned to watch over her today. She knew one of the Bond Agency investigators lurked about the grounds and surrounding streets.

She also knew it wasn't Brogan.

Mr. Verity, the agent protecting her that first day, had told her Brogan hadn't volunteered for the duty.

She plucked up the book again, tapping her thumb on its spine, and tossed it back down. "I'm going for a turn about your gardens," she told Hy. "Do you want to come?"

Without looking up, Hyacinth said, "It looks like rain. I think I'll stay inside."

Juliana nodded and stood. She passed Mr. Butters's office on her way to the rear door and waved to him at his desk. It was much more pleasant staying at the Butters's house as an invited guest. She shook her head. All the subterfuge and secrecy of before felt a bit foolish now.

She'd almost made it outside when the butler found her.

"Lady Juliana, you have a caller." He tugged on his lapels. "Your brother's here to see you."

"Snowdon?" She chewed on her lip. She and Snow had much to discuss, but it wouldn't be a comfortable conversation. She'd thought about Brogan's suspicions, about how Snow's friends could be using him, and come to the conclusion that he might be right.

She hated to admit that a man who had his head up his rear end on so many other issues could be correct in this one, but there it was.

She blew out her cheeks. And delaying an uncomfortable conversation did no one any favors. "Can you show him to the folly?"

The butler nodded and hurried away.

Juliana slipped outside the back door and made her way to the mock Roman temple. The folly seemed out of place in a London townhouse garden, but the Butters enjoyed its frivolity, one of the reasons why Juliana liked the family so much.

She sat on one of the stone benches beneath the portico and arranged her skirts—and her thoughts. Her brother didn't take well to being shown he was wrong. She had to approach this carefully. Try to make him come to the conclusions himself.

"Jules?" Snowdon hopped up the steps to stand before her. "What are you doing out here? It looks like it might rain."

She smiled. If only he'd shown an interest in her best friend, maybe all of this could have been avoided. She would have had a sister she adored, and her brother, a wife he could trust. But, alas, even over several meetings, there was no interest on either side.

"The weather will hold," she said. "It's good to see you, Snow. It's been too long since it's been just the two of us talking."

He circled his hat in his hands. "Yes, it has been. I'm leaving for Bluff Hall soon. Come back with me, Jules. Don't you think you've pursued this nonsense long enough?"

Her spine snapped straight. "Our father's life isn't nonsense."

He frowned. "I thought since you broke off relations with the Bond Agency that you'd realized our father's life wasn't in danger."

"You heard about my fight with Mr. Duffy?" she asked.

Snow rocked onto his toes. "Oh, yes. Half of the Ton has heard about that argument. Sir Williams is saying what poor form it was to fight at his house in such a public event, but secretly he's delighted his home was the hotbed of a minor scandal." He smirked. "It sounds like you gave that tosser a what for."

"Brogan isn't a tosser," she said through gritted teeth. Stubborn. Infuriating. A right pain in her rear, yes. But he wasn't ill-bred. She gripped the edge of the bench, the cold stone chilling her palms. "I had thought your association with Miss Lynn had changed your attitude about the working class."

"Yes, well." He cleared his throat. "Miss Lynn doesn't control my thoughts. I'm still my own man, sister."

Juliana let out of breath. That was good to hear. It could make this easier. "Her ideas, while well-intended, can lead to much destruction. I'm glad you don't agree with her on everything. She is a unique thinker, though. I credit her with that."

A small smile tilted his lips. "Miss Lynn is unique in every respect."

"Are you two close? Are you..." She hesitated. "Are you going to ask her to marry you?"

Snowdon studied her. "Perhaps. Does the idea of her as a sister bother you?"

"Yes." A small niggle of jealousy wiggled beneath her breast, but she stamped it out. Her brother marrying a woman of his choice, one in a lower class, had no bearing on her ability to do the same. Brogan would be a mule about their relationship no matter what Snow did.

"And here I thought you believed in equality," her brother said.

She stood and grabbed his arm, squeezing. "I don't object for the reason you think. I only worry about you. About the kind of woman she is." Even though no one was around, she lowered her voice. "Don't you find it odd that father's accidents began after you became acquainted with Miss Lynn?"

"What are you saying?" He snorted. "You think she's behind it?"

Juliana shrugged. "She says she doesn't object to violence to achieve her ends. If she were to make you an earl, think she could control you, what wouldn't a woman like that be capable of?"

Snowdon threw back his head and howled with laughter.

She tapped her foot until his amusement trailed off. Her reasoning was sound. He didn't have to be a jackass about it. "I can see you disagree with my assessment of your paramour."

He clapped her shoulder. "Not at all, sister dear. I laugh because of the irony. You worry about what Bella has done, but you've never once questioned what I am capable of."

Juliana's fingers tingled. "What do you mean?" She took a small step away from her brother, uneasiness sliding up her spine.

Snow slid his hand into his coat pocket. "Come with me to Bluff Hall. We can have a nice, long talk about everything that worries you. You've imposed upon the Butters family long enough."

She glanced at the back door into the house and took

another half-step away. "Mr. Butters has assured me I'm welcome for as long as I like. What do you mean 'what you're capable of?'"

"Perhaps he's just being polite."

"I don't want to go to Bluff Hall." She stuttered over the words. The same feeling of dread that filled her veins when she entered their home was starting to swamp her now.

"Why do you always have to make things difficult?" he asked. "All my life it's been, 'Isn't Juliana clever,' and 'Why can't you help the tenants like your sister does?' Do you know how annoying it is being your brother?"

Juliana stumbled back. "What are you saying? You can't mean..."

"I'm tired of this family holding me back." He slapped his hat on his head. "Bella's shown me who I can truly be. How much change I can make in the world with the Withington title. How renowned the name Withington, my name, can be. I'm not going to let you stop me."

"It's not your title, not yet."

"Soon." He gazed around the gardens.

"You tried to kill father," she whispered. Her skin crawled, like hundreds of spiders skittered across her body. It was monstrous, beyond her comprehension. She shook her head, trying to clear it. "I don't understand."

His eyes snapped to her face. "You wouldn't. You wouldn't understand how infuriating it is being smarter than every man in the room yet still hearing them talk down to me like I were a child. How can they expect me to have any accomplishments when I'm only a viscount? It's not fair. Society sets up all these expectations for men like me then throws up barriers to achieving them."

She pressed a hand to her stomach. If he had stamped his foot, he couldn't have presented a better picture of a spoiled child in leading strings defying his nanny.

He slipped a small pistol from his coat pocket and waved it in front of her. "We're going to Bluff Hall. Don't make a fuss. You won't like the results." He slipped his hand back into his pocket but kept his fingers wrapped around the pistol grip.

She placed her hand on a stone column, leaning against it. This couldn't be happening. It couldn't be true. There had been affection between them growing up. It still existed, at least on her part.

"Oh, Snow, what will come of you?" She'd thought Pickens had met an ignoble end in prison. How much worse would her brother, a viscount, fare? Would he hang? Would her father hush it up, send Snow away somewhere?

"Come on." He jerked his head toward the front of the house. "The carriage is waiting."

She stumbled down the steps of the folly, her mind swirling. Perhaps he was ill. A disease could affect the mind as well as the body. There was no other explanation for a man to try to kill his father. Their father had given them everything they needed, never had a harsh word for anyone.

"This is going to devastate Father," she said. His son, his heir, trying to kill him.

Snowdon grabbed her elbow with his free hand. He tugged her along the garden path that ran the side of the house. "Don't worry. He won't even know what hit him."

Her knees gave way. She would have fallen to the gravel if Snow hadn't jerked her upright. Here she'd been thinking of the awfulness of her brother's actions. Of their family's shame and heartache. She hadn't thought ahead to where he might be successful.

"I won't let you hurt him," she said. Her voice sounded far away.

Snowdon pushed her against the garden gate, freeing the latch before grabbing her again. "What are you going to do, little sister?" He pushed her through the opening. "Write an essay to stop me? Give a little speech like you do at the salon?" He snorted. "No one there likes to hear them. They won't be any more effective now."

A couple in a small curricle laughed as they rolled past, the man flicking his whip in the air.

Juliana saw his wrist moving, saw the cat's tail snap, but didn't hear the crack. It was like a wet blanket had been thrown over the sounds of the city, leaving only a dull rushing sound in her ears.

Another man hurried down the street, his face buried in a paper, swerving around her and Snow as he passed.

She blinked. How did the rest of the world keep moving while hers was falling apart? Brogan had been more right than even he knew.

"You're all right, mum?"

Snowdon's fingers dug into her flesh as they turned to face the agent striding down the pavement. It was Mr. Hurst today. A nice enough man, but when all she wanted to see was Brogan, he was a poor substitute.

"Everything's fine," Snow said. "Nothing for you to be concerned about." He towed her toward the carriage which stood ten feet away.

Juliana recognized the driver on the box. Surely the servants wouldn't help Snowdon with his plot. They all respected her father.

But doubt rooted in her breast. If even Snowdon could be so evil, who was to say who else could be involved? What a little bit of money wouldn't seduce someone into doing?

"Lady Juliana?" Mr. Hurst shifted his hand to the back of his trousers.

Snow cut her a look. "You know him?"

"An investigator for the Bond Agency," she said. "I haven't cut all ties as you thought."

A giggle burbled up her throat. Their plan had worked. They'd uncovered the villain. And now she wished she'd never had this harebrained idea. She wanted nothing more than to go back in time fifteen minutes, when she didn't know the truth.

"Tell him everything's fine," Snowdon hissed in her ear, his grip on her arm going even tighter.

"Everything's fine," she repeated. "My brother and I are

just..."

She blinked. What was she doing? Was she willingly going to leave with Snowdon like a lamb to the slaughter?

She jerked her arm away. Turning, she looked up at her brother. She traced the familiar lines of his face with her gaze. Had his eyes always been so mean looking? His jaw always so soft? He looked a stranger.

In truth, he most likely always had been.

"No," she told him.

The pistol in his pocket bulged against the fabric. He chuckled. "My sister and I were to leave for home, but it seems as though she's changed her mind. Are you certain, Jules?"

The familiar nickname burned into her skin like a brand. She wanted to smack his mouth.

No, she wanted Brogan to smack his mouth. He had the skills to make her brother hurt. Make him bleed.

"Father is arriving at Bluff Hall soon," he continued. "It will just be he and I alone together if you don't come."

She pressed her hand to her side. Her breath came in short bursts. She'd laughed with her brother, played silly games with him, cried on his shoulder when their mother died.

And now he was trying to blackmail her into going with him, so he could kill his entire family with no one the wiser.

She took a step back. Another. Until she felt the presence of Mr. Hurst's body behind her.

"I guess she's changed her mind." Snowdon shrugged. "You know how women are."

The agent slid in front of her, never taking his eyes off Snow. Instinct must have told him something was wrong between brother and sister. That, or Brogan had told him her brother wasn't to be trusted.

"I know what this woman is like," Hurst said. "She has a good head on her shoulders. If she doesn't want to go with you, she has a reason."

The cloth covering the gun barrel shifted.

Juliana held her breath. Even after everything Snowdon had told her, after all the attempts he'd made on their father's life, she couldn't believe he would pull the trigger. Shoot her in cold blood. She didn't want to believe it.

She saw every expression that crossed her brother's face. It seemed like she could see every strand of his hair as a soft breeze ruffled his locks. She knew the moment when he made his decision.

"I'll see you around, Jules." He pulled his hand from his pocket and tipped his hat. He turned for the carriage.

It wasn't until it had rolled halfway down the block that the sounds of the street came roaring back.

Mr. Hurst turned to her. "Are you all right?"

She nodded, numb.

"Can I get you anything?"

Brogan. She wanted Brogan. Wanted him to wrap his arms around her, hold her tight, tell her everything would come out right in the end.

She swallowed.

Nothing would be right again.

Her brother was a killer. And Brogan... Brogan wasn't there to offer her comfort. He didn't want to be the man to help her pick up the pieces of her soul.

"I need to speak to the agent in charge of my investigation," she said, her voice hollow. "I have new information to disclose."

Chapter Twenty-Four

Brogan slapped the flat of the blade of his whittling knife against his palm.

He wanted to slap it against something else. Juliana's brother deserved that and more.

Wil brought Juliana a cup of tea as she sat before Hurst's desk. Her head was high, her shoulders back, but she was pale. More shaken than he had ever seen her.

"Tell me what he said again." Wil crossed his arms over his chest. "Try to repeat your brother's words as exactly as possible."

Hurst sat across from her, his pen poised above an inkwell. He'd already written down her statement, but Brogan knew it was effective to have the witness go over it several times. Memories were funny things, and shock had a strange effect on them.

"I told you." She put the cup on the desk, untouched. "He wants to be earl. He thinks he'll be able to do great things as Lord Withington." She swallowed, her throat rolling. "I guess he's no longer willing to wait until nature takes its course. I must get to my father. I must tell him." Her voice broke on the last words.

Wil squeezed her shoulder, and Brogan squeezed the handle of his knife.

He should be the one offering her comfort. But comfort led to other emotions, to an increase in her expectations. Comfort led to heartbreak later.

"Your father's up in Leeds?" Wil asked. "With this poet fellow?"

Juliana fiddled with the lace on her left cuff, her fingers ceaselessly moving. "They've been good friends for twenty years now. And Mr. Rose is more than a poet. He's written political essays and given lectures to several members of the House of Lords. His ideas could change England forever."

Hurst looked up from his notes. "I'll take her. Verity and I can both go. I'll make sure this gets sorted." He scowled. "I knew I didn't like the look of that brother."

Brogan stabbed his blade into his desk, leaving it upright in the wood. All right, that was it. He stood. "I'm taking her."

Yes, this idea was stupid. Yes, it went against everything he'd just been telling himself about keeping his distance. But no way was he trusting Juliana's safety to anyone but himself. Even the past few days, when other agents had taken their turns at her friend's house to watch over her, he had remained close by, always ready to intervene.

Juliana started, as though she'd forgotten he was there. Which was something else that got under his skin. He didn't want her to be heartbroken now they were no longer together, but did he slip her mind that easily? There wasn't a moment she wasn't invading his thoughts.

"Why?" she asked. "Are you still working my investigation?"

"Of course, I'm still on your investigation," he said sharply. "I was never off it." She had received a large shock, been betrayed by a close family member. That could be the only excuse for her thinking he would leave her security to anyone else.

"That's true." Wil tilted his head and eyed Brogan. "Mr. Duffy is still lead investigator. He just had some personal matters to attend to these past couple days." He raised an eyebrow. "Are you certain the personal matters are now resolved? We do have other agents who are more than capable of—"

"I'm sure." He circled his desk and went to stand in front of Juliana. "Your brother has returned to Bluff Hall?"

"That's where he said he was going."

"We have some time then." Brogan rubbed his temple. "Tomorrow morning we'll leave for Leeds. Have a chest packed and be ready for me. Early."

She nodded and stared at her hands. "This will devastate my father. I don't know how he'll ever recover."

"Will he believe you?" Wil asked. "You're a very sensible sort of woman, but if it came down to your word against your brother's, who will your father believe?"

She blinked. "I... I think me." She licked her lips. "Snow said Father respects me more, and much as I hate to think a parent plays favorites, I think he's right. Father does ask my opinion before Snow's. It's one of the reasons he h-hates me." A shudder ran through her body, and Brogan fought the urge to drop by her side, pull her into his arms.

He flexed his hand instead, and visualized the broken nose he would give Snowdon. The meaning of her words filtered through his anger, and he frowned. "Your father trusts your judgment over your brother's?" The man hadn't when Juliana had told him she thought his life was in danger, but suspicions were different than relating a first-hand conversation with her brother. Withington might think Juliana was mistaken about the attempts on his life, but if he trusted her to not outright lie about what she'd learned...

"Yes, that's what I just said."

Brogan didn't mind her testy tone. He liked that a bit of temper brought some color to her cheeks. "Then is it likely that your brother would return to Bluff Hall, give you time to speak with your father, time to bring the authorities down upon him? If I had admitted to such a dastardly plan, I would hardly kick my heels up at home, waiting for my end to come."

"What are you saying?" Juliana asked.

Wil ran his hand through his hair. "I'll send a messenger ahead. He'll ride like the wind to get a warning to the man."

"What would the message say?" Juliana jerked out of

her chair and started pacing. "I *think* my father will believe me, if I talk with him, face-to-face. If the information is relayed in a letter, that his son is trying to kill him, even if signed by me?" She shrugged. "He won't accept the seriousness of the situation from a message. Why would he when he doesn't even believe anyone has tried to kill him before?"

"Do we have any men around Leeds who we can send to watch over him?" Hurst asked.

Wil rubbed his thigh, then found a chair to sink into. "Perhaps. But to what end? If Withington won't believe him, and our man doesn't have access to the house the earl's staying in, our avenues of protection are limited."

"I need to speak to him," Juliana said. "If Snowdon is trying to get to him first, we must leave now. Immediately."

Brogan nodded at Hurst. "Whatever is in the wardrobe closet that would be appropriate for travel, put it together for us, will you?"

The agent nodded and hurried to the back room.

Brogan rested his weight on the balls of his feet. The calm that came right before a fight dropped over him like a veil. "Well," he said to Juliana, "it looks like I'm finally going to meet this famous poet and philosopher you talk so much about."

And since such an introduction held the potential for bloodshed, it was a meeting Brogan for once looked forward to.

* * *

Leaning her temple against the carriage window, Juliana watched as the last building of London rolled out of view. The coach rattled over a rut, and she bounced, her head nearly hitting the ceiling.

They were taking the fastest carriage the Bond Agency owned, with four horses out in front running hell for leather. This trip had a single purpose, and the niceties, like comfort, no longer mattered. It was a race, who would reach her father first, one she and Brogan had to win.

She traced a seam in the wood paneling near the window. One would think that in such an important matter that she would feel more interest. That her pulse would be racing, her stomach turning over.

Instead, she felt nothing. Nothing but duty to do her best to save her father.

Brogan leaned forward and rested his palm on her knee. "It will be all right."

She looked at his face, dropped her gaze to his hand. It was such an intimate gesture, his desire to console her. He must think her quite out of her senses if he was willing to risk such unprofessional behavior. He'd made such a point of denying them anything else.

He snatched his hand back, as though she burned.

Yes, that was more like it. She looked out the window again. It was worse being in this carriage with Brogan. She wished it had been any other agent who had come with her. She wanted to stay in her little cocoon, remain numb as long as possible. But every word from his mouth, every look, threatened to drag her out.

"I don't require reassurance," she said. "We can keep this completely professional. The way you want."

He loosed a deep breath. "None of this is what I want."

"But this is what you've created." She tapped her fingers on her thigh. "If it's not what you want, then why have you made it this way?"

"Because it's what is best. Someday, you'll see—"

"Please, be quiet." Heat rose up her chest. She didn't want to hear how someday she'd be thankful. Or happy. Grateful that he'd put an end to their relationship. He might think he was saving her to marry someone better, someone of her own station.

She couldn't imagine marrying anyone. Not if it wasn't Brogan. Why didn't he want to save her from heartbreak? From loneliness?

Brogan leaned back, his nostrils flaring. He plucked his hat from the seat, gripped it, then chucked it into the corner of the coach.

Brogan would marry. He wouldn't be lonely. A man like him deserved a good wife. Her heart pinched, and she placed her hand over it.

She'd always thought jealousy a foolish emotion, reserved only for the simpletons who didn't trust their partners. But Brogan was under no obligation to her, he'd made no vows. There was no trust to break, yet jealousy still clogged her throat until she thought she couldn't breathe.

She hated the woman he would marry. The woman who would share his bed. Hold his hand when he was sick. Laugh with him. Tease him.

For just a moment, she understood her brother and what he was capable of. Understood how passion could turn ugly, drive someone under its spell to do something horrible. If Brogan whispered in her ear, promising her forever if only she'd commit some dastardly deed, how tempted would she be? One bad act that would give her everything.

That would give her him.

But Brogan would never ask her to do something immoral. He was no Miss Bella Lynn.

The carriage jounced again, so hard she nearly fell off her seat. She cried out at her sharp landing on the springs.

"We can't slow down," Brogan said.

She smoothed her hands down the stomach of her gown. "I didn't ask you to."

"Come here." He patted the seat next to him. "I'll make sure you don't bounce away."

"I'm fine." She clenched her teeth together at the next rut in the road so she didn't bite her tongue clean through.

His eyes narrowed. "Don't let your anger keep you from getting more comfortable. I promise—"

"No." Whatever it was, she didn't want to hear his promises. Not if they didn't include keeping her forever. "Cuddling up with you wouldn't be professional, regardless of the circumstances. And we do want to keep things professional."

He cursed, his hands fisting and opening the way they only did when he was truly irritated.

But his irritation was no longer her concern. She turned on her hip and stared out the window. Stared at anything other than him.

Then squawked when he lifted her from her seat and plopped her down beside him, his arm banding around her waist.

"What do you think you're doing?" She pushed at his chest, but he was immovable. The carriage hit the next bump in the road, and he squeezed her to his side, keeping them locked together.

"Making sure you don't break your fool neck out of pique." He tucked a strand of her hair behind her ear. "Let me hold you, Juliana. Please."

She stopped squirming, sagging against him. There was no fight left in her. The warmth of his body seeped into her side. She didn't want to like being pressed against him so much, but for the first time in days, she felt safe.

She felt like she was home.

She dropped her head to his shoulder. "What am I going to do? My brother..." Her voice broke.

"I know." He ran his hand up and down her arm. "We'll figure it out. You're strong. And I'll be there to help you. As your friend."

The last word was the one that broke her. Tears slid down her cheeks before ugly sobs tore from her throat.

Her brother wanted to kill her father, to kill her.

And Brogan was only her friend.

She felt like she had fallen down a dark hole, and she saw no way to ever climb out.

Chapter Twenty-Five

Brogan jumped from the carriage, turning to give his hand to Juliana. The trip had been grueling, in more ways than one. The breakneck pace and little sleep had made all of his muscles ache.

Being confined with Juliana made something else inside of him ache even more.

"We're finally here." Juliana climbed down the steps and pressed her hands to her lower back, arching. She gazed at the house, worrying her bottom lip.

It was a two-story stone structure with elegant side wings. It seemed like a more impressive house than a man who wrote lines about love should be able to afford, but what did Brogan know? Juliana admired Rose; the man must be good.

She closed her eyes and took a deep breath. "What am I going to say to Father?"

He shoved his hands in his pockets to keep them from doing something stupid, like pulling her in for an embrace or rubbing the soreness from her back. "The truth." He cleared his throat. "You'll tell your father the truth. What he does with it is up to him."

She swallowed. "This is the end of my family. No matter what happens, nothing will ever be the same."

Someone like her poet would have found the words to comfort her. Said something to give her courage and lift her spirits.

Brogan had nothing. Nothing but honesty. "No, life will never be the same for you. But you'll survive."

She nodded and smiled as a butler approached. "Let's get this over with," she said. She introduced them to the butler and told him she had an urgent need to speak to her father.

"Of course, mum." He took their coats. "I'll have one of the lads see to your horses and your driver. You can follow me." His smile included Brogan in the invitation, but it wouldn't have mattered if it hadn't. There was no way Brogan was leaving her side. He'd seen her through the investigation this far. He would see her through to the end.

Their footsteps echoed down the long corridor. Colorful paintings lined the walls, along with bookcases crammed full of books sticking out every which way.

The man must do nothing but read. And this was the type of man that Juliana admired. This was the type of man who deserved her.

The butler opened a door and shuffled inside, but Juliana paused at the entrance.

The blood drained from her face. "I don't know if I can do this," she whispered.

Brogan smiled sadly. She didn't know it, but she could do just about anything. All she needed was a little push. He placed his palm on her back and guided her inside.

They had been announced, so the four men were already on their feet. The two older men were her father and who Brogan supposed was Rodger Rose. The sight of Snowdon, smirking at his sister, sent fire racing through Brogan's veins. But it was the fourth man that halted his steps.

Juliana hissed in a breath at the sight of her brother. Snowdon murmured something to their father then laughed.

How much had the bastard poisoned the well against Juliana? Seeing that Snowdon had beaten them here was a punch to the gut, but perhaps it was for the best. It was better to see the snake than wonder where it was.

The larger problem for Brogan was the fourth man. He

was a veritable giant, someone Brogan had only seen once, but not a man to forget. Was he friends with Snowdon? And if so, why hadn't Brogan been informed?

"Juliana," her father said. "What a delightful surprise. What on earth are you doing here?"

She took a step forward, swayed. But she stayed on her feet. "I came to speak to you, Father." She stared at Snowdon. "It's most urgent."

Her father hurried forwards and took her hands. He looked nearly as wobbly as his daughter, with tiny beads of sweat dotting his forehead. "What is it, child? Are you all right?"

"Yes," she said, "I'm not the one in trouble." She spoke to her father, but her gaze remained on her brother. Betrayal was visible in every line of her body.

She shook herself and squeezed her father's hand. "But how are you?" Her eyebrows drew together. "You look flushed."

He waved his hand. "I'm fine. Just a bit under the weather today. Now what did you need to speak to me about?"

"How rude we are," Snowdon interrupted loudly. "Lord Dunkeld, Rose, this is Mr. Duffy and my sister, Lady Juliana Wickham. Rose, you, of course, already know Lady Juliana. Duffy, Jules, this is the Marquess of Dunkeld. With such inspired company, perhaps we should wait until later for any family discussions."

The enormous man, Dunkeld, hooked a thumb in the pocket of his tartan-patterned waistcoat. He nodded at them and gave Juliana a curious look. He must have felt the uneasiness of the newcomers. The man's body tensed as though preparing for a fight.

Which wasn't a surprise from what Brogan had heard about him. The marquess was someone even a professional boxer would be leery of facing in a ring.

"This is quite the coincidence," Snowdon continued. "Dunkeld, do you know, Mr. Duffy? He does work for you after all."

"Is that right?" Dunkeld stepped forward, hand outstretched. His faint Scottish burr warmed his voice.

They shook. "Yes, sir. I'm an investigator with the Bond Agency." And the Marquess of Dunkeld was one of its five owners. What Brogan did now, in front of the man, could establish his position...or end it.

"Is this visit for pleasure?" his employer asked.

"No." Brogan's heart beat sluggishly. "We're here on business."

Snowdon snorted. "This is the man I hired to find my sister. And find her he did. And now the two seemed joined at the hip. A bit unconventional, don't you think, Jules? Even for you."

Dunkeld narrowed his eyes. He cut his gaze over Juliana's family, and Brogan could see the gears turning in his head.

"While this is all delightfully interesting," Rose said, "my gout is acting up, and I need to sit. Come join us," he said to Juliana and Brogan as he eased himself down in his chair and plopped his leg onto an ottoman. He leaned an brass-handled cane against his chair.

Juliana walked stiffly to the open space next to her brother on a settee. Brogan grabbed a chair by the wall and set it next to her. He wished he could wedge it between her and Snowdon. The man's very presence tainted the air. Juliana shouldn't be subjected to his nearness.

"I was just speaking to your father about you, Lady Juliana." Rose picked up a cheroot and took a puff. "I read the essay you sent me on poverty alleviation programs. The writing needs a bit of work, but the underlying arguments are interesting. There might be a spot for you in my debate society after all."

She rubbed her temple. "That's nice?"

Her father chortled. "Nice? You've been blathering on about wanting to go on tour with Rose for a year." He flapped his hand in the air, trying to dispel the cheroot smoke, his mouth twisting. "Here's your chance."

Rose tapped his ash into a bowl. "Now Withington, I didn't say it was guaranteed. I'd want to see some more of her work before it's settled. But that shouldn't be a problem for such an accomplished young woman, should it?"

Juliana opened her mouth, but no sound emerged.

Brogan's chest burned. She was finally getting the recognition she wanted, the opportunity she craved. And she couldn't feel pride in her accomplishment because of her fuckwit brother. "It won't be a problem. Lady Juliana has many good ideas."

She frowned at him. "I'll do my best," she finally said. "Father, can we—"

"How long are you planning on staying?" Snowdon asked her. "Father and I are returning to Bluff Hall in two days. You should join us. It will give you time to write something that will really impress Rose."

"Why wait?" Rose shifted his leg and grimaced. "With the people I have staying here now, I'm sure ideas will be gushing from Lady Juliana like water from a geyser."

"Who all is here?" Brogan sat at the edge of his chair. The more guests, the harder it would be to keep track of Withington, to keep him safe. That's if they weren't ejected from Rose's house after Juliana told her story.

"Us, Dunkeld's lovely wife." He nodded at the Scotsman. "She has become one of our most engaging speakers on natural sciences."

"She enjoys your meetings whenever we're in Town," Dunkeld agreed. "My wife is quite the woman of science. She's increased our harvest four times over since she's moved to Kenmore Castle." Pride spilled from the man's words.

"Anyone else?" Brogan asked.

"What?" Rose rubbed his leg. "Oh, yes, that self-assured young woman who joined us about a year ago. A Miss..." His face cleared. "Ah, here she is now, along with the marchioness." He nodded to the door, and Brogan turned.

Miss Lynn and a tall, sturdy woman entered the room, each carrying a book in her hand.

"Did you find my greenhouse to your liking?" Rose asked the marchioness.

"Lovely." The woman crossed to her husband and pecked his cheek. "Though I did give your gardener some advice on soil additives. I hope you don't mind."

"What's she doing here," Juliana hissed at her brother as she glared at Miss Lynn.

Rose started. "I received a note that Miss Lynn was in town, so of course I extended an invitation. You know I have an open-door policy for my salon members."

"Of course." Juliana's breathing increased, her chest rising and falling rapidly. "Father, I really must sp—"

"Miss Lynn, there is room for you here." Snowdon scooted over and patted the space between himself and Juliana. The look he shot his sister was too smug by half, and Brogan fisted his hands, wanting to knock the pompousness right out of him. Juliana practically sat on the armrest of the settee to put as much distance between herself and Miss Lynn as she could.

Dunkeld glanced at Brogan's fists and arched an eyebrow. Brogan forced himself to relax. Miss Lynn appeared to be an intimate of the marquess's wife. How would the man take accusations against her character? All the other investigators said their employers were fair men, but none of them had accused one of the owner's friends of criminal acts. And this owner had a known temper. Perhaps his fairness had a breaking point.

Snowdon laced his fingers together and rested his hands over his belly. "There now, isn't this nice? A cozy gathering of intimates. Isn't this better than running off on your own, Juliana? Being surrounded by family and friends? I do hope you'll give up the queer ideas that have taken hold of you lately and rejoin the family. You should—"

Juliana leapt from her seat. "Shut up, Snow, you swag-bellied maggot pie!"

The room froze. Even Brogan stopped breathing. Those insults were minor by a man's standards, but coming from his usually composed Juliana, shocking nevertheless. Her face was red and her limbs shook with rage. If ever there was a person who had been pushed too far, Juliana was an exact portrait of her.

He stood, ignoring the impropriety, and cupped her shoulder, pulling her into his side. "Take deep breaths," he murmured into her ear. "In and out. There you go."

She relaxed fractionally under his hands. Her face remained red, though whether purely from anger or if embarrassment was now added to the mix, Brogan didn't know.

"Juliana." Withington struggled to his feet, his face grey. "What is the meaning of this? Get hold of yourself, girl."

"I apologize, Father. Mr. Rose." She pressed a hand to her stomach. "But I have something I need to tell you. About..." Her gaze flicked to Snow.

His jaw was clenched and his eyes narrowed to slits. Miss Lynn sat beside him looking as unconcerned as an angel before heaven's gate.

Withington raked his hand through his hair. "While family matters should usually be conducted privately, you've publicly insulted your brother. It is only fair to him for you to say your piece here."

Dunkeld stood and subtly placed his wife behind him. He nodded to Brogan. "Perhaps we should go outside. Have our own talk as they have theirs."

"I'm not leaving Juliana's side."

Withington's eyes flew wide at Brogan's use of his daughter's first name.

Dunkeld's face went grim.

Snowdon and Lynn watched with a glee more appropriate for spectators at a scandalous play.

Rose frowned, a deep divot forming in his forehead. "I won't have nonsense in my house, or my salon. We gather to discuss high ideas, not gossip and use base language."

Juliana squeezed her hands together. "I do apologize. But I must speak to my father. And if he won't speak with me alone..."

Then she would make a fool of herself in front of her idol. Ruin her chances for her spot in his debate society. Her one chance to make a difference in the world, or so she thought.

Brogan's stomach hardened. He couldn't let her do it. If her father wouldn't make it easier on his daughter by removing himself for a private conversation, Brogan would remove him with his own bare hands.

Perhaps he should have remained a boxer. His first instinct was always to use his hands. He shot a glance at his employer. Soon, Dunkeld would realize the mistake he and his partners had made hiring an ex-bruiser.

His spine straightened. But there was nothing for it. His job, no matter what Juliana had paid the agency for, had been to protect her. And he wanted to protect more than just her life. He wanted to protect her future, as well.

"Lord Withington," Brogan said, "we will be retiring to a private room for your conversation with your daughter."

"See here, Duffy," Snowdon began.

Miss Lynn patted his arm. "Not now. Can't you see your father is distressed?" She rose and hurried to the man. "I'm sure your daughter's behavior has come as quite a shock, although those of us who've spent time with her recently have seen she must be suffering from an attack of nerves. But you have been away and missed her alteration. Let me get you a drink to help calm you."

Withington placed his hand on the back of a chair and leaned against it. "I don't feel well. A drink won't sit right."

"I know something special for upset stomachs." Lynn gave his arm one last pat before hurrying to the sideboard.

"I believe Juliana needs to rest, Father." Snowdon bore down on his sister. "She's been allowed too much free rein to traipse about unattended and the stress is getting to her." He reached for her arm, and Juliana jerked away.

"How did I never truly see you before?" she asked. "How have I lived with such a snake and never known?"

"Juliana." Her father's voice was sharp. "What are you saying? What could he have possibly done to deserve such censure?"

"Here you are, Lord Withington." Miss Lynn sashayed up, carefully holding the over-full glass. "This should set you right up."

Without looking at her, Withington reached for the glass. He wiped his forehead with his other hand.

Brogan eyed the drink, watched as Miss Lynn's lips tilted upward as he raised the glass, observed the man's pallor, his sweaty brow.

He reached for the glass, intending to grab it away, but Withington pulled back at the same time, splashing the liquid over his waistcoat and trousers.

"Good lord, man!" Withington shook the wet from his hand. "What do you think you're doing? What is going on here?"

"I apologize for my investigator." Dunkeld's brows drew down. "I presume he has a good reason for his actions here today."

Juliana gave one last longing look at Rose then squared her shoulders. "They're trying to kill you, Father. Snow and Miss Lynn. I know it sounds mad, but Snow admitted it to me in London when he tried to force me to Bluff Hall. He wants to be earl. He doesn't want to wait."

Withington loosed a disbelieving chuckle. "Is this a jest of some sort? How can you say such a thing?"

"Really, Lady Juliana." Rose scowled. "There's no call for this nonsense in my home. No call at all."

She lifted her chin. "I say it because it's true. All those accidents, all those little mishaps that could have cost your life. He was behind that. He and his"—she glared at Miss Lynn—"friends."

Miss Lynn pressed her fingers to the base of her throat. "Her mind has truly broken. Lord Snowdon, you must see to your sister. She deserves good care. Don't be too harsh on her. It's not her fault if her mind is diseased."

"There's nothing wrong with Juliana's mind," Brogan growled. Oh, the woman was good. He could see how she had insinuated her way into Snowdon's life. Wrapped her claws into his mind. But the hint of playfulness that lingered in Miss Lynn's eyes gave her away. It also made Brogan question how serious she was about her revolutionary ideas. Was this a game to her or was she in earnest?

She was willing to kill to achieve her ends, but he bet that she had kept her hands clean, that she'd made Snowdon do all the dirty work.

Juliana took her father's hand and held it tight. "I know this is unbelievable. That this is the last thing you'd ever want to hear. But I'm not sick. I'm not lying. He admitted to this as he pulled out a pistol to kidnap me. And then he raced up here to get to you first. Please, Father." She pressed his hand to her heart. "Please, you must believe me. Your life depends on it."

Withington swung his head back and forth. His eyes were glossy, his mouth slack. "But what you're saying..." he mumbled. "It's monstrous. It would mean that your mother and I have produced a monster. It can't be."

"Of course, it can't be." Snowdon strode forward and jerked his father's hand from Juliana's grip. "You know me, Father. You know I could never do anything like this. All I've ever wanted to be was a good man, be as good an earl as you are when the time comes. I've worked my whole life towards that end."

Withington staggered back. "You've never cared about being earl, good or otherwise." He clawed at the knot of his cravat. "Whenever I tried to instruct you in your duties, you never paid me mind."

Snowdon's hand twitched, and he shoved it into his pocket. "You can't listen to her. She's a liar. She's never wanted what was best for me. She's always tried to hold me back."

Withington shook his head, blinking rapidly. "No. I know that's not true. Juliana always tried to encourage you in your duties. I've seen it." He swayed. "Why would you lie? Is this true, Snow? Do you hate me so much?"

"Of course, it's not true." Miss Lynn hurried to Withington's side and grasped his arm. "Your son has been a true friend, a good man. I know he could never do anything so..." She trailed off.

Brogan turned his head to follow her gaze.

His blood iced his veins when he saw the pistol in Snowdon's hand.

Pointed straight at Juliana.

Chapter Twenty-Six

"Son, what are you doing?" Her father's voice was broken, worse even than when he'd told her and Snow that their mother had died. "Put down the weapon."

Snow's hand shook. "You had to get in my way. You couldn't let me have this one thing."

A burble of laughter escaped Juliana's throat. She pressed the back of her hand to her forehead. "Let you kill father? You think you're entitled to that?" She shook her head. "You're mad." She almost wished he truly was mad. That his eyes were wild and he had the disease of mind that Miss Lynn had accused her of.

Then this would make sense. Then she could have sympathy, and still love her brother.

"Is it mad to want to fix this broken world? Mad to see the oppression rife in England and want to fix it?" He jerked his index finger at his face. "I could have been the one to fix it. Father does nothing in the House of Lords, but if I were earl, I would make changes. People would listen to me."

"I'm already tired of listening to you," Rose grumped. "This is insufferable, young man."

Aside from a twitch in Lord Dunkeld's lips, everyone ignored the poet.

Juliana stepped forward, then stopped short when Snow waggled the gun at her.

Brogan growled.

Snowdon's aim wavered between Brogan and herself. Panic clogged her chest. Everything was wrong. Her life was torn apart. But Brogan was still whole, healthy, and wonderful, and there was no way she was going to let her brother hurt him.

It wasn't Brogan's fault he'd become mixed up with the likes of her. That his first case entangled him with a woman who came from such a broken family.

She wanted to make a difference in the world? Keeping Brogan safe was the best thing she could do.

"People would listen to you?" She huffed. "You think you would walk into the House, one of nearly seven hundred members, and people will trip over themselves to hear what you have to say?" She shook her head. "I know you've always been spoiled."

Her father stiffened at those words, but she pressed forward. There would be time to comfort her father, hopefully. First, they had to survive.

"You're never told no," she said. "All our nannies would praise you, the future earl, for the smallest accomplishment. But praise without merit is a toxic combination. Even you can't be so deranged as to think that with no skills, no discernable talents, that you can change the world."

Snowdon looked to Miss Lynn. "It only takes a very small group of determined people to make change." The words came as if by rote, as though they'd been spoken by Snow a hundred times over.

Or heard by him.

Miss Lynn pressed her fist to her mouth, her eyes flying wide. "What have you done, Snowdon?" She gasped dramatically.

Juliana pressed her lips together. The woman's acting was a bit overwrought in her opinion, but it seemed to work on many people. What did Juliana know about the effectiveness of a woman's wiles? She'd rarely tried to employ them.

"Violence is never the way," Miss Lynn continued.

Snowdon's forehead wrinkled. "But... you know that action needs to be taken. That eggs need to be broken in order to make an omelet, as the French say. I'm only doing what you want."

Miss Lynn clasped her hands together and frowned, looking like a disapproving nursemaid. "You knew that my brother was hurt in the Durham riots. I can't stand the thought of anyone's pain. There's too much misery in the world as it is."

Another snort of laughter escaped Juliana. She must work on controlling that reaction. Not only was it inappropriate for the circumstances, but it was such an indelicate sound. What would Brogan think of her?

And that made her want to laugh harder. They were facing death and she was worried about appearing lady-like in front of her love? It was absurd and amusing all at the same time.

It must be the dire circumstances that were making her act so. She had hoped she would be the type of woman to keep her head in a tense situation, but apparently she was the kind of woman who snorted.

"How quickly your admiration of the French Revolution has evaporated," Juliana said, "now that it has come time to face justice for your own actions. Did you not shrug your shoulders at the heads that rolled in the streets of Paris because you thought the cause was just? My brother would not have thought up this scheme on his own. Snow is not only spoiled, but he's too simple-minded to conceive of it. There was a viper speaking in his ear. That viper was you."

Miss Lynn's face darkened. "You don't know what you're talking about. But I'm not surprised. What else should I expect from an aristocrat?" She turned to Rose and raised her hands, palms up. "Their kind always covers for their own. Even the ones who join your salon, they might speak of equality, but they don't mean it. The Beau Monde will always look out for their own. Look for people like you and me to take the blame for their own actions."

Rose sniffed. "Don't include me in your melodrama. I've had quite enough of the lot of you, regardless of class." He grabbed his cane from his chair's arm and stabbed the carpet at his feet, to emphasize his point. "Though I do feel most badly for you, Withington. Such nonsense you have to put up with."

Juliana's spine hardened. She was part of that nonsense. Her chance of ever joining his debate society was well and truly sunk. And she couldn't even feel badly about it. It was something else that made her want to laugh.

Why had she spent so much time caring about Rodger Rose's opinion of her? Debates and discussions and lectures were all very nice, but they weren't life. Keeping one's family safe was life. Having and holding the ones you loved. Those were the things that mattered. She'd been such a fool.

"It isn't rank Juliana's trying to preserve." Brogan fisted his hands, his knuckles going white. He inched forwards, his intended path putting him between Juliana and her brother's gun. "She's saving her father, honoring him by risking everything. She believes in justice and truth and doing what's right, even when it's hard. But you wouldn't know about that. A woman like Juliana can't even be conceived of in your imagination, the two of you are so far apart."

Juliana's throat went thick. She loved him for thinking so highly of her, and hated him for putting her up on that pedestal he didn't feel worthy of touching. If they survived this, she was going to have a strongly-worded speech to deliver to him.

"I'm the one holding the gun." Snow waved it in the air. "I'm the one who decides justice here. And I want all of you to be quiet so I can think."

The handle of Rose's cane glinted in the afternoon light. Juliana's breath caught in her throat. She circled away from Brogan, ignoring his scowl, and inched towards the poet's side.

"Snow, somewhere deep inside, you know this is wrong. You know you could never be earl enough to make a difference." Taunting her brother most likely wasn't her smartest idea, but as it was her only one, she went with it. "Even your Miss Lynn knows that having control of a man such as yourself would gain her very little towards her revolutionary ideals."

The toe of her boot nudged the leg of the side table next to Rose. A brandy glass atop it rattled, and she froze. She cleared her throat. "You and your friends, you're not filled with hopes for equality. You're filled with resentment. You know you're too weak, too pathetic, to change the world for the good, so you've decided to tear it all down instead."

Snowdon's arm swung from Juliana to Brogan to their father and back to her. "Shut your mouth, Sister."

"Does the truth hurt?" She took another sliding step towards the poet's chair.

Brogan followed her movements like a hawk watches a hare.

She jutted her chin towards the cane, trying to tell him her intent without words. And probably not succeeding. "I know you. I know how as children, when I built a taller, grander sandcastle, you stomped through the sand, destroying it instead of trying to build yours better."

Her skirts brushed Rose's sleeve. "I remember when Father hired a fencing instructor for us, that after the first time I bested you, you bent all the epees so I could never win again instead of applying yourself to have a better form. Even in Rose's salon, when a discussion occurs on a subject you don't know, you mock and belittle the experts instead of trying to learn from them. You've always made fun of my aspirations, but I'd rather try and fail than give up as you have. It's easy to destroy. It takes a strong man to build."

A shadow flickered across her brother's face. Juliana hoped he was considering his actions. Realizing what he'd done and who he'd become. If her brother could feel even a little remorse, there'd be hope for his redemption.

His next words buried those hopes. "You're jealous," he told her. "You've always been desperate to make a difference, to make a name for yourself in this world, always knowing that it would never happen. Now, when I finally stand up, take action, you can't bear it."

"Take action?" Their father swayed. "Killing me? That's what you call taking action?" His knees gave way, and Brogan and Dunkeld leapt forwards to catch the man's arms. They lowered him to a chair.

"I'm not going to stand here and listen to any more of this," Miss Lynn said. She lifted her chin. "This family is full of criminals and liars." She glared at Snowdon and Juliana. "If I never have anything more to do with you, it'll be too soon."

She turned on her heel, her skirts flying.

And froze when the decided click of a pistol hammer being cocked ricocheted through the room.

"I thought you loved me," Snowdon said. "You said you loved me, that you'd stand by me."

Juliana's heart squeezed. Even now, she felt sympathy for her brother. She took another sliding step towards Rose. His cane was almost within arm's reach.

Snowdon swung the pistol back at her.

"Put the gun down," Brogan ground out through clenched teeth. He stepped forward, and Dunkeld gripped his shoulder, holding him back.

Juliana looked at the gun, at the cane, at Brogan. If she were going to die today, she wanted Brogan's face to be the last thing she saw. She traced the bend in his nose that spoke of all the blows he'd taken, and all the times he'd climbed back to his feet. The stubborn angle of his jaw that charmed her when it wasn't so irritating. The clarity of his ocean blue eyes that seemed to see deep into her soul.

She didn't want this to be her last moments on earth. She wanted to spend hours laughing in bed with Brogan, making babies with him, growing old in his arms. But if it wasn't meant to be, if her eyes closed forever on his face, she would die content.

She and Brogan locked gazes. She rolled her eyes to the

cane and back.

He shook his head. To tell her no, or that he didn't understand?

It didn't matter. She had one chance to end this, to protect the people she loved.

She nodded once, and took a deep breath, steeling herself. How badly did a bullet tearing through flesh hurt? Her heart raced. She could do this. If only she could make her limbs move. The barrel of the pistol looked huge. There was no way Snowdon would miss.

She drew her shoulder blades back. She'd wanted to make a difference. Well, now was the time.

She sucked down another deep breath, her muscles tensing.

But before she could make her move, all hell broke loose.

Chapter Twenty-Seven

Brogan rolled onto the balls of his feet. It was a stupid, foolish, brave idea Juliana had. If he could have stopped her from implementing it, he would have. But there were several feet between them, and, besides, she never let anyone get in her way.

Damn, fool woman.

Since he couldn't stop her, he needed to help. Her chest was bobbing up and down like pistons at full speed. As nervous as she was, he was surprised she didn't swoon. Her hand twitched towards the cane's head, and his time to work on a plan was up.

He whirled, swinging his fist straight at the marquess's face.

Dunkeld's eyes flew wide a moment before Brogan's hand connected.

Brogan hadn't used full-force, but pounding into the Scotsman's thick jaw bloody hurt.

Dunkeld stumbled to one knee, and Brogan towered over him. "You're in on this with Snowdon."

The marchioness gasped and dropped next to Dunkeld, glaring at Brogan. "How dare you? You'll pay for striking my husband."

Dunkeld blinked up at him, his left eye already beginning to swell. Every other eye was turned toward Brogan, too.

Including Snowdon's.

Juliana reached out, snatched Rose's cane from under his hand, and grasped it tightly. With a move sure to make her former fencing instructor proud, she whipped the cane over her head and brought it down on her brother's wrist.

Snowdon howled.

The gun dropped to the carpet.

And Juliana practiced a few more moves, walloping her brother over and over until he collapsed to the ground in tears.

As she was smacking the fleshy bits of her brother, areas that wouldn't cause permanent damage, Brogan saw no reason to end her fun. Juliana had a lot of anger to release, and beating the source of it seemed fair to Brogan.

He picked up the pistol then turned to offer Dunkeld a hand up.

The Scotsman grunted, and got to his feet without Brogan's assistance.

Brogan sighed. There went his job.

"No good... two-faced... sap skull..." Each oath from Juliana's lips was accompanied by a sturdy swing of her cane.

Brogan studied her form, frowning.

Dunkeld stepped beside him. "She's dropping her left shoulder with each swing."

"I see that." He could work on that with her later.

Snowdon pressed one hand into the floor, pushing his upper body upright. "Jules, please..."

Juliana threw the cane down and made a fist. "You don't have the right to call me Jules." She pulled her arm back.

Brogan leapt forwards and caught her hand just in time. He kissed her knuckles. "You're more likely to hurt your hand than his head with an untrained punch, my love."

Her chest heaved. Her eyes were wild. And she was the most beautiful thing he'd ever seen.

"It's over," he told her. "You did it. Your father is safe." Brogan darted a glance at the man. Withington was slumped in his chair, his face grey and haggard. He looked caved in, broken, but such a shock would do that to a person. Juliana would help him recover.

"While I'm quite happy no one is going to get shot, what do you think you were doing hitting my husband?" The marchioness planted her hands on her hips and glared at Brogan.

Dunkeld rubbed his face. "I believe I was the unwitting distraction he provided for Lady Juliana to grab Rose's cane."

Brogan shrugged. "You're big enough to take a punch."

Lady Dunkeld's eyes went even squintier. "How dare—"

Her husband ran his hands up and down her arms. "Don't trouble yourself. I've been hit harder by children," he said archly.

Brogan ignored the insult. "Will you send for a doctor?" he asked Rose. "There's a chance Snowdon and Miss Lynn put something in Withington's food or drink that affected his health."

Rose stood and shuffled to the bell pull. "And the dramatics continue." He made his way to Withington and squeezed the man's shoulder. "Of course, I'll send for a doctor. Along with the magistrate."

A servant entered. Over much protesting on Snowdon's part and sneering on Miss Lynn's, Rose directed the servant to have them held in the stables until the magistrate arrived. The appearance of several burly grooms as escorts put an end to their complaints.

Brogan shoved his hands in his pockets. His job was done. As was his short-lived career as an investigator. When he returned to the ring, there was an even smaller chance of ever seeing Juliana again than he'd had before.

His employers were aristocrats. Somewhere in the back of his mind he'd thought perhaps he might run into her while performing a task for them. See her at an opera if an investigation took him there. But as a boxer, their paths would never cross.

He let himself enjoy one more moment of weakness and tucked an errant strand of Juliana's hair off her cheek. His fingers lingered on her smooth skin. "You'll be all right now. Goodbye, Juliana."

She blinked. "What?"

"My job is over. It's time I got back to London and looked for new employment. Your life is here, with your father."

"New employment..." She looked at the raising bruise on the marquess's face, her face clearing with understanding. She pointed a finger at the Scotsman. "You'd better not be thinking about dismissing Brogan. I don't care how high up you and your friends are, if you end his employment, I will make it my life's mission to destroy your agency's reputation."

Brogan rocked back on his heels. "Uh, Juliana, that's not necessary. I'll just—"

"You'll do nothing of the sort." She included Brogan in her finger jabbing. "If you think I'm going to let you lose your job for such a trifle—"

"A trifle!" Lady Dunkeld huffed.

"—then you haven't been paying attention to the kind of woman I am." Juliana whirled on Rose. "I know you don't like scenes. I suggest you leave now if you don't want to witness the one I'm about to make."

Rose grunted. "You saved your father. I suppose your behavior can be excused just this once."

"Juliana..." Withington reached out, and Juliana took his hand, kissing it.

"Don't worry, Father. I'll take you home soon and we'll work together to get past this."

Brogan's chest went tight. This really was the end. She'd sputter and fight for his job a few moments longer, then she'd disappear into Bluff Hall and he'd...

He swallowed around the lump in his throat. He'd be fine. His life had been tolerable before he'd met Juliana; it would be tolerable after she was no longer in it.

With one last squeeze to her father's hand, Juliana stomped towards Dunkeld, her expression transforming into a terrifying scowl. Brogan almost felt bad for the marquess. Confronting an enraged Juliana was like facing an angry cat. Your chances for survival were decent, but you wouldn't escape without several deep scratches.

"Juliana," Brogan began.

She put her hand up, palm in his face. "We'll talk later. Right now, your employer and I have—" She squawked as Brogan banded an arm around her waist and lifted.

He carried her out of the room, her squirming and cursing the entire way. At the door, he turned and nodded to their audience. "My apologies. I'll return her later."

"Put me down." She clawed at the walls, as though that would stop their progress through the house.

Brogan kicked open one door, startling a maid, and continued down the hall. He kicked another door, and stomped inside after seeing the room was empty. He placed her down in the middle of the library, between floor-to-ceiling bookcases, and planted his hands on his hips. "Just what do you think you're doing? There is a small chance you can still join Rose's debate society. But squawking like an angry hen isn't going to help you."

She prowled around him. "The debate society? Who gives a fig about the debate society? This is your career we're talking about. I'm not going to let you be dismissed for doing your job."

He ran a hand up the back of his head. "I hit my employer. Of course I'm gone." The dread he'd expected to feel wasn't there. It had been worth it. He might want to show people he was more than just his fists, but when it came down to it, those were his best tools. Juliana had needed a bruiser, and he was happy to fill the role, regardless of the consequences.

"Why, exactly, did you hit Lord Dunkeld?" Her circling about him made him the slightest bit dizzy. She truly was like a cat, stalking her prey.

Brogan didn't know whether to chuckle or take a wary step back. "It was a distraction, like Dunkeld said. If you were going to do something as foolish as disarm your brother, you needed as much help as you could get."

She threw up her hands. "You couldn't think of any other distraction besides punching your employer!"

He scratched his jaw. "I thought if I punched your father you'd be angry."

She stopped pacing and dropped her face into her hands. "Unbelievable." She looked skyward. "Why did I have to fall in love with an idiot?"

Brogan stilled. "Don't say that. Don't say you love me."

She dropped her gaze to his. "Why not? It's true."

"Saying it aloud will only make it harder on yourself." On him. He barely had the strength to walk away from her now.

She smiled, but there was no amusement in it. "If you think I won't be anything other than devastated if you walk away, then you are sorely mistaken." She reached for him, then dropped her hand. "I'm willing to fight for you. Fight for us. Against any nay-sayers or cuts direct. But..." She swallowed. "I won't push myself where I'm not wanted. Do you love me, Brogan?"

He snorted. "Loving you isn't the issue."

She blew out a wavering breath. "Can you say the words? Can you do that for me? Sometimes a woman needs to hear the words."

He grabbed his hair, tugging. "I love you, damn it. Now how does that help anything?"

Her whole body sagged, as though she hadn't expected him to admit to it. He narrowed his eyes. Or hadn't known that he'd actually loved her. But if she didn't know that already, then she was the idiot.

"You said it for me." She beamed.

He stepped close and gripped her shoulders. "Damn fool woman, don't you know I'd do anything for you? That's why I broke things off. To protect you."

"If you'd do anything, then live for me. Live with me. You think I won't be happy with you? Well, make me happy."

He gave her a small shake. "It won't work." A sharp pain thudded behind his temple. Why wouldn't she listen? She had to be wrong. Didn't she?

"It could be embarrassing for you, joining with my family." She placed her hand over his heart and rubbed small circles. It felt better than he wanted to admit.

"What? Your father's an earl."

"And my brother is a criminal." She shook her head. "By the standards of decent society, you'd be the one marrying beneath you."

"That's asinine." The toes of his boots nudged the toes of hers. "I don't care what your brother is."

"And I don't care who your father is." She lifted her chin. Her lips hovered inches beneath his.

"It's not the same thing." But he could feel his resolve crumbling. Everything he wanted was right before him. Was he an idiot to refuse it? Couldn't he make it his life's work to make her happy?

"No, a moral failing is much worse than an accident of birth." She leaned forward, the tips of her breasts pressing against his chest. All his muscles tensed. He ground his teeth so hard his jaw ached. "Your mother is a god-fearing woman," she said. "When she hears of what my brother's done, she'll look at me like I'm tainted. Like I'm nowhere near good enough for her son. Like—"

Brogan shut her up the only way he knew how. He kissed her.

Her mouth opened beneath his. She eagerly met his tongue with her own. She wrapped her arm around his neck and held him close, as though afraid to let him go.

She needn't have worried. His fight was gone. If Juliana was willing to risk a life with him, then he wasn't able to say no any longer.

Being his wife would be an adjustment for her. But if he couldn't buy her a new dress each year, he would make it up to her in other ways.

He angled her head and took the kiss deeper. Better,

more pleasurable ways.

A sliver of guilt niggled at him. Perhaps he should give her one more chance to change her mind. He pressed his forehead to hers, sucking down air. "Think carefully. Once you become my wife, there's no going b—"

Juliana leapt at him with a squeal. She clung to his shoulders and kissed him hard.

He staggered back, gripping her waist and holding her tight.

Well, all right then. He'd given her every opportunity to do the right thing. He could hardly be expected to persist past the lady's desires, not when acceding to them would make him deliriously happy.

No man was that strong. Not even a hardened ex-boxer.

And all it took was one spunky lady to bring him to his knees.

Chapter Twenty-Eight

Juliana stiffened her spine as she stooped through the low door. The cells, little more than fortified rooms in the magistrate's basement, were dark and dank, and Juliana pulled her coat more tightly about her. It was late in the evening, but she hadn't wanted to wait until morning to have this conversation with her brother.

Snow jumped up from his pallet at her approach and leapt for the cell door. "Jules, I knew you or father would come. This chastisement has gone on long enough. Let me out."

If Brogan hadn't been at her back, she might have lost her courage. He squeezed her shoulder, and she nodded.

"Father asked me to come. He's too distraught to look at you." She turned away from her brother's expression. It was filled too much with pique and not enough with guilt. "He will pay for an attorney for you. It won't be the best attorney; father can't afford the best. But he'll be better than you deserve."

"Attorney?" Snowdon whined. "He isn't going to actually press charges against me, is he?"

A brittle chuckle came from the next cell over. "Shut up, Snow," Miss Lynn said. "If I had to be arrested, why did it have to be with you?"

Juliana took a step towards the disembodied voice. Brogan's fingers flexed on her shoulder. She patted his hand, and with a sigh, he released her.

She peered into the next cell. "Why?" She had to ask. This woman was the cause of her family's ruin. If she and

Snow had never met, her brother would never have acted so odiously. He would have lived a life of banal decadence, accomplishing little, but he would have been free.

He wouldn't have broken his father's heart.

Miss Lynn's influence didn't release Snow from responsibility for his own actions, but Juliana's gut burned standing in front of the woman who had sown such destruction.

Miss Lynn's dark eyes appeared at the small window in the door. "Why what?" Her tone was mocking. "Why did I work so hard to free my brothers and sisters from their chains?"

"The only chains you'll encounter are the ones that will wrap about your wrists soon." Brogan grunted. "Life for most is hard, but it doesn't excuse this."

Juliana stepped forwards. They were nearly face to face, only a thin bar separating the women. "Do you truly care about improving society, or do you only revel in the chaos you create?"

"Can't it be both?" The edges of Miss Lynn's eyes crinkled devilishly. Even facing prison, and who knew what else, the woman had brass. Was it her mind that had something wrong with it? No one should react such to the future she faced. "You should be more understanding," Miss Lynn said. "You've always wanted to make a name for yourself. History isn't made by meek women."

"It isn't made by shrews, either." Juliana hadn't only wanted to become renowned. She'd wanted to be known for doing something good, improving society. Her name would be whispered far and wide now, with a brother accused of trying to kill his titled father. Her family would make good grist for the gossip mill. And the fame she knew was to come turned her stomach.

But it didn't matter. Her father was alive. She loved Brogan. Nothing else compared. "It gives me some comfort to know that history won't be made by you."

Miss Lynn narrowed her eyes. "My life isn't over yet."

"No, and you might even get to enjoy some of it if you provide the courts with information," Brogan said. "Your brother was involved in the Durham riots?"

"I already told you that." Miss Lynn gripped the bar in the window. "Lord Stanhope was starving his tenants, not letting them hunt on his land. That riot was the beginning of the end for England's aristocracy. Mark my words."

Brogan leaned his shoulder against the wall. "And does your brother hunt with a firearm?"

"No. Bullets are much too dear..." Miss Lynn pressed her lips tight. The glare she sent Brogan would have made lesser men turn tail and run.

"He hunts with a sling, does he not?" Brogan waited for an answer, but when he turned to Juliana with a shrug, it was clear he hadn't expected one.

At least the woman had loyalty to someone. For Snow's sake, it was too bad it wasn't him.

"So, he's the one who tried to take off my head." Juliana shoved her hand in Brogan's coat pocket, hoping to warm it.

"It will be hard to prove." Brogan took her hands and chafed them between his own.

She rested her temple on his shoulder. "I don't even care any longer. As long as he stays away from me and my father, I don't mind that he's not in prison."

She rubbed his chest as a low grumble vibrated through it. Of course, he wouldn't agree. Brogan would want to hunt down anyone who had tried to hurt her.

And she didn't mind that, either.

"Jules, you're my sister." Snowdon stretched his hand out to her. "You can't leave me in here. People like me don't belong in places like this."

She took a last look at her brother. She would remember the affection she had for him as a child. Remember the times they'd laughed together, and nothing else. "Goodbye, Snow."

Brogan wrapped his arm around her waist as her

brother's shrieks filled the basement. He nodded to the magistrate as they left his house. He helped her into a cart and turned the wagon for Rose's home.

It was a quiet ride back. Instead of a groom, Lord Dunkeld met them at the stables. He helped Juliana down then turned towards Brogan when he jumped to the ground.

Her muscles tensed. She had hoped she was done fighting for the night. There wasn't much left in her. But if the marquess thought he could—

Dunkeld stuck out his hand. "I'm happy to know my and my friend's little agency is doing some good."

Brogan rubbed his jaw before slowly reaching out to shake. "Does that mean I'll get a reference?"

The Scotsman crossed his arms over his barrel chest. "Are you looking for new employment?"

"I thought, after hitting you, that I'd have to look for another job."

Dunkeld laughed. "My wife is still hopping mad, but I hold no grudges. It was a good play. And you," he said to Juliana, "wield a mighty fine cane."

Juliana bounced on her toes.

Brogan tapped his fingers against his leg, as effusive a sign of excitement as he was liable to give.

She wouldn't have minded marrying a boxer or a woodworker or whatever Brogan had decided to do, but marrying an investigator...

They'd worked well together on her case. Would he let her work with him again on others?

She'd have to work on her debating skills if she was to convince him.

Dunkeld turned for the house, and they fell in step beside him. "My wife and I will return to London with you, Duffy. I know Wilberforce will want a full report of this investigation, and I want to speak to him and the others about improving communications at the Bond Agency. I was here with Withington, one of the subjects of our cases, and I didn't know. I could have been protecting him." The marquess's nostrils flared.

Juliana placed her hand on his arm. "The doctor says my father will be fine. He wasn't poisoned. It was just too much plum pudding."

Dunkeld nodded tersely. "Nonetheless, we need a better system. At least one person who knows where all agents are located and the elements of each current case so nothing like this falls through the cracks again. We were lucky this time."

"Agreed," Brogan said.

The marquess rubbed his chin. "I must say, your little tap to the jaw has reminded me how much I miss getting my hands a bit dirty. I might ask for a case of my own when we arrive."

Brogan chuckled. "I'd be happy to assist you."

Juliana reached for Brogan. "But you'll come to Bluff Hall as soon as you've finished?" She rubbed her breastbone. How quickly she went from thinking she'd never see the man again to expecting him to be by her side at all times. Even a week of separation seemed interminable.

"The very moment I've given my report, I'll return to you." He laced their fingers together.

"I hear congratulations are in order," Dunkeld said.

"Yes, my father is looking into getting us a special license." He'd seemed happy to have a task to focus on. Anything to take his mind off Snowdon.

Brogan's hand clenched around hers. "I can't believe he gave me his blessing. It was unfair to ask for your hand when your father was in such a state of mind. Perhaps I should ask again when he's recovered from his shock."

Dunkeld stopped in front of the front door. "Don't be a daft fool. When given a gift like a woman to love, you grab onto her with both hands, and fight anyone who would try to take her away. Ask again." He huffed out a breath. "What nonsense."

Juliana looked down at their clasped hands. From his grip on her, she didn't think Brogan letting her go was going to be a problem. And his uneasiness over their marriage would disappear when she greeted him each day with a smile, and each night with a naughty kiss.

And speaking of...

"Gentlemen, if you will excuse me, I believe I'll turn in for the night." She dipped a curtsy to the marquess, and gave Brogan the sauciest look she knew. And when she sauntered away, she made sure to inject a bit more swing into her hips than was technically necessary.

It had its desired effect. Within moments, Brogan gave his own excuses, which she was sure didn't fool the marquess in the least, and his footsteps pounded after her.

He caught up when her hand was on her bedroom's handle. He herded her through the door and muffled her laughter with his mouth. He pushed the door closed with her body.

"You little minx." He ran his hand over her waist to the back of her thigh and tugged until she wrapped her leg around his hip. When he pressed forward, his hard length nestled right where she needed it.

She nibbled on his jaw. "I can't wait to be Mrs. Juliana Duffy."

"Truly?" He lifted his head to gaze down at her. His eyes flicked back and forth over her own, as though trying to read her deepest thoughts.

"Truly." Gripping his neckcloth, she pulled him back down. Their lips brushed. "Only an ex-boxer turned investigator will do. Someone strong enough to help me through my family's troubles. Smart enough to keep me safe. And stubborn enough to stick with me even when I'm irritating the stuffing out of you. You're perfect for me, Brogan Duffy. Imagine how bored I'd be with a toff."

He grinned. "One thing I can promise, my love, is you'll never be bored." He took her mouth, the kiss sealing the promise better than anything else could do.

It took running away from home, being chased down by an investigator, and solving a crime in order to discover what gave her life meaning. And loving the man in front of her was a very big part of that.

Life was a mad, marvelous thing.

And she was going to enjoy every moment of it.

* * * *

About the Author

Like almost one-third of all romance writers, Alyson Chase is a former attorney (okay, maybe a slight exaggeration, but not by much). She happily ditched those suits and now works in her pajamas writing about men's briefs instead of legal briefs. When she's not writing, she's probably engaged in one of her favorite hobbies: napping, eating, or martial arts (That last one almost makes up for the first two, right?) She also writes humorous, small-town, contemporary romance novels under the name Allyson Charles, and paranormal romance as A. Caprice.

Connect with Alyson at:

www.alysonchase.com
www.facebook.com/AlysonChaseAuthor
Twitter: @1alysonchase
Email: alysonchaseauthor@gmail.com

Made in the USA
Columbia, SC
12 May 2024

35587019R00133